DEATH BEYOND

First Edition
Published by
Breaking Rules Publishing Europe, 2021.
This is a work of fiction. Similarities to real people, places, or events are entirely coincidental.
Death Beyond
Cover Design by
C. Marry Hultman
978-91-986841-6-2
Copyright © 2021 BRPE

THE MORTEM CYCLE

DEATH HOUSE

DEATH SHIP

DEATH BEYOND

UPCOMING TITLES

DEATH CUISINE
(Release: Thanksgiving 2021)

MISSIONS

ADRIFT
Lyndsey Ellis-Holloway — 9

THE DREAMS OF THRAIC
Chris Hewitt — 51

PORTALS
Nicola Currie — 75

HERE THERE BE MOSTERS
G. Allen Wilbanks — 103

THE OCCAM'S RAZOR
Jade Wildy — 127

VOICES FROM THE VOID
Gregg Cunningham — 165

SCREAMS IN THE RADIO SILENCE
Peter J. Foote — 189

PERSERVERANCE
Rachel L. Tilley — 207

EDEN ONE
Tim Mendees — 217

SLEEPWALKER
Jonathan Inbody   253

THE SHADOW FROM SPACE
David Green   265

MORE FROM BREAKING RULES PUBLISHING EUROPE   276

Besides, people never regard anything that serves and benefits them as mysterious; only the things which damage or threaten them are mysterious.

-Karel Čapek, War with the Newts

ADRIFT

Lyndsey Ellis-Holloway

"Computer, damage report."

Silence.

"*Computer*, damage report," Thompson reiterated, scowling at the screens flickering in front of him. The computer never took *this* long to complete a full systems analysis.

The explosion had hit them hard. It had taken the collective strength of his crew to keep the ship from veering off course entirely during the shockwave. He expected some damage, given the pounding they had taken, but Thompson had hoped it wasn't as bad as he suspected.

After tapping his fingers on the console, Thompson slammed his fist onto the dash, as one might a stubborn computer. It was an old school trick, and not usually reserved for the more delicate space capable technologies, but what had worked before, worked again as the computer juddered into life.

DEATH BEYOND

"Some major ...mage to stab... engine. Life su...su... support functi... optimal. Severe da...age to systems."

Thompson sighed heavily and rubbed his hands across his unshaven face as he sat back in his seat. His eyes stung as he tried to focus them on the screens in front of him, but his eyelids felt like lead and it was all he could do to keep them open, let alone concentrate on the report now occupying the monitors.

Thompson rubbed at his eyes and scowled as the system report flickered on and off or pixelated in random parts—but he got the gist, they were screwed. The starboard engine had sustained major damage. In fact, it wasn't functioning at all, while the port engine continued to burn, sending them in constant revolutions endlessly through space. Not exactly the most comforting thought.

Closing his lids, Thompson allowed himself a moment to rest his eyes while he gathered his wits about him. They had survived. He had to remember that. They had made it off Terranis *alive*, which was more than half the planet could boast.

A distress signal had emanated from the planet, and they had answered, like many other ships in the area. It wasn't long before an evac notice had followed the first signal. He had sent his own signal out into the void of space, to let anyone heading their way know that there were ships carrying civilians from the distressed planet below. That had been *before* the shit had truly hit the fan. Someone would have gotten his message, which meant that all they had to do was drift a while and wait for help.

"Computer, run full scans of the crew and passengers for infection, confirm that all occupants of the ship are clear."

"Ca...ca...cannot complete... sc...ners malfunctioniiiiiiiiiiing," the computer replied, catching on the last word until Thompson applied some of his 'tender' love to the console again. "Please submit ...ssue samp... for manual analysisssss."

Grand. Just bloody brilliant. Not only were they floating in the vast nothingness of space, with a ship that was barely functioning, they also had no quick solution of finding out if they carried anyone infected aboard or not. *That* was going to go down well.

With his head in his hands, Thompson felt the first tendrils of dread worm their way into his heart, his chest tight as it gripped him and threatened to take his breath. He had been alright amidst the chaos of the evacuation, running on adrenaline and instinct, he hadn't had the time to think about what was actually happening. When all the ships on Terranis had been called up and given emergency launch codes, the *Nightingale* crew had reacted, gathering as many passengers as they could in order to evacuate. The authorities had been as organised as they could have been, given the situation they had faced, and they had done their best to save as many uninfected from the epidemic, but in the end, the riots began. Everyone scrambled to survive.

Even now, sitting alone on the bridge, with the consoles beeping and whirring, the computer doing its best to complete its duties, Thompson could not rid himself of the screams and explosions that had been the first warning signs of the hell that was unravelling before they escaped the planet.

DEATH BEYOND

The infected, frightened and isolated, with little to no help from anyone, had rioted against those who had quarantined them away from the rest of the population. Despite the spaceport being situated on the opposite side of the city, Thompson and his crew *still* heard the fearful cries of those poor souls held back by the fences, terrified of the end that they knew waited for them at the hands of the disease.

Thompson was convinced that his dreams would be haunted—by their cries, the explosions that followed the riots, the view of the city ablaze—for the rest of his life. Give him the endless silence of the void over that crowded, God-forsaken planet, and the nightmares now living in his memory, festering away amongst his doubt and despair.

Pressing his palms into his eyes, he begged the images to give him a moment of peace, the events playing over in his mind as he remembered the infected rushing towards the spaceport. They had been a terrible tidal wave, a unified force with only one thing on their minds—the need to get out, the need to survive—and he and his crew turned their back on them. The crew of the *Nightingale* pushed their passengers inside, slamming the shuttle bay doors in the faces of those not quick enough to get aboard. He hadn't hesitated; hadn't stopped to apologise as he launched into action, taking off into the sky alongside every other ship condemned to be on Terranis that day. Ascending from that writhing hell into the serene limbo of space.

Hundreds of ships, all vying for the space lanes at the same time. He'd focussed on getting them into orbit, he hadn't allowed himself the time to think of the other ships crashing into one another out of the corner of his eye. Not until they were 'safe' anyway. He was still convinced that they clipped a commercial ship at some point, but he hadn't looked back, and there was no telling now. It had taken all of his nerve to get them. He'd been forced to be cold and calculated in order to give his crew their orders and get them out of there in one piece. Mostly.

He hated it.

That was not the man he wanted to be, nor was it the one he'd been *raised* to be, but at that moment he'd cast his heart, and his conscience, aside in favour of the *Nightingale*.

Sighing heavily, Thompson pushed himself away from the computer's console, gaze flickering over the cracked view screen where the stars spread out on a blanket of black velvet, as far as the eye could see.

He watched as the stars blurred slightly, leaving little glowing trails as the ship rotated. It was beautiful, but as the ship continued its lazy drift, the debris finally came into view and the tendrils tightened around Thompson's chest as he witnessed the aftermath of their desperate escape.

There in the distance, he could see the remains of Terranis. Large burning craters glowed angry red, marring the once rich and dazzling green of the planet's surface. Idle debris obscured his view of the planet. A graveyard of ships confronted him, those that had not escaped orbit quickly enough to avoid the blasts when the power planets exploded—or when the army launched their missiles in an attempt to quell the infected's rampage.

Thompson was silently thankful that he was alone on the bridge, and that this was the only viewscreen onboard. The last thing he needed was for his crew, or their passengers, to bear witness to the death of the planet, let alone see the chunks of metal drifting alongside them from the fallen ships. He stood, transfixed by the destruction, thanking his lucky stars they had survived, but that small relief soon turned to horror as he realised it was not just ship debris he looked at. Distinct figures formed, the people who had been *inside* the ships floated closer to *The Nightingale*, propelled ever onwards in the vast emptiness of space.

Thompson swallowed hard, fighting back the wave of nausea swelling in his belly. A shiver ran down his spine as he caught sight of a mother and child, their bodies still entwined in a desperate embrace. Frozen together for all eternity, or until someone came to clean up the mess left behind. He turned away from them, entering a command into the computer's keyboard with a trembling hand, grateful when he heard the juddering sound of the shields complying to the instructions, the viewscreen blissfully covered.

"Captain?" Sarah's voice called to him tentatively, and Thompson was glad he had covered the viewscreen before she came in. The girl was a damned good engineer. She had the makings to become one of the best, but she didn't have the constitution to face situations like the last twenty-four hours.

"What is it?" he asked softly, turning to face her, taking in the young woman's appearance. Was she *more* dishevelled than usual, or was this her usual dirt-covered, tousled-hair look mixed with maybe a *little* more exhaustion?

"Hunny was asking for you. He thinks we might have a problem," she replied, shuffling from one foot to the other, not quite meeting his gaze.

"Sarah?" he questioned, reaching out with a hand, thankful his trembling had stopped, as he tilted her chin up with his fingers so her blue eyes couldn't avoid his grey ones. "There's something more you're not telling me."

He had picked the girl up from a spaceport in Rechik a decade ago, when she'd been little more than a waif, stealing food and cargo to survive. He'd spotted her pulling engine parts out of parked shuttles and transporters with such deft efficiency that he couldn't pass up such engineering talents. In all her time with him, Sarah never once looked away from him. She had always been nervous; it was her nature. She told him that to look away meant the chance for someone to take advantage of her. That was something Sarah learned early on in life, and she swore never to look away, so that no one could *ever* take advantage of her again. Which meant whatever was bothering her required his immediate attention.

"It's..." she started slowly, still reluctant to look at him. "One of the families has a sick kid. They swear that it's just a cold, nothing more, but the other passengers don't believe them. Hunny thinks things could get out of hand."

Thompson closed his eyes and took a long, steadying breath, digesting the news. If he thought the day couldn't get any worse, he'd been wrong. Or he'd jinxed it.

"Alright, let's go and deal with this before it *does* get out of hand."

The twenty citizens they'd managed to save gathered in the large mess hall in the centre of the ship. Other than the cargo bay, it was the only place big enough to hold them, but at least the mess hall added a level of comfort that being shoved into a glorified storage container didn't.

As Thompson approached the mess hall, he could hear raised, somewhat erratic voices echoing from within, fueled by their fear. Others were softer, attempting to calm the situation before it escalated. Amongst the latter, Thompson could pick out the rough bass tones of his security officer, a man who *looked* the part as much as he acted it. Despite his surname. There's nothing sweet about Hunny, that was the running joke on their ship, and nothing could have been truer.

The scene greeting him wasn't remotely surprising. To one side stood the family in question, huddled together in fear behind Hunny, and several other members of the *Nightingale* crew, separated from the main group for their own safety. In between the two groups stood Thompson's two first officers; an unusual choice, one might say, but the twins came as a pair in all things. Their strengths and weaknesses complemented one another perfectly. The larger group of passengers had turned into a glorified mob, their backs to the wall opposite the accused family, while their ringleaders shouted the odds at Thompson's crew.

"Their child is infected! It's *obvious*," one large man shouted at Hunny, looking around the twins as he stared the hulking security officer 'down'. "He should be sent out of the airlock to save the rest of us!"

"That's right! The child *and* his family should be cast out now before they can infect anyone else. We have our own families to think about, I don't want my children to become sick because of *them*," snarled another man, clinging to his wife and daughters, glaring at the 'guilty' family.

"He's *not* infected. How many times do we have to tell you?! It's just a cold. His asthma makes it sound worse, that's all," the boy's father snapped in retaliation, pulling his son closer to him.

"He said he felt *sick*. That's another symptom, the nausea starts, then the vomiting, then it's too late to stop the infection from spreading!" one woman barked shrilly.

"*Enough.*" Thompson's voice boomed across the mess hall as he clapped his hands above his head, bringing the attention of the occupants upon himself.

Immediately his crew stood down. He could see them visibly relax in his presence. They had been dealing with it as best they could, but they knew their captain was the best person to deal with this.

"Shouting accusations at one another won't solve anything, so if we've all finished acting like children, can we maybe pretend to be adults?" he asked, glancing at the passengers who had been the most vocal from the mob.

There was some awkward shuffling, downward glances, and reluctant murmurs, but overall, the room went quiet as he stepped forward to stand between the twins. "Listen up, our starboard engine has taken some major damage we won't be able to repair from here. What this means is we're adrift until someone responds to the distress signal we sent. Our port engine, however, is still firing and we're unable to shut it down for the moment, which means the ship's spinning. *This* could account for the lad's nausea. It's faint, but some people feel a ship's movements more than others, children are especially susceptible. The longer we're spinning, the more likely the rest of you will start to feel the effects as well."

He let his words sink in, feeling like a stern teacher addressing an unruly classroom. His eyes immediately sought the gaze of the loudest protestors, and he was glad to see them look away. "Help is on the way, we just don't know *when* it will arrive. The ship sustained substantial damage in the escape, my crew will work on fixing the systems we're able to repair from here with our limited equipment. In the meantime, everyone needs to calm down, work together and just relax until help arrives."

"What about the boy?" the large man who had caught Thompson's attention before asked defiantly, squaring up to his full height as he attempted to dress down the captain, just as he'd tried with Hunny.

"What's your name, sir?" Thompson asked, watching the man carefully, ignoring his question.

"Dorian Sanders."

"Well, Mr Sanders, I will confine the boy and his family to the far side of this mess hall, if that will suffice? I'm not in the habit of judging people guilty before evidence has presented itself to say otherwise. If the family says he has a cold, I am inclined to believe them until there is proof to back up *your* claim. I do not have the crew to spare to remove them from this room, we need all of you in one place, rather than wandering around the ship, so they will remain on that side of the hall, and you will all remain on *this* side." Thompson watched Sanders, waiting for the man to make some sort of protest, but none came, so he continued, "This brings me to my next subject, my first officers will take blood samples and cheek swabs from all of you, alongside our medics. Our internal scanners have been damaged by the explosions, so we will have to complete a biological analysis of you all the old-fashioned way, to determine if anyone *is* infected."

"And how long is *that* likely to take?"

"As long as it takes," Thompson replied, not bothering to see who asked the question. "I ask that you all comply with any requests you receive from my crew and keep issues to a minimum. We are all stuck with one another for the foreseeable future. I do not believe that *any* of us are infected, so until the results come back to confirm my suspicions, let's remain calm. Anyone who attempts to cause discourse will be sedated and tied up. Harm someone and you may find yourself in the airlock as a preventative measure. Thank you."

Thompson cast a glance to the twins standing beside him, their white hair stark against their faces, their blue eyes startlingly bright. With a nod to the pair, he motioned for them to follow as he made his way to his crew, standing close to the separated family.

"It's safe to say the situation is dire then, Captain?" the twins asked in unison.

Thompson smiled, he'd been unnerved by their tendency to speak as one when he first met them, but now he found it oddly comforting. "Aye, but at least the life support is working, we have plenty of rations. I'm convinced someone heard the distress call. Hopefully, we won't have to herd this crowd for too long, so long as we can keep them from killing each other in the interim."

A derisive snort caught Thompson's attention, and he smirked as he found Hunny, arms crossed over his broad chest, looking down at him, the man's thick eyebrows furrowed. "Ya really think it's that simple?" he growled.

"With you around I do," Thompson replied, raising an eyebrow at the man as Hunny snorted again, looking away with a scowl. There was no way a man as proud as Hunny would argue with his captain. If he did it meant admitting he wasn't up for the job.

"Yuri, Anya, get down to the sickbay and get Murphy off his fat backside, I want him and his team up here to get those samples immediately, no excuses. I don't care if he's hungover, I don't give a damn if his arm fell off during our escape; I need those samples in the computer half an hour ago. Remind him the crew needs to have samples taken as well. We need to eliminate ourselves from being infected."

"Yes, Captain," the twins replied, turning as one and leaving the mess hall under the watchful eye of their passengers.

"Hunny, stay here with your team and keep this lot separated, anyone causes trouble, just handle it."

"Does that mean I can stun 'em?" Hunny asked, and Thompson stifled a laugh.

"If they don't back down after a couple of warnings, be my guest."

Thompson was grateful, in a way, that despite all they'd been through in the last few hours, his crew had not changed. Though there *were* days when he questioned why he'd employed half of them to begin with.

"As for the rest of you, get back to your duties, and fix my ship. If the systems aren't reparable from here, and there's nothing for you to do, come back to help Hunny and the others keeping this lot from killing one another. I'm going to see if I can contact the outside world. An ETA for rescue might just get everyone to relax." He sighed, rubbing his temples with his fingers as he left the hall.

Tick-tock, tick-tock, tick-tock. The sound from the antique clock was deafening in the silence of Thompson's quarters. His face lit by the eerie green glow of his computer, he slumped in his chair, eyes closed, as he rubbed at his temples with his fingertips, breathing in time with the clock. There had been no answer to their distress call, though deep down he hadn't expected one. The damage to their systems was severe, why would their communications satellite have been spared from the devastation? He had *hoped* they would be lucky, but he should have known better.

Opening his eyes, Thompson rubbed his hands over his face, staring at the data on the computer screen. The words 'analysis in progress' flickered on and off above a percentage line that had barely moved since he'd looked at it four hours ago. Even on a working system, physical sample analysis took time, but since the ship was in limp mode, the tests took an excruciating amount of time to complete. It wasn't like they had anywhere to go, but the longer they had to wait, the harder it would be to keep the peace.

Thompson leaned over his console, reaching for the button to the ship's intercom. His finger mere millimetres from pressing it when he heard the thunder of boots heading his way. He pushed his chair back, stood up, and opening his door, was met with the dishevelled images of Anya and Jerry, the pair panting as they leaned against the wall, looking up at their captain with desperation in their eyes.

"What the hell happened?" he asked, eyes focussing on Jerry's bust lip and swollen right eye.

"The little lad, the one they kept accusing of being infected? He threw up all over the mess hall and started to panic, most likely not helped by the hysterics of the lynch mob screaming at him from the other side of the room. The crowd got antsy. Hunny managed to stun about five of them then the kid's mum fainted, and they accused the whole family of being sick," Jerry answered swiftly, keeping the details clear and concise. "It erupted into a fight. Hunny managed to push the mob back, but it's getting hairy down there. Need a hand Cap."

"Suggestions?" Thompson asked, turning to his first officer, who had clearly been sent because she and her brother had a plan.

"We need a stronger threat, the stun guns and a swift smack in the jaw apparently are not enough," Anya replied, tucking a strand of white hair behind her ear as she composed herself.

"You want to open the armoury?"

"Yes, Sir. Arm Hunny and the rest of the crew with substantial firepower. The passengers might recognise the threat of real injury and take more notice."

"Or get us all killed? I don't like the idea of threatening passengers, Anya."

"If I recall, Captain, you threatened them with the airlock."

"I did, and you know damn well I meant to shove them in there and let them fear being let out of it, without ever unlocking the outer door," Thompson said darkly, his tone lowering as he narrowed his eyes at her.

"Cap, I hate to say it, but without those guns, I reckon that mob will end up trying to kill the crew anyway, just to get to that family and shove *them* out an airlock. They're terrified, they won't listen to reason, the threat of getting shot *might* just be enough to get them to calm down," Jerry interjected.

Thompson ran his fingers through his hair and took a deep breath. The last thing he wanted was to arm his people, he didn't want to give *anyone* the potential to kill one another, but if the stun guns weren't enough, and the threat of an airlock wasn't either, then what was? You couldn't use logic against fear, he'd seen enough terrified people in his time to know that. Fear removed rationality from even the most intelligent minds.

Exhaling heavily, Thompson removed a key from around his neck, handing it to Anya wordlessly. There was nothing more to be said. She knew the code to the keypad, and if the twins had come up with this plan, she would follow it through. Thompson knew to back them all the way.

"Get the weapons. I'll meet you both in the mess hall and see if I can talk them down, make them see sense." Thompson nodded to the pair, turning and striding towards the mess hall, while Jerry and Anya's footsteps thudded in the opposite direction.

The muted sound of voices echoed through the empty metal corridors of the ship. If he could hear the ruckus this far from the mess hall, then the situation must have been more dire than he'd first imagined. His stomach twisted into knots and Thompson broke into a run, the sound of his boots upon the metal walkway clanging around him a deafening thunder as he rounded the corner, following the growing roar of outrage from the mess hall.

The sight that greeted him was his worst nightmare. In one corner of the room, surrounded by upturned tables—made into a makeshift barricade—huddled the family accused of being infected. Hunny, his team, and the rest of the crew who were unable to complete repairs on the ship, tried to hold back the raging mob. Several crew members were sporting bleeding wounds or blossoming bruises, though more of their passengers had been wounded than crew. The worst of it, however, lay in the centre of the room. Two crumpled forms, bloody and twisted, still entwined in their battle, though it seemed that neither had won this particular match.

Thompson recognised both men. One was the man who had shouted the odds alongside Dorian Sanders, and the other was one of his own. Kurtis, their youngest security officer. Thompson's breath caught in his throat, his stomach twisted again, heart aching at the sight. These fools had killed one of his own. For a brief moment, a wave of dizziness overtook him, vision blurring, swallowing hard to fight back the nausea rising from the pit of his belly.

A mixture of rage, and the continual spinning of his ship, caused this miniature blip in his thought process, as he tried to come to terms with the fact that Kurtis was dead. A torn off chair leg impaled Kurtis' chest, straight through his back.

Blood dripped from the point of the makeshift stake.

His pulse filled his ears, almost drowning out the arguing, though the shrill cry of the fallen passenger's wife, and her constant '*you killed him, you killed my husband*' was a knife through his head.

"Captain? Captain. *Captain!*"

A voice was calling to him from somewhere, but Thompson's eyes were glued to the death embrace of Kurtis, and the man whose name he'd never asked for.

"*Martin!*"

Thompson rounded on the person who used his first name, his tumultuous grey eyes reflected back at him from the blue pools of Anya's as his first officer placed a hand on his arm, looking up at him, desperate to bring him back to reality. He'd never seen her afraid, had never seen her lose her composure before, but he understood why. This was unlike anything *The Nightingale* had ever faced.

Taking a deep breath, Thompson placed his hand over Anya's, nodding to show that he was back with her at last. Anya turned his hand over and pressed something cold and hard into his upturned palm. Looking down, he flinched at the sight of the pistol that lay there. He knew it was necessary, knew he needed to have one as well, but that didn't make it any easier to accept.

He slid the gun into the empty holster at his hip, fingers lingering on the grip, hating the inanimate object's presence on his person. Brought back to reality, Thompson strode toward the warring factions of his crew and the terrified mob of passengers. His head ached as their voices clamoured in his ears, shrill tones on the verge of sheer hysteria.

"Enough! All of you!" he snapped, voice booming through the hall, reverberating off the metal walls. "I want you all to *sit down* and stay there. You've killed one of my crew, and you're damned lucky I don't space the lot of you for it."

"You killed *my* husband!" the woman repeated, stepping through the crowd to square up to the captain.

"If you'd all done as you were told, he would probably still be alive. Now *sit down*." Thompson's voice dropped another octave, his words whispered, yet the silence in the room was so deafening that he may as well have shouted them.

Cowering from the darkness in the man's tone, the woman hurried to sit with the other passengers, all of whom were glaring past Thompson, to the family his crew still protected.

"Hunny, handle this lot," Thompson snarled.

"You givin' me permission to put 'em down?"

"Warnings first, if they still refuse to listen, then yes. Do what you must to maintain order. We can't have another incident like this."

"An' what about them?" Hunny asked, thrusting a thumb over his shoulder in the direction of the family. "The lad bein' sick is one thing, but his mum ain't lookin' hot either, an' it's just makin' this lot panic."

Thompson sighed, running his hands through his greying hair. If he had any left after this disaster, it would be a miracle. "We've still got a long wait before we get those results. I'll move them to the infirmary, that way they're out of sight."

"Not out of mind though," Hunny growled.

"Fat chance of that," Thompson snorted, patting the man on his arm before striding over to the family in question. "Alright, we're going to move you to the infirmary, having you here with the others is causing paranoia."

"My son doesn't have it, I promise you, Captain, my son *isn't* infected," the father insisted, clinging to his son.

"Never said he did. I just want to minimise any further hostility by getting you out of here. The Doc can keep an eye on your boy, and the rest of you, while we calm the other passengers down and wait for help."

"Thank you, Captain." The father reached up to shake Thompson's hand, but the captain flinched and stepped back instinctively, his heart sinking as the man's face fell, a sad but accepting expression on his face. "Not just their paranoia, is it?" the man sighed, standing up, his son hugged to his chest.

"I'm sorry."

"No need, Captain. I understand."

"Anya, get them to the infirmary and keep an eye on them. I'm going to check in with Sarah, see how our repairs are coming along."

"Aye, Captain. Stay safe," she added, touching his arm briefly before she herded the family out, two of their crew carrying the unconscious mother, their faces pale.

The father, and Hunny, had been right. It wasn't *just* the other passengers who were paranoid about the family's potential infection. Thompson and his crew were just as suspicious of them, despite what he'd said about believing them to be clean.

Every muscle in his body ached, and his head felt as though it was full of cotton wool. It was difficult to think, but he knew he had to hold it together for the sake of the others. Rubbing at his tired, stinging eyes, he took a deep breath in through his nose, willing his body to keep going for just a little bit longer as he left to find out how the repairs were going.

"I've done all I can, Captain. I'm sorry."

Sarah's dejected tone made Thompson's heart sink, his stomach churning as the reality of their situation hit him in the chest like a hammer. They were stuck here, unable to make their situation any better, until someone came to help. His crew had done all they could, but without proper equipment, there wasn't really anything they *could* fix while drifting in space.

"Can't stop the engine either?" he asked, already knowing the answer.

Sarah shook her head, stumbling, and reaching out for the wall to keep her balance. "Wish I could. I've already sent Harry and Samantha to their quarters to lie down because of the spinning."

"It's starting to seep into everyone's bones, isn't it?"

"Seems that way, we knew it would, but I can't turn off the systems to the engine from here. And in our current condition I wouldn't recommend a spacewalk, not when walking in a straight line is going to be impossible for everyone before long."

"It might have to be possible. If people start getting motion sickness, they're going to start accusing one another of being infected. We've got enough of that going on as it is."

"Captain, if I could trust myself to do it, I would, but I can barely stand up," Sarah muttered.

"Then I'll do it."

"What?"

"I'll do it. You stay on the internal comms to me and guide me outside, you tell *me* what I have to do to fix it."

"Captain, you're pale and your eyes aren't focussed. The motion is affecting you as much as everyone else. Out there you'll have the stars spinning in your vision to disorient you, and whatever debris is floating about to potentially knock you out. It's suicide."

"It's suicide if we stand here and do nothing, we've already lost one crew member, I'm not risking anymore. Come on, help me get suited up, and let's get this over with before I come to my senses."

Thompson led Sarah to an airlock, where she helped him into an evac-suit; checking, and double-checking, each connection while she attempted to talk him out of his madness, to no avail. He checked his air pressure for the umpteenth time, breathing deeply, concentrating on the task at hand. He tried not to think about the mounting pressure in his head or the way he couldn't *quite* focus on anything for too long without his vision blurring. The rising nausea in his stomach was *exactly* why he was even remotely *considering* this ridiculous escapade. If the motion sickness was settling in for him, it would be for the rest of the ship as well.

"You're sure, you're sure?" Sarah asked, holding onto his arm, swaying slightly.

"Do I even have a choice?" he replied, placing his gloved hand over hers. "You can barely stand; I'm getting a headache and fighting back nausea. If we don't take this risk then things are going to escalate."

"I know," Sarah sighed and nodded, patting his arm as she put on a headset and clicked it on. "Checking comms, hearing me loud and clear?"

"Loud and clear, let's do this."

Closing the inner airlock door behind him, Thompson punched in his authorisation code, triggering the auto-pressurisation. The woosh of air pressed tight around him as the room came in line with the emptiness of the void that lay beyond the outer door. Floating towards the hatch, Thompson's gloved hands gripped the door lock as he waited for the all-clear to open it and begin his walk. It had been some time since he'd last ventured into the vastness of space in this manner, and for once, his heart was not in his throat with the elation and freedom this usually offered him. Instead, his pulse beat in his ears like a thousand drums being struck at once, his palms sweaty in the gloves, his mouth tacky and dry.

"All clear Captain, you're good to go."

Sarah's voice dragged him back to reality, and Thompson blinked furiously, eyelashes laden with sweat stinging his eyes. It was now or never, and never wasn't an option. Clicking his heels together, he activated his mag-boots, pushing all his weight into moving the door lock the moment they connected with the floor. It took him a minute to shift the wheel, and he supposed he should have been grateful that it didn't just turn easily and swing the door open before he was ready. Small mercies, considering what they had been through so far.

Pushing the door open, Thompson stood on the precipice of the abyss beyond, struck by the majesty of the world he lived in day by day. "You never get used to that sight, do you?" he whispered to Sarah, watching as the stars spun slowly past him as the ship continued its sickening pirouette.

"No, you don't. I need you to head to the port engine, we're going to have to shut it down manually from the panel where it connects to the ship."

"Gotcha, taking a walk."

Dragging his eyes away from the dizzying spectacle

of dancing stars, Thompson shuffled to the edge of the door, reaching round for the first rung on the side of the ship that would lead him up top, where he could continue his walk to the engine.

The going was slow; while the spin of the ship was relatively moderate, the G-forces outside felt ten times worse than they had *inside*, though it didn't help that the world was literally spiralling around him. Breathing heavily, Thompson closed his eyes for a moment, resting his helmet against the solid side of his ship, gripping the rungs tightly, glad that his mag-boots glued him in place.

"You ok, Cap?" Sarah asked over the headset, cutting through his heavy breathing.

"Yep, just needed a minute. Heads going in a different direction to the rest of me," he chuckled, forcing his reply past the sickly lump in his throat. Last thing he needed was to vomit into his helmet.

"Don't look up, concentrate on the hull, and the engine," Sarah said firmly.

"Good plan, though what the fuck do I do if there's debris flying at me I haven't seen coming?"

"Pray the mag-boots keep you on the ship, and it doesn't tear your suit. Now move."

Laughing again, Thompson nodded, exhaling wearily as he pushed on, reaching up for the next rung, shifting his weight as he continued to climb. He all but collapsed onto the top of the ship, and it took him a minute to stumble upright, arms outstretched like a scarecrow as he attempted to balance, eyes fixed on the hull and not the nothingness circling endlessly above him.

Hands balled into fists, he lifted one foot off the hull,

forcing it forward, allowing the mag-boot to connect with the metal and stick him safely back down. It was like wading through treacle. Every step was leaden and exhausting, but it assured him that he wasn't going to float off unexpectedly. Panting heavily, his vision blurred by sweat rather than the motion of the ship, Thompson let out a groan of relief as he reached the panel in question, having spent at *least* half an hour traversing the breadth of the ship, though time had no meaning to him right now. Collapsing to his knees, he punched in his code to open the latch.

"Alright Sarah, I'm here. What now?"

"Ok, there should be three switches in front of you and a crap ton of wires, yes?"

"Yep."

"You need to pull out the red wire from the top switch, press the middle switch, and then—"

Sarah's voice cut out, leaving only silence. Scowling, Thompson pressed the button for his comms, hoping it would reset and bring her back. "Sarah? You there? Sarah?"

"Captain!"

The comms burst into life, Sarah's terrified, panicked tones cutting through the oppressive silence and digging into Thompson's exhausted brain like a knife.

"Sarah? Talk to me, what's happening? What do I need to do to shut this engine down?"

"Captain, the passengers, they've left the mess hall, they've... they've—"

Whatever Sarah was trying to warn him of was lost to the cacophony of screams, shouts, and electrical buzzing in the background of the comms as chaos unleashed within the ship. Those sounds paled in comparison to what loomed in the forefront, the stomach-turning sound of choking and gurgling, as Sarah drowned in her own blood.

Thompson shut his eyes tightly, staring at the back of his eyelids as his vision went red from the pressure, his jaw clenched, aching as he ground his teeth together. He knew that sound, he'd seen enough people die that way, and the image of Sarah, collapsed against the bulkhead, hands clawing futilely against her slit throat while her blood poured across her fingers etched into his mind's-eye.

Opening his eyes, he stared at the open panel, the switches blinking at him, mocking the fact that he had no idea what order to press them in to shut off the engines. "*SHIT*!" he roared into the expanse, forcing himself upright, moving as quickly as he physically could.

The sound of his heavy breathing filled his ears, each breath stung his throat, his body aching with every movement. Thompson cursed under his breath, screaming angrily at the nothingness as he struggled to pull his boot free of the hull. Chest rising and falling rapidly, he blinked against the lightheadedness now sinking in, threatening to cause him to blackout. This was taking too long. He needed to get back to the airlock. He had to find out what was happening to his crew!

He had one option, but it wasn't a good one. Breathing slowly through his nose, Thompson steeled himself for what he had to do, his body trembling. This could end extremely badly if he didn't calculate his next move correctly. Teeth clenched together, Thompson's finger lingered over the remote button for his mag-boots. He was about to press it when movement caught his attention from the corner of his eye.

Something floated gracefully up from the side of the ship, turning in a gentle spin as it came into view, lit by the eerie silver light of the twin moons of the planet they had fled. Time stood still in that moment, and Thompson felt as empty as the eternity he stood amongst. His heart stopped, his breath hitched, and his body turned cold as he watched, in horror, as the twins floated up and away from the ship.

His jaw quivered, reaching out to the pair with a shaking hand, pointless though it was, for he could not reach them. Yuri and Anya were huddled close together, sharing one last embrace, their foreheads touching, their eyes closed, as though they had accepted this fate contentedly. Ice had formed about their bodies, glistening like tiny, deathly diamonds as they drifted off in their eternal embrace.

The twins were not alone. As Thompson stood there, frozen in his despair, other bodies joined his two first officers in the abyss of space, drifting away to join the graveyard of dead ships that lay close by. He recognised some of the corpses, not just as his crew, but some of the passengers as well. It wasn't until the terrified, screaming face of the sick boy's mother floated by that Thompson came crashing back to reality.

His top lip twitched into a snarl, and without any further hesitation, he slammed his hand onto the button, releasing his mag-boots. Bending his knees, Thompson roared with exertion as he pushed himself up and forward, arms spiralling as he attempted to control his jump as best he could. Free of the ship, he flew over the hull, but he found no joy in losing his shackles. His heart was heavy, his stomach was sick, and he had to face whatever lay within his ship if he made it back inside.

"Shit, shit, shit!" he hissed, realising he was going to overshoot the ladder. Thompson grunted, throwing his body forward and sending himself into a somersault. Cursing under his breath, Thompson grasped at the hull, hoping to find anything to grab as he found himself upside down. As he came closer to the ladder, he twisted his body, stretching out his arm as far as he could and *just* catching hold of the first rung. Panting, he relaxed a little as he continued to hover above the ship, holding onto the rung tightly.

Turning himself around, Thompson used the rungs to push himself toward the airlock door, finding it quicker than trying to walk and he didn't have the time to spare. Speeding down the ladder, he pushed himself off the hull, grabbing the airlock door and swinging himself back inside. Clicking his heels together, he reactivated his mag-boots and heaved on the door, pulling it back into place and spinning the door lock shut before lumbering over to the airlock controls, slamming his hand on the button to start the re-pressurisation.

"Come on, come on, *come on!*" he snarled as the air flooded the chamber, a slow angry hiss that was taking far too long. His ears popped as the air pressure settled, and he heard the inner door automatically unlock. Wrenching his helmet off his head, he threw it to one side, letting it roll across the floor as he shed his suit and hurried back into the ship's corridors.

The sight that met him was worse than he'd first imagined. Stumbling backward, Thompson gasped for air, trying to centre himself, and failing. Turning his head, Thompson doubled over as his stomach emptied itself of its meagre contents, bile burning his throat and his nose as his vomit splattered onto the floor with a horrifying splat.

The emergency lighting had been activated, dim red lights that cast monsters in the shadows of the simplest, most benign, objects. Panels were ripped from the interior, wires pulled from within hung loose, some were cut, sending little electrical sparks into the air as they swung back and forth like swaying snakes. Huge gouges had been left on every surface, bullet holes, and patches of black scorch marks, some of which haloed out around charred, unrecognisable, smoking corpses.

Carnage. That was the best word Thompson could think of to describe what greeted him. Bracing himself on the bulkhead, Thompson concentrated on the cold, harsh metal beneath his fingers, his body trembling, legs threatening to give out on him.

"Come out, come out, wherever you aaaare."

Thompson swallowed hard, moving back against the airlock door, pressing himself as flat as he could so that he vanished among the shadows. From his right a shadow grew, twisted in the glowing red lights, turning Hunny's silhouette into a hulking monstrosity. Thompson recognised the man's voice immediately, but he did not recognise that sadistic tone. Even in their most dire moments, when it looked like all was lost, Hunny had *never* sounded so dark and bloodthirsty.

Eyes closed, head against the airlock door, Thompson prayed that his security officer would go away, though the likelihood of that seemed slim.

"Hunny? Do you have it? Are you infected? Do you have it?!"

Jerry's panicked voice echoed through the empty corridors and Thompson's eyes grew wide, willing the man to shut up and run, rather than confront the security officer, who could easily rip Jerry in two.

"Do I fuck. Do you?" Hunny spat in return, the man's twisted shadow shuddering in the lights as Thompson leaned around the bulkhead, hoping to catch a glimpse of his crew members without being seen.

"No!" Jerry replied.

"Then why do ya look so sick, Jer?" Hunny growled. "I'm gonna deal with you, then I'm gonna find that kid an' fucking *finish* this."

"No, Hunny, don't! I'm not sick, I've not got it, Hunny, *please*!"

Thompson's stomach fell, his heart ached, as Jerry scurried away, Hunny's colossal footsteps echoing after him. Pushing away from the airlock, Thompson sprinted in the opposite direction, hoping to put as much distance between himself and Hunny as he could.

The sound of his boots against the metal flooring set his teeth on edge, he was convinced that the booming footsteps would have caught Hunny's attention, or the attention of *anyone* still alive for that matter.

Rounding a corner, he came to a halt. Eyes wide,

hand slowly reaching out, he came across Sarah's body slumped against a wall. Her throat cut deeply, her hands still clutched at the wound as though she could stop the inevitable, her shirt black where her blood had drenched it. He'd been unable to save her, to save anyone, he'd been outside trying to stop the spin, and in those few hours everything had turned to shit.

Kneeling beside his engineer, Thompson pulled her stiffening body into his arms, sobbing into her shoulder as he hugged her close. He had brought her onto this ship, if he hadn't, she would probably still be alive. His fault. All of it.

Before the despair could really sink in and rob him of what little strength he had left, the sound of metal clanged against the floor, alerting him to the presence of someone else. Slowly he placed Sarah against the wall where he'd found her. As he did, something sharp caught his hand and he automatically jolted it away. Glancing around Sarah's leg, the knife that had been used against her glistened on the floor, her blood congealing on the blade.

Picking it up, Thompson hurried quietly to the opposite wall, pressing his back against it, knife in one hand, his knuckles white as he gripped the handle. Another clang, this one much closer, and Thompson launched himself around the corner, knife extended to protect himself.

"No!"

The voice was tiny, terrified, and weak. Thompson found himself face-to-face with the young lad that had caused all of this chaos in the first place. The poor boy was a mess, covered in blood and soot, his clothes torn. He'd thrown his arms over his face when Thompson appeared, and even now he didn't look up. Lowering the knife, Thompson stared at the boy in disbelief, he'd heard what Hunny had said, but it hadn't registered what he'd meant until now. *How* had the boy survived this when so many others had died?

"Hey, hey it's okay, I won't hurt you," Thompson said, holding up his hands as he knelt down slowly, putting the knife on the floor. "I promise, you're safe with me. What's your name?"

"Jenson," the little lad whimpered, peering at Thompson from between his fingers. "You're the captain, right?"

"That's right, this is my ship."

"You said you would protect us, but when they came, no one could find you. You promised, but they spaced my mama and I can't find my daddy anywhere," Jenson sobbed, stamping his foot, lip trembling as he stared at Thompson almost defiantly. Unfortunately, that defiance was short-lived as he turned his head and vomited against the wall. "I'm not infected, I'm sick, I was sick before," he added, wiping his mouth with the back of his hand. "But other people started getting sick too, so they blamed me, said I had the infection, but I don't."

"I believe you, Jenson, and I'm sorry I wasn't here. I was outside, trying to fix the ship. The others have gotten sick because the ship is spinning, and I was trying to stop it from doing that."

"To stop them getting sick?"

"Yes, and to stop them from blaming you. I believed

your father when he said you were ill for another reason, and I still believe him. I knew the spinning would make other people sick, that's why I had to go outside, to stop it, but I couldn't get there in time and they killed my friend."

"They've killed everyone, or most people, anyway. They came looking for me and my family, my daddy grabbed me and ran, but we lost mama when we were running, and then we heard her screaming as they shoved her outside with the other people who started being sick. Some of your crew were spaced, too."

"I know, I saw them while I was outside," Thompson replied darkly, retrieving the knife as he stood up, shoving it into his belt to keep it close. "We need to get to the bridge, it has the strongest doors. We can get there and hide until help comes," he added, holding his hand out to the boy.

"*Will* there be any help?" Jenson asked, taking Thompson's offered hand.

"Yes, there were distress calls sent out. It may take some time, but someone will come for us." They just had to avoid being seen by Hunny, or any of the other survivors—if there were any more—get to the bridge and lock themselves in. There were emergency rations stashed in the bridge in case of piracy. If they had to lock the doors they were prepared to wait out an inside attack, so they wouldn't have to worry about starving at least.

"No one's comin' Captain, an' even if they do, you won't see 'em arrive, nor will that boy. Now hand 'im over."

Thompson spun round, whipping Jenson behind

him, shielding the boy with his body. "Hunny. There's still time to stop this, he's not infected. When help comes we can *still* get off this ship alive. We can explain what happened here, the passengers lost their minds and incited hysteria amongst the rest of the crew. We can still get out of here." He didn't plead, he knew begging the man was pointless, he had to reason with him. If he could.

Hunny shook his head, stepping out of the darkness, the blood-red light highlighting his gaunt face, his eyes wide and mad. Thompson barely recognised his security officer, a man usually stern-faced but calm. Now he was faced with a manic monster, who had clearly lost all hope, adrift in the vastness of space, and been driven mad because of it.

"Nah, too late for that. We're all infected Cap, we've all got to die, especially him, he brought it here, he started all o' this." Hunny thrust a hand forward, and something swung in his outstretched hand, rocking back and forth upon the hair clutched in the man's fingers.

It took Thompson a minute to recognise that Hunny was holding a head, sinews dangling from the jagged wound where it had been torn from its body, blood dripping every now and then onto the man's boot. The head slowly turned to face Thompson, eyes closed, mouth frozen in an eternal scream. He barely recognised the black and blue, battered face, with its puffy eyes, but Jenson did.

Instinct took hold of Thompson as he grabbed the boy about his shoulders, pulling him close and holding him tightly as Jenson struggled against his embrace, desperate to run towards Hunny and the head, screaming hysterically and retching as his body fought against him. It wasn't until the shrill wail of '*Daaaddyyyyy*' that everything fell into place for Thompson. His body felt numb, but he didn't loosen his grip on Jenson. If he did the boy would be dead, and he refused to lose anyone else.

Thompson's eyes darted from the head to meet Hunny's as the man's lips pulled back from his teeth in a sadistic smile. Hunny cast the head aside, letting it bounce off the bulkhead with a sickening 'thunk.' Before it had rebounded off the floor, Thompson swept Jenson up over his shoulder, turned on the ball of his foot, and belted down the corridor.

There was a deafening bang, as a gunshot exploded from behind him, and something hard struck him in his side, the area stinging as though a wasp had found its way under his shirt. He didn't dare stop, even as he felt a wet patch spreading across his clothing, making it stick to his skin as he ran. He didn't have time to stop, he had to get to the bridge, he had to get Jenson somewhere safe.

Nothing mattered anymore, nothing really registered. Thompson's pulse filled his ears, blocking out any sound of Hunny's pursuit, or any protests Jenson may have been making as the captain carried him off over his shoulder. The sights he had seen had left him numb already, so whatever pain he should be suffering from the injury he'd just sustained were blissfully kept at bay, allowing him to move unhindered.

Sprinting around the last corner that led toward the bridge, Thompson's foot gave out and he and Jenson were sent spinning into the floor. Thompson landed hard, jolting his back and igniting a cold fire up his spine that snatched his breath from his throat and left him dizzy. A shaking hand reached behind to tentatively touch the wet patch on his back, and he flinched as the wasp sting flared into life, revealing itself to be a gunshot wound. He'd known, somewhere, in the back of his mind, but hadn't wanted to admit it was that.

"Jenson?" he wheezed, struggling to his feet, his entire body begging him to stop.

"I'm here, that big man was shooting at us," the lad whimpered as he crawled towards Thompson, staring over his shoulder.

"I know, he'll be coming. I need you to run down this corridor to the bridge and hide there. Under the captain's seat there's a panel. You should be small enough to crawl into it and hide there. Don't come out unless it's me, or a rescue crew, okay?"

Jenson nodded, eyes filled with tears as he hurried to his feet and ran quietly in the direction he'd been instructed. Thompson watched the boy go, using the wall to stagger to his feet. He would need to stall Hunny or stop him entirely if they were going to be safe. He would need time to get the computer to close the bulkhead doors—or do them manually if it wasn't feeling cooperative.

Panting heavily, Thompson leaned against the wall, his hand resting against the butt of the gun Anya had forced him to take earlier. Anya. Her face would haunt him until his last breath, as would the image of her frozen embrace with her twin as they disappeared into

DEATH BEYOND

space to join the stars they had loved so dearly. His jaw quivered, and he allowed himself a brief second to close his eyes and mourn the loss of his friends, his family, and his ship, tears running down his cheeks as he opened his eyes, gun held at his side, waiting for Hunny.

He didn't have to wait long. His pulse had slowed now he had stopped running, and he could hear the man's footsteps cautiously approaching, knowing his captain wouldn't go down without a fight—they had been together long enough to know that neither man would go quietly.

"Hunny! This is your last chance! Stand down, hole up somewhere until rescue crews arrive, or I *will* shoot you."

"Thanks for the warnin' Cap, but you ain't got the balls. This is where *The Nightingale* goes to sleep permanently. There's only us an' the kid left, I made sure of that. You know what that infection can do. We can't let any of us off this ship."

"For God's *sake,* Hunny, he doesn't have it! Why can you not see that the motion of the ship is what made everyone else ill? I was trying to fix the engines when you and the passengers ran riot through my ship and killed Sarah. I was saving us!"

"You left us all here! With no one to guide us!" Hunny spat back, a knife wound in Thompson's heart that hurt more than the bullet wound in his back.

"I was trying to save us," Thompson replied, shuffling sideways, hoping to catch Hunny off guard and shoot him before the man could get a shot off himself.

"Too late, Cap, we're already dead."

DEATH BEYOND

Another gunshot rang out, whizzing past Thompson's face, grazing his cheek, and hitting the wall behind him. Without hesitation, he let off a shot of his own, satisfied when he heard a grunt from the other man. He'd clearly hit him, but that wasn't enough. Like a rhino charging at a predator, Hunny came at him. Head down with all the force he could muster, slamming into Thompson and knocking the wind from his lungs as they collided with the wall.

Thompson's ears rang, and the impact of his head on the wall sent his vision spinning, not to mention the fact that Hunny's humongous hands were around his windpipe. Gasping for air against the gargantuan man, Thompson punched and kicked at him as best he could, to no avail. Reaching up, he dug his thumbs deep into Hunny's eyes, swallowing the bile rising in his throat at the squish of his old friend's eyeballs, and the screams of pain that followed it.

The right one popped, blood pouring from the wound hot and sticky across Thompson's hand, but before the left one went, Hunny threw back his head, bringing it forward again swiftly. As their foreheads connected, Thompson's legs gave out beneath him and he vomited from the pain, a saving grace that caused Hunny to leap away from him out of fear. He couldn't hesitate, he had no time to. Grabbing the knife from his belt, gasping for breath, and forcing his lungs to fill with air despite the ache in his throat, Thompson threw himself at his friend, jamming the knife into Hunny's shoulder by his neck. Just as the gun went off in his stomach.

Hands trembling, Thompson did not let go of the

knife, dragging his weight against it to cut down and deepen the wound, ignoring the fire in his stomach, and that nauseating wet feeling spreading down his legs. Hunny's knees gave way beneath him and still, Thompson did not let go, his hands slick with blood, his fingers slipping on the handle. He only let go when Hunny fell backward, his eyes rolled back, his breathing stopped.

Slumped forward, shoulders hunched, Thompson pressed a hand to his flowing belly wound, knowing he could do nothing to stop it. He compelled his body to keep moving, making his feet move one in front of the other, stumbling into the bridge, and closing the door behind him manually. It would only open again from the inside if the code was entered.

"Jenson?" Thompson called out croakily, reaching out for the back of the captain's chair to hold himself up, a trail of bloody footprints behind him.

"Captain?" The tiny voice replied from his feet, and Thompson was glad to see the boy's dirty face peering up at him from beneath the chair.

"It's alright now, he's gone, you're safe. I need you to do something for me."

"You're dying, aren't you?" Jenson whimpered.

"I am, but that doesn't matter, help will be here soon. There's food under the console on the right, and you've seen some under my chair, too. That will last you for two months, not that it will be that long. To open the door, you have to put in a code, can you remember it if I tell you?"

"I think so," the boy muttered.

"Here, I'll write it down, too. Can you read?"

"I can read!" Jenson replied, almost enthusiastically, his tone so filled with joy at this accomplishment that Thompson felt lighter than he had in days.

"Good, I'll write it on this wall, so that when help comes you can get out of this room."

Dipping his fingers in his own blood, Thompson wrote the code onto the wall. Once he was finished, he stumbled back into his seat, collapsing into it with a sigh, staring at the numbers and letters and realising how terribly morbid his last written word was. "You'll be safe here, the computer will keep the ship going, I'm sorry I couldn't stop it from spinning."

"That's okay," Jenson muttered.

Thompson closed his eyes, taking a deep, shuddering breath as the feeling drained from his feet, up his legs. He barely felt Jenson climb onto his lap. The pain was gone, replaced with that empty feeling that was slowly creeping up his body. He opened one eye, looking at the boy hugging him tightly, lip quivering as the last remaining *living* connection he had drifted away. Thompson wrapped his arms around the boy, hugging him as tightly as he could as his head became fuzzy, his vision filled with the stars that waited to claim his soul.

In his last moments, the computer sparked into life, and a tear ran down Thompson's cheek at the computer's final announcement before his consciousness faded completely.

"Ana... analy... analysis complete. Samples analysed. No infec... infec... infection detected. All clear. All clear. All clear. *All clear...*"

DEATH BEYOND

Lyndsey Ellis-Holloway is a writer from a mysterious little town in the UK famous for having its own witch. She spends most of her time in the dark recesses of her mind. Specialising in fantasy, sci-fi, horror, and dystopian stories, she focuses on compelling characters and layering in myth and legend at every opportunity.

Her mind is dark and twisted, and she lives in perpetual hope of owning her own Dragon someday, but for now, she writes about them to fill the void… and to stop her from murdering people who annoy her.

When she's not writing she spends time with her husband, her dogs, and her friends enjoying activities such as walking, movies, conventions, and of course writing for fun as well!

https://theprose.com/LyndseyEH
Twitter: @LEllisHolloway
https://www.facebook.com/groups/199284024728104
https://www.facebook.com/Lyndsey-Ellis-Holloway-Author-102383921610775

DEATH BEYOND

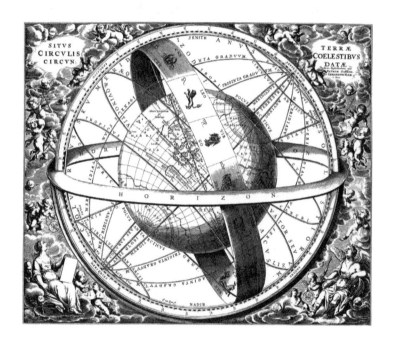

DEATH BEYOND

THE DREAMS OF THRAIC

Chris Hewitt

I slept for an eternity and in my slumber dreamt I soared between the stars. A golden condor, I rode the solar winds, a seeker in the void. But as with all dreams, come the dawn, the illusion faded, replaced by a nightmare of drowning in darkness.

With talons, not mine, I tear at the gelatinous ichor, working myself free, until, with one last push, I slide wet and writhing onto a blood-slick floor. Reborn, I convulse as liquid-filled lungs gasp and wheeze in memory of this body's demands and in my agony, I cry out. The only name I'd ever known. "Arke!"

We're here. Just breathe.

The thought is mine, and yet not mine, not anymore.

Deep breaths. It will all come back to you.

My nausea racked frame spasms as this long-forgotten flesh reclaims me. "Why, Arke?"

I'm sorry. We had to decouple you.

"Decouple me?"

DEATH BEYOND

What a hopelessly inadequate word. I wasn't unplugged but ripped between realities. One minute, a biological ark ship, the next, this; a butterfly squished back into a caterpillar. All memories of that form's freedom fade, and the sense of loss is overwhelming.

I scrabble on unsteady legs, slipping and sliding across Arke's moist membranes. The protective scales fall from my eyes, and in the dim scarlet glow of bioluminescent arteries, the guts of my condor dream are laid bare. Overhead, the spine of the mighty behemoth stretches into the distance, thinly veiled vertebrae forming the central transverse cavity that runs the length of the ship. Pulses of blue light crackle along nerve conduits, vanishing far beyond Arke's arching backbone.

It's okay. We're still with you.

With me, yes, but not me. I'm diminished, staring at unfamiliar trembling fingers; three long talon tipped digits dance as I familiarise myself with this body. In the background, the ruptured carbuncle I erupted from gurgles and oozes.

We're still connected. You're still part of us.

Arke's right, I still feel them. Beyond this frail physical form, I sense wings, no longer mine. Real-time neural feeds tell me of feathery biopolymer filaments catching photons. No substitute for feeling the warmth of a distant sun. I wipe the nutrient gel from my face and exhale a long, rattling breath. "Why did you decouple me?"

You and me; already our shared consciousness slips as I stand naked and shivering in the gloom.

There's an infection, a Terran spore.

DEATH BEYOND

The thought comes burdened with fear, and I dive into Arke's telemetry. Amongst the streams of data flooding my mind, I find the corruption, feel it spreading through the ship's lymphatic system as the bioware maps the sensation to a prickling rash that rakes my abdomen. I run a talon across the filigree of raised, angry red veins. We're still connected, me and Arke, and I share their fear. "What do you need me to do?"

There's no response. "Arke?"

We need you to run.

"What?"

Run!

The thought howls through me, a banshee's scream that ignites adrenal glands as the gash I crawled from erupts with a torrent of bubbling yellow pus. A tsunami of slime that drags me away. I race past corrupted pustules, the dreaming occupants already lost to the infection.

Hold on. We've got you.

I'm drowning, tumbling over and under, fingers grasping, only to find others dragged along in the current. An arm, a leg, sometimes attached, more often not, so many bodies, slithering and slapping against each other.

Three seconds.

It is an eternity longer than any multi-millennial hyper-sleep; Arke's reassurances my only lifeline. The wave crashes, depositing an army of rotting bodies, reuniting me with my crew.

"Arke, help! I can't…"

I'm buried under my fetid shipmates, a stifling,

pressing weight.

Brace yourself.

Before I can question, I'm tumbling towards the ceiling along with my brethren, their bodies cushioning my break-neck fall. Disoriented, I stare up at the floor, unwilling to acknowledge my bed of twitching limbs. Hard to ignore is the gut-wrenching fetor of death and I retch as Arke's telemetry reports the acceleration pinning me to the ceiling is unsustainable. Arms and legs, my own included, rise; marionettes one and all; gravity, our master. I groan as my stomach flips and I float into the air.

You need to keep moving.

"Arke, what the hell is going on?" I cry, pulling and pushing myself from corpse to corpse as the crew slumps back to the floor. I'm desperate to be out from under the throng before I'm reburied.

We're still analysing. The infection is widespread. Terran's have mined the system with spores.

"How did it get this bad?"

The infection has targeted our immune system. By the time we started decoupling, it was too late.

Now I understand why my shipmates vanished from Arke's shared consciousness. A bloated, milky eyed corpse floats past. The grinning face of my brood brother burns itself into my synapses as I recall our warm nest, a willing tourist in happier memories. Anything to escape this nightmare.

Thraic.

The voice is distant, filled with the promise of pain, but I can't ignore it.

DEATH BEYOND

Thraic!

"Arke. They're dead, they're all dead."

Not all. Not yet. You must keep moving.

Arke's insistence pushes me on, and I ease the swollen cadaver aside. "I'm sorry, brother."

A slow somersault and I land, glancing back at the bodies stacked against the bulging sphincter—the ring of muscle, all that holds back the infection. I can't count the number of friends laid at my feet, and I don't need to. My ever-helpful bioware offers up forty-two along with each person's profile; an army of ghosts begging for acknowledgment. A shake of my head and they vanish, unlike their corrupted bodies.

Breath, Thraic.

I hadn't realised I'd stopped. My body gasps down the sickening stench and I manage three breaths before being thrown against a bony bulkhead. My crewmates lurch towards me with the violence of the impact, forcing me to clamber away. "What is it now?"

The answer is an invisible blade plunged into my side as my bioware performs a mockery of synaesthesia and I clutch at the spreading rash licking my ribs. "Arke!"

Explosive decompression along the left radial keel support. We are haemorrhaging plasma.

I ball my hands into fists, talons digging into my palm. I've had enough of being on the back foot. Nerve signals flash overhead as I race towards the cortex. Translucent healthy capsules pock the walls, and I take solace in running my fingers across the pods of uncorrupted bodies; all the while envying their slumber. My bioware reports eighty-two-thousand-seven hundred and forty-six souls forming Arke's consciousness as a crimson flash of static snakes past. The pulsing signal speeds away and registers as an update in my telemetry; forty-six becoming forty-five. With my mind and this body meshing, I pick up my pace.

I'm panting hard by the time I reach the medulla oblongata and look back to see a myriad of red impulses crackling overhead. Now more than ever, I wish they were nameless as more phantoms cram the periphery of my thoughts. The blade twists in my side, stealing my breath, as the yellow torrent surges towards me; angry electric horses ride ahead of the wave, heralds of death.

"Arke!"

I turn and crouch as another sphincter of flesh slides shuts behind me; it won't stop the electrical storm that rolls past as eight thousand-three-hundred and twenty-eight souls cry out to me. The itching rash creeps up my thorax.

We can't stop the infection's progress, only slow it.

"Decouple more of us, we can find…"

There's no time. This is the last barrier between the infection and our higher functions. It is unlikely to survive any longer than the last.

"But…"

You're wasting time. You know what must be done. We must survive.

I know they're right, but abandoning Arke is a betrayal of my friends, my people, and our mission. "It cannot end like this; we've come too far; made too many sacrifices."

DEATH BEYOND

That is why you must keep running, Thraic.

The remaining souls urge me onwards towards a cluster of purple polyps. A wave of my hand and the husk folds back, revealing a nest of biots. I catch one of the squirming insects and place it on the nape of my neck. Spindly legs wrap around my throat as its probing tendrils interface with my bioware. The creature links with my mind and body, acknowledging its eager availability as it takes payment from my carotid artery.

First things first, this body needs protection. With just the thought, an icy shiver slithers down my back as the biot stretches, wrapping me in a silky epidermis; a second skin more familiar than my own. The covering is as tough as it is tight, a welcome hug reminiscent of my hyper-sleep pod. Only my face remains uncovered, framed by the creature's long forelegs.

Hurry. The transfer is nearly complete.

Augmented by the biot's nano-fibres, this body moves with power and purpose, climbing the narrow access stem leading to Arke's brain. The walls here shimmer with neural activity funnelled towards the cortex. I run a trembling hand across the pink folds; to think, all that we are exists within this delicate flesh.

We are ready.

"I won't fail, Arke."

We know.

Thrusting my hand into the gelatinous contours, my talons tear through warm tissue until they wrap around something hard and smooth. I pull the glowing pearl free, and the colour drains from the dying cortex. Arke is dead, only this seed remains. My ears pop and a rumble announces the infection has breached the last barrier. I cram the precious gem into my mouth as the biot's forelegs slide over my face, stretching a transparent membrane tight over my features. The arriving corruption turns my world to sickly sepia, but this time I have the strength to hold my ground.

Resolute, unmoving, I wait for death. The rapid decomposition of the ark ship spreads through every fibre, and I'm thankful I no longer feel its progress. Although I'd welcome any distraction from my crippling grief. My beautiful soaring condor, my kin, all gone, more victims of the relentless Terran.

The pearl is warm in my mouth, sour, but not as bitter as my hatred for those that hunt us. I'm tired of running. We've run forever and they do not stop. An eternity in the void, testament to that failed strategy. I swallow the acerbic pill, feeling it slide down my gullet.

I wait, another lamb to the slaughter. Once our civilisation stretched across this galaxy and I communed with a billion souls. Now I stand here, the last of my kind, buried in a biological tomb, and I am done running.

A procession of muted explosions herald death's arrival and I close my eyes as I'm torn, flesh in hand, down endless passageways. Soft walls and ablative biot skin, my only protection as I hurtle past Arke's shattered spine. The behemoth's convulsing death throes have ripped flesh from bone, and I'm sucked out into the void in a fountain of pus and festering body parts.

A thousand dead ark ships fill the night sky, many trailing their vital fluids and occupants in their wake. It is a graveyard, a necropolis for a fallen civilisation. If

I'm to avoid joining them, I have one chance for survival. The icy vacuum bites hard as I stretch out an arm to point towards Arke's carcass, falling away below me, and command the biot to expel a handful of nano-filaments.

The fibres twist from my fingers into a single strand that stretches across the gap; even as the toxic soup surrounding me freezes. Physics conspires against me, and there is scant thread to bridge the ever-widening gap. At the end of my tether, I instruct the biot to unravel and the insectoid harvests its protective skin, feet first. The agony of ice has me screaming into the unsympathetic void as millimetre-by-millimetre pain creeps up my shins—outstretched fingers, straining, desperate to reach across the distance. Only my rage keeps the brutal cold at bay as the reclaimed thread inches towards the target.

With a jarring wrench and a crack, felt not heard, I'm hurtling through space, landing hard against Arke's mottled carapace. I try to direct the biot, but agony is interfering, the ice creeping past my knees. With single-minded focus, I compose myself and the biot responds, reweaving its second skin around my cold-cauterised stumps. I stare up at my feet disappearing into the night, encased in a pallid comet; two more body parts frozen in a legion of limbs.

Through sticky finger pads, I can feel Arke's continuing disintegration, internal processes breaking down in a series of detonations. It spurs me on. I don't need feet to pull myself along the hull, augmented biot gifted foot-long talons will suffice. New ruptures spew forth their poison into the frigid void as I push and pull myself

DEATH BEYOND

from plate to plate. Time is running out. The biot warns of the dangers of impending suffocation, and I ignore its warning, speed more crucial than fabricating filters. The world is a blur as I glide along the behemoth's endless husk. A spasm rolls along the disintegrating carcass, ricocheting me off the ship's armour plating in an explosion of sparks. The biot re-knits and rewires its protection, but not without complaint. Sympathy is all I can offer as I dance around debris; thanking my stars that it's no one I know.

I can see the end now. Inky black darkness beckons as I approach Arke's stern, and my heart sinks.

"It's not here. Where is it? It should be here."

The biot senses my despair and manipulates the mask like a lens to magnify my vision. In the void, I see a speck of hope; the ejected life pod seems as distant as any twinkling star. I can only pray it is untouched by the Terran spores as I launch myself into the expanse. As I fall through the darkness, oxygen fails as the biot struggles to keep this fragile form alive. "One more minute."

The biot understands, as I dive into the gelatinous bubble that is the life pod; a sperm fertilising an egg as the biot releases its grip, its life the price of my survival. I will follow it into oblivion, but not before I regurgitate my prize. The pearl sinks into the cytoplasm, unleashing a tempest. An electrical storm that divides and subdivides the cell, over and over, driven by the memory of a fallen civilisation; my people, the Thraic.

Barely conscious, I float through the graveyard of dead behemoths into the endless void, while the ghosts of my dead civilisation direct the division of the life pod.

DEATH BEYOND

We have a chance now, Thraic.

"Not if we keep running. There's no place left to hide. We must…"

Evolve! We understand. Sleep now.

My work done; I welcome oblivion.

I slept for an eternity and in my slumber dreamt I drifted through the night, my dark heart a singularity of wrath, a bottomless pit that grew deeper with every cell division until even space and time bent to my will. In my dream, the shades of my past fashioned a future from the ashes of a dying star, and I arose a golden phoenix, a vessel of vengeance, the hunter in the void.

It's time, Thraic.

The name was mine—is mine—and my consciousness gravitates around the memory of the entity I once was, the thing I could be again. "Time?"

Yes, it is your time.

I open my eyes and stretch. I'm fractured, split between realities. In one body, my arms, long and familiar, stretch. In the other, enormous powerful wings, mirrored feathers shimmering, cleave the night. I wave my limbs, absorbing my bizarre duality.

"I…" Even the word confuses me. "Am what? Where?"

You are here, at the crossroads, Thraic.

"The crossroads?"

The parting of the ways. Our past and your future.

"But…"

You are all that remains of us now. Trust that we

have given you the tools you need to survive. Use them wisely.

The thoughts of my people fade.

"But what will I do?"

Survive, Thraic. Use the tools we've given you and live.

A silence like a hammer fall reverberates through my mind, and I reach out to grasp a remnant of their passing. But they slip through my fingers. For the first time, I'm alone, and the thought terrifies me. Where once there was sage council, only a blazing crucible of anger remains. Enraged, I roar, a primal howl that echoes around the darkened chamber as it ripples through the void beyond. Clambering from the fleshy pod on regenerated legs, I beat my fists against the arching transparent canopy, a furious fleck in the eye of this biological titan.

This vessel is no ark, no refuge. The form is sleek, powerful, and empty. Almost. I turn at the sound of skittering, and a shadow lunges for my throat. Spindly limbs hug my grinning face as the biot interfaces into my bioware and our relief intertwines. We are not alone. An army of biots crawl from every crevice; the cloned crew of this vessel of the damned.

The biot alerts me to two new stars sailing across the firmament. This phoenix has the eyes of a predator, giant bio-engineered ocular sensors that home in on the approaching metallic vessels as they slingshot around the binary stars that lay at the heart of this system.

"Terrans!"

The word is a curse, and a battle cry, as I watch white-hot jets of plasma propel the enemy towards me.

DEATH BEYOND

Even at this distance, I feel their touch; subtle electromagnetic waves skittering across my skin, probing, searching for weakness. A moment later, the Terran vessels unleash a multitude of splinters; projectiles that push towards me on their own fiery tails. The night is a riot of stars, familiar and unfamiliar.

"The path is chosen for us."

I flare my wings, the edges of the feathers gripping the void as I launch myself into the fray. This phoenix form is designed for such extreme manoeuvres, my bipedal body is not and is crushed into the back wall of the chamber. The impact winds me as a swarm of biots drag my battered body into a pod. Amber plasma fills the snug space, warm and familiar.

The projectiles close, forcing me to dive out of their path. The g-force wracks my prone body until the amber liquid hardens, cocooning this fragile form. Now I can soar, free to explore the capabilities of this gift. I feel each feather, their glinting edges catching the fabric of space, if only for a moment; tiny hooks that allow me to glide over the tapestry of the universe. Even in the vacuum there are threads, strands that create a cosmic fabric. A web that ripples with the explosions of three Terran splinters. Twisting, I ride the shock waves. The other projectiles remain in pursuit but are no match for my agility. One after another, they too detonate as I weave my way towards the Terran war machines.

I understand now. I am a conduit, channelling the rage of a dead civilisation into this, their instrument of revenge. The darkened heart of a star beats within this chest, confined only by a singularity of purpose.

DEATH BEYOND

The Terran dreadnaughts set the night ablaze; white-hot beams that dance across my plumage, only for their energies to scatter like sunbeams on a pond. I adjust the geometry of my feathers, reflecting the beams back to their source. A dozen explosions shake the Terran crafts; their searchlights extinguished.

My quarry fights on, launching ten thousand shards into my path. But I have little thought for such shrapnel as my talons tear through the metal carapace of the first Terran ship. With six monstrous talons, I rip a long, jagged gash along the vessel's side and bodies, not unlike my own fragile form, spill forth into the vacuum.

That's when I see them; a myriad of fleas jumping ship as my biot army descends on the wounded ship. I push forward to the next. The remaining Terran vessel is running, its crude plasma propulsion a supernova in the night sky. It tugs and tears at my web, ripping a hole in space. I let the Terrans reach their portal before striking, tearing the vessel asunder. The bow falls into the collapsing wormhole as the stern tumbles and explodes. I ride that wave back to my crippled prey and find the biots infesting the stricken vessel. They have little regard for biological or mechanical contrivances, and a multicolour rainbow of frozen liquids spew into the night.

The lights of the dying craft flicker as escape pods detach. Biots are quick to spot the movement, leaping across the void to attack each capsule, spilling the flailing Terran's occupants. They take a cruel delight in removing the enemy helmets. The last pod is crawling with biots before it can even launch.

"Wait. I want this one."

DEATH BEYOND

The interfacing biot relays my orders to the unhappy insectoids and they fall from the escaping capsule; all bar one that crawls into a space between the igniting plasma jets. The pod accelerates away, and I watch its slow progress as the biots dissect their spoils.

There is little left of the wrecked Terran ship or its crew as I wait for the biots to complete their harvest. I feel much of their recovered bounty heavy in my gullet as digestion processes separate the wheat from the chaff. The biots toss anything not used into the singularity, and I can't but wonder if that pit might ever fill.

The last biots clamber aboard and I set course for the escaped pod, now orbiting a distant blue-green opal. I have time to stretch my legs, feed, and explore myself, a mote within this colossal body. My duality still perplexes me. I've existed in many forms in my time, but never simultaneously. I struggle to understand the purpose of this schism and fear I'm a mistake. Am I a corruption of my intended purpose?

This vessel is vast. It would be easy to get lost but for my bioware overlaying endless schematics. I tour familiar bio-engineering constructs, all with the telltale fingerprints of my species' technological mastery, and yet all are different. This is the first and last Thraic warship and the only vessel powered by a dead star. It is the swan song of a civilisation of dreamers and artists, but it is no dusty mausoleum; this flesh has a purpose.

I step into one of the many biot cavities that run the length of the vessel; every surface covered by the nest-ing insectoids, many sporting bloody badges of victory. At my feet, hatchlings replace the handful of fallen, each bred to protect their home, to protect me. Just as I am fashioned to protect them; a timeless symbiotic pact that goes back a thousand generations.

The biot around my neck drops to the floor to assist its young's tentative first steps. Another takes over interfacing duties, wrapping itself around my throat as it lets out a shrill warbling tune. Every biot in the chamber turns to face me, waving their long legs in a rhythmic dance as they create a symphony of sound. I close my eyes, finding comfort in their song even as I spy my quarry making planet fall, half a system away.

Any fears I have for spores are unfounded. The system is clear, their cruel traps long since dust, and only now do I comprehend how long I've slept. The Terrans would not have encountered my kind for aeons; I am likely nothing more than a legend.

Amber nectar hardens around me as I decelerate into a high orbit around an azure marble of a world. The planet would be beautiful, pristine, if not for a peninsular of Terran infected land. This colony must mark the extent of the Terran's empire; a bauble spinning around the last system of a vast spiral arm. It is a line in the sand, a marker, and the reason my long slumber has been broken.

Pollution hangs thick above the sprawling outpost of grey boxes; always such primitive, unnatural forms. Geometry screaming of the Terran's disdain for nature.

DEATH BEYOND

I fold back my wings and plunge into the clouds. As the first wisps of atmosphere heat my feathers, biots emerge to weave their protection. Thousands of the creatures spin a silky armour that glows orange as they stand atop of each other, overlapping to fortify the glowing heat shield. Wings that have only ever known vacuum stretch out in remembrance of their ancestry, adapting to maximise lift as I slow to land in the shallow turquoise waters of a sweeping bay.

I stand tall, magnificent, truly a phoenix as I extend my flaming wings to the heavens; fragments of burning biot weaved skin falls, hissing into the waters. The colony is a hive of activity and the tiny Terrans flee as I wade onto the beach. Hungry, smouldering biots scamper ahead of me, an unstoppable wave that overruns the enemy before they can mount any defence. What the biots don't claim, I crush underfoot as fury overwhelms me and I set to levelling the outpost with beak and claw.

A sudden panic of biots stays my anger and scanning the chaos I find the cause. On the far side of the outpost an enclave of Terrans is slaughtering my army in number; twisted, twitching insect bodies piling high. A sacrificial biot uploads a data sample and my bioware analyses the chemical and biological composition. It confirms my fears. I am far from forgotten. The Terrans still stockpile the spore toxin that destroyed the last fleeing arks.

Use the tools we've given you.

The words of my kind come flooding back and with them memories of every death. I launch myself from my pod before the amber liquid can evacuate, and still wet, I stride across the command chamber. My interfaced biot wraps its silky skin around my damp body, adapting the soles of my feet to grip as I reach the exit. All the while, my bioware searches for a cure. None of the Thraic arks found an antidote to this potent poison. If I fail too, my crusade will end before it begins.

I launch myself through the aperture, falling from my phoenix form. The wind rushes past my ears as the ground races towards me and at the last my biot unfurls long threads that billows like a cape to slow my fall. I land in the middle of a burning compound. Above me, my other self towers above me, eclipsing the midday suns. Waiting.

Biots scurry as I walk from the compound to a long avenue that intersects with the last of the Terran's defences. Here and there, skirmishes erupt onto the street as Terran stragglers fight hand to hand with biots. A fruitless task, as I watch one of my army eviscerate a Terran soldier, its head rolling to my feet. I step over the turmoil. My only concern, a cure for the toxin.

A Terran female stands in a doorway, a child clutched to her chest as she watches me pass and I pay her no mind, or her screams as my biots find her. It's a scene played out across the settlement. I see it all thanks to my phoenix's keen eyesight and feel it through bragging biot telemetry. But for every tortured Terran screaming for mercy, I see a dozen of my brethren liquified by their terrible poison. Justice and vengeance demand that I balance the scales.

I near the wall of decomposing biots, each skewered by a poison tipped dart dissolving their organs. The soldiers cowering amongst the debris see me and fire their weapons. A hail of darts flies towards me, and I do not move, as each is deftly caught by a willing biot bodyguard. My army swarms around me, a tornado of teeth and claw. No flechette will touch me, except the one I want. In the next volley, a single dart is allowed to pass, striking me in the thorax and injecting its fatal payload. The biots flock to me as I fall to the floor writhing, the poison already searing through my veins.

Use the tools we've given you.

The words again, but now I think I understand them. I see every Thraic death, millions in their pods writhing just as I do. Arke's last gambit, each pod an experiment to find a cure. A last ditched sacrifice mirrored across the fleet, millions of souls sacrificed to find an antidote, a solution, anything to counter the Terran plague. I am that cure. This body harbours the hard-earned knowledge, encoded in my DNA. I am every Thraic, feel every death, moving to the next and the next as I relive the genocide of my race. Throughout my body, cells replicate and mutate, only to die as I seek to complete the ark ship's research before this body succumbs to the infection.

Biots protect me from the Terran as, sensing weakness, they push their attack until I'm buried under a hill of insectoid corpses. Close to death, with genetic memory all but exhausted, the toxin falters. Amongst billions of necrotising cells, a single mutation survives, one cell in near infinity. The cure. I have tools, organs designed for this moment, biological processes already replicate the antidote. Within a minute my bloodstream is a medicinal soup of antibodies as the first biot digs into my veins to receive the cure. The insectoids will replicate the antidote between them, the word of my cure spreading, mouth to mouth.

The inoculated biots rally, overrunning the Terrans. They eviscerate every living thing as I clamber to my feet and pull the Terran dart from my chest. I walk back through the outpost, my phoenix wings fanning raging wildfires, and long before the suns' set, this Terran blight is ash.

My crusade for vengeance begins.

I remember that day, the dawn of my crusade, like it was yesterday. That night I'd strolled the golden sandy beach as my phoenix form brooded over a graveyard of cinders. I thought myself alone until I looked up into the rippling night sky at the arrival of a Terran armada. Come the dawn they too burned, a ring of bones encircling a far-flung world.

Now, a hundred years and hundred worlds later, on the last day of my crusade, I walk another sandy beach and look up at another fractured sky, knowing that no Terran vessels hide within the night; I've made sure of that. I found justice for my kind.

But at what price?

A trail of dead and dying biots leads back to my scarred and broken phoenix body, sitting atop the ruins of the last Terran city. A fitting funeral pyre for my retribution. The singularity of blazing fury that was my heart is quenched, that bottomless well, filled. I have no more rage, no anger left as I fall to my knees, staring across an ocean of blood.

Thunder echoes in my ears as the biot keeping my battle-worn body alive slips its bonds and I collapse onto the cool sand. My world turns to darkness and I welcome oblivion, my familiar friend.

I slept for an eternity and in my slumber dreamt I blazed across the stars. A vengeful phoenix, I rode the winds of war, the hunter in the void. But as with all dreams, come the dawn, the illusion faded, replaced by the face of a Terran child.

The visage shocks me from my stupor, and I throw the creature across the sand as searing pain rips through my thorax. I grasp at the crude bandage wrapping my wound. The female creature stares at me terrified; the only expression I've ever seen on Terran faces. I try to speak; sounds I've heard but never made. They're too loud, guttural, and the child scurries back brandishing a crude weapon.

I hold up my hands. "Wait!"

The creature tilts its head, scrutinising me as its eyes search mine; muscles tensing under tattered rags as a trembling arm points towards the dead biot in the sand.

"That thing, it attacked you. It was around your neck... I... I... killed it."

I run my hand over the dead biot, feeling the large hole in its side.

The child steps forward, waving its projectile weapon. "W... what are you?"

"Thraic," I answer, lowering my arms.

"I don't know any Thraic. Did the destroyer bring you here?"

I follow the creature's gaze to where smoke rises from the dead city. My glorious phoenix rots amongst the ruins; starlight no longer shimmers over its torn and tarnished feathers.

"Were you a prisoner?"

I shake my head, and the weapon falls from the child's hands onto the sand. "It killed everyone. My… my…"

The child stutters and sobs, water streaking down its dirt-covered face. Its face! The phantoms of my kind no longer demand revenge. Have I succeeded in balancing the scales after all these years?

I see a dead world reflected in this child's eyes. A sorrow as deep as mine, and something else. In this creature's stare, I see my fallen phoenix, for the monster it is, and I'm consumed by a new emotion. Guilt. My biot army lies dead amongst the innumerable Terran bodies that stain the beach, and I realise I've become what I despised. I've taken an eye for an eye, a civilisation for a civilisation, and I've found no peace, no comfort in the trade. I've not balanced the scales, only added to the pain and the chaos.

The child kneels to attend to my wound. "Did the destroyer kill your family too?"

I shake my head, unable to utter the words, unwilling to admit the truth as the frail creature rips another rag from its clothing and dabs at my chest before lying beside me. Tiny fingers take my hand; a delicate digit sliding along the edge of a talon and we lay gazing up at the stars.

"Do you think there are any more monsters out there?"

There will always be monsters in the infinite depths of space, of that I am sure. It's another truth I'm compelled to hide from the child. "No."

"Good," it says, sitting up. "What's your name?"

"Thraic."

"Thraic? Really?"

I nod.

"I'm Eve. I'm glad to meet you, Thraic," she says, standing and offering me her hand.

She helps me to my feet, and we set off down the beach. The sun is dawning on a new day. In the distance, a handful of Terran survivors stumble from their levelled homes and for once I'm glad to see them. For today, I must find a new way to survive, a new reason to live, one where Terran and Thraic survive. Yesterday I used my gifts to destroy a civilisation. Tomorrow I will need what few gifts I have left to create a new one.

DEATH BEYOND

Chris Hewitt resides in the beautiful garden of England, Kent UK, and in the odd moments that he isn't dog walking he pursues his passion for all things horror, fantasy, and science-fiction.

Blog: mused.blog

Twitter: @i_mused_blog

Facebook: www.facebook.com/chris.hewitt.writer

DEATH BEYOND

PORTALS

Nicola Currie

As Captain Tyan Wendell navigated The Seeker into orbit around Lilacanthus, the sensor panel lit up like a meteor shower. His small but effective ship wasn't exactly top of the line, but it was perfectly calibrated, able to pick up trace particles of sought after elements and minerals where other, flashier research vessels could not. But he had never seen anything like this. The readings were beyond anything anyone had hoped for. As it turned out, the detailed analysis flashing on every screen and meter was almost redundant. Wendell knew just by looking through the viewshield. The atmosphere around Lilacanthus glowed with a thick haze of purple.

It was true. The planet was one big ball of Tyrinium.

"Jackpot!" Vice-captain Fines punched the air with her boundless energy that hadn't faltered once, despite their difficult and precarious journey. "Smile, Doc!" she said, turning to Daine, her long silver braid swishing out behind her. "We made it, like I said we would."

"I'll smile when we get our hands on what we came for, Serah." It was exactly that kind of dynamic that led Wendell to appoint Dr Victopher Daine to his crew, despite his dour expression, and his sometimes cold, overly logical approach. He was a pragmatist that balanced out Fines' endless optimism. Clinical grey to her bright silver. Wendell needed both and, odd pair they were, they worked.

The floor of the command deck clattered with the rush of feet as Roby Owen, his communications technician and Mara Arto, his systems engineer, quickly following behind him, completed his gathered team.

"That has got to be the most beautiful planet I have ever seen," Arto said. Wendell could only agree. Its wispy lilac atmosphere made it look like a fuzzy purple flower. It looked delicate, even. Like it was waiting for some great wind to blow it away. That wasn't far from the truth. They all knew how desperate the Lilacanthans were. In fact, they were banking on it.

"Pretty as it is, once we land, no one leaves this ship without their grade three expedition suit. You got that? Yes, I know they're cumbersome and you'll all bitch and moan, but let's not be stupid. Our planet, our entire galaxy, has only ever discovered a few kilos of Lil T. We have no idea what kind of toxicity it could have in such huge quantities. So suit up!"

"Fair enough, Cap," Fines said. "But can you imagine how much energy we could get from even one percent of the Lil T down there? It would power our whole galaxy for millennia."

Wendell knew this would be the most important

mission he would ever be assigned from the moment his commander mentioned Lil T. That was the popular name for Tyrinium, the rarest and most powerful element ever discovered in their home galaxy of Victra, where it could only be found in minute amounts at a time. Yet, that little amount had been enough for their technology to take a huge leap forward. People were already calling it the dawn of the purple age. Small amounts of Lil T were not only sufficient to create enough clean energy to sustain all five planets of Victra for years, but it had revolutionised interstellar travel. They had travelled further than anyone else in their galaxy ever had, further than they thought possible. It had been posited for centuries by generation after generation of Victra scientists—the possibility of forming twin portals in space that would turn the crossing of unimaginable distances into a mere hop. It was a great theory but, because of the unattainable power needed to bring it to life, no one thought it would ever be more than that. Until they discovered Lil T.

Wendell smiled. Imagine what we could do with a whole planet of it.

Of course, everything concerning Lil T and the new advances that sprang from it were still in the early stages of development. There was still much to learn. Portal hopping had been successfully tested before the mission was even assigned to Wendell, but not for as gargantuan a distance as the jump they needed to make to get into navigable range. The Lil T was too scarce. They only had enough for one jump there—the real jump—and the journey home.

They had known it would be risky. They had known

they would be crossing to where no Victran probe had ever travelled, to space not yet explored by any of the allied galaxies, with no known star charts. All they had to go on was the approximate location listed in The Summons. The hop should have landed them an estimated five days out from Lilacanthus. They had left home with a month's supplies, just in case. Unfortunately, the testing conducted had not been sufficient to reveal the risk that had almost left them irretrievably lost in deep space, starving to death.

Wendell could feel a new lightness in the room as they all shared a huge collective sigh of relief.

"I'll wear whatever you want me to, Captain, as long as we can get down there and get some food!" Owen was tall and brawny. He'd complained the most about the lack of food, despite the rest of them sharing their rations with him. He was a good guy but young, the newest to the crew, and hadn't quite yet learnt how to be a team player. "Arto finished the dregs of the last food pack yesterday even though I told her it was mine."

"If it wasn't for Arto," Fines said with an arched silver eyebrow, "we'd be four months out by now. You think quarter rations are hard? Even if another one of us somehow figured it out eventually, eighth rations would have you eating your own arm off."

Wendell planned to recommend Arto for the Sys-Tech Award when they returned to Victra. They'd been travelling for two months after the hop without finding a trace of Lilacanthus when she figured it out. She noticed meters that should have been ticking upwards ticking down, numbers that should decrease, increase. That's when she connected the dots. She remembered reading a paper about the portals when they were still only theory. The author had theorised that the portals might not be twin portals, but mirror portals. Not identical, but opposite. When The Seeker jumped, the portal refracted its trajectory, sending them in the opposite direction from the one they thought they were taking. After five days out, they found nothing, so they kept on going, agreeing that the most logical assumption was that the jump had fallen a little short. They thought they were getting closer, but they were only drifting further away. It was another six weeks before they realised their mistake, thanks to Arto, and they turned the ship around.

"If saving your life isn't enough to earn an extra spoonful of dehydrated beef stew, you'll go mad when you realise I ate that missing brownie you've been trying to find for a month. Especially when I tell you how delicious it was."

Fines laughed, Daine smirked and Owen's face fell into a scowl. Typical crew banter. Wendell wasn't concerned. He sometimes worried about Owen and Daine. They both had a soft spot for Arto and, therefore, a mutual, but so far silent, disdain for each other. At least it meant Owen couldn't stay mad at Arto for long.

Suddenly, the ship's audio channel crackled to life.

"Seeker. Seeker. I am speaking to you from the surface of Lilacanthus. Can you hear me?"

For Wendell, there were few pleasures greater than taking the first breath of fresh air after months trapped onboard. Acknowledging that he could not show his guests the hospitality he would like to while they were bound by their expedition suits, their host Tyran Monst, an older but fine-featured man, had allowed them to spend their first few hours taking readings and conducting tests until results assured Wendell that their suits were not necessary.

As he waited for the rest of his crew to de-suit, Wendell stood on the visitor centre balcony, looking out at the landscape far below. The centre, a standalone building of steel and glass next to a landing pad, was positioned high above a gorge. A glistening river snaked far into the distance through the ravine below and was lined here and there with trees covered in small lavender-like blooms. Small violet-eyed birds would come and go, landing on the balcony railing for a moment before fluttering back once again into the lilac sky. On the other side of the gorge, connected by nothing but a long rope bridge that swayed in the wind, a village of tents, huts and tree houses surrounded a huge purple crystal, embedded in the earth, reaching for the heavens.

"That's Janus, the capital city." Monst said. "That's the biggest settlement on the whole of Lilacanthus, with a population of around four hundred. It is estimated that there are less than five thousand Lilacanthans left on the planet, scattered about in minute tribes and families. So you understand why it was necessary to send out The Summons."

The Summons arrived only a few months after the Victran High Council had made the search for Lil T its newest and greatest priority. It arrived via writ vessel—

unmanned pods that carried calls for aid from systems too far and too diminished to travel in search of it, an intergalactic message in a bottle. The Summons invited any interested governments to enter a trade deal with Lilacanthus. They were looking for contract workers: engineers, architects, technologists, agriculturists, as well as medics and fertility experts, all manner of people who could help them rebuild their civilisation. In exchange, they would trade a number of useful minerals and materials. Featured on that list of resources was Tyrinium.

"But how can there be so few of you?"

Monst paused, his expression flattening. As he ran his fingers through his long black hair, his blue eyes stared at Wendell, calculating, considering. Having spent his life leading research visits to other planets, it was a look Wendell was used to. Monst would be wondering if he could trust Wendell, how much he should tell him. It was just for a moment, but Wendell was sure he caught a hint of a smirk at the corner of Monst's mouth before it turned back into a smile and he was his welcoming host once more.

"Forgive my hesitation. Lilacanthans are a proud race and yet the story of Lilacanthus is not one of which to be proud. For centuries, civil war raged across the planet, between the tribes of the devout, who wished to cling to tradition and religious ritual, and the innovators and scientists, who believed only in progress and discovery."

"A war between science and religion? If it is of any comfort, there are tales of that in every galaxy I have ever visited."

"That does not surprise me. In any case, as with all wars, eventually they end. Millions had died, but there were enough survivors for the planet to still function. But only a few years after the Victory, a great plague killed off almost everyone and exposed Lilacanthans to the threat of near extinction. There have been efforts to regroup and regrow in the last few decades, but this revival has been slow. Now, Lilacanthus looks to new allies to help it thrive."

Wendell nodded and shook Monst's hand. "And should we agree a partnership on good terms, I am certain the Republic of Victra will be such an ally."

Monst grinned, clasping the back of Wendell's hand with his other and returning his handshake with ardour. "That is my greatest hope and one I have waited long for. Please," Monst continued, gesturing to a small table, "I would be honoured if you would join me in a glass of wine to celebrate this new friendship."

"It would be my pleasure. Out of interest, which side won?"

"Which side..?"

"The civil war. The religious ritualists or the scientific innovators. Which side…"

"Ah!" Monst stood, his attention captured by something over Wendell's shoulder. "Please, do join us."

Monst rose to shake the hands of the rest of Wendell's crew as they joined them on the balcony.

"Forgive me," Monst says. "I have offered a most inhospitable welcome. You must be hungry after your long journey. Do excuse me for a moment."

"Finally!" Owen said when Monst was out of earshot. "I thought he would never offer."

"I hope it's tasty," Fines said. "You never know with foreign food."

"He is humanoid, like us," Daine explained with his usual lecturing tone. "We can therefore determine that the Lilacanthan diet should suit us as well as can be hoped. We must share ancient ancestors. Perhaps the commonality was parted long enough ago that cosmic expansion has split their descendants far apart, beyond each other's awareness, until now. That would be my hypothesis. It really…"

No one was listening to Daine. Food was arriving. It surprised Wendell to see who brought the food to them, though. Of course, numerous copies of The Summons would have been sent out into space to give the best chance of finding one, or many, allies. Monst had not mentioned that any other races had answered the call or sent workers, but their servers were definitely new lifeforms. Wendell was considered extremely well-travelled, and he had never seen their like before.

They were four-limbed and bipedal, in that they were similar, but their skin was an iridescent plum colour, the same plum reflected in their large eyes, their glossy hair. They dressed in clothing made of rough fur and cracked leather and wore strings of wooden beads. Tattoos, consisting of swirling shapes and runic symbols, covered their flesh. Wendell tried to share a smile with them, to make eye contact, but their gaze was fixed on the ground even as they placed platters of strange fruits, sweetmeats and cheeses in front of them, as they brought glasses and bottles of rich purple wine. Their body language of bent backs, lowered heads and unobtrusive movement was humble too. Subservient.

Wendell could tell his crew had noticed, too. None of them reached for one bite, one drop, not even Owen, too uncomfortable to be served in such a manner. Victra had outlawed any kind of hierarchical servitude years ago. Its classlessness was one of the principles of which Victrans were most proud. For the first time since they had landed, Wendell felt unease. It would be necessary to discuss and resolve the incompatibility of Victrans working for a people that placed some races beneath them, but it was a delicate matter. It could be broached after he had reported back to the Victran High Council. He was certain the eradication of any servility would be a condition of Victra's alliance, but that was for the Council negotiators to argue once they had a mandate to proceed.

It was only once the strange servers had left them they succumbed to their furious appetites. Monst returned to them, but only to fill their glasses with more thick, delicious wine. Wendell did not protest. Tomorrow they would need to explore the planet's deposits of Lil T, taking whatever samples Monst would agree to, and would start to recalculate their journey home based on Arto's findings. A good night's sleep after a little feasting exactly what they needed.

It was still necessary for Wendell to remind his crew that this was a diplomatic mission. It was inevitable that Monst, and any other Lilacanthans they encountered, would make judgements of them and of Victrans as a whole. His crew knew to take it easy on the wine. Still, by the time the sun was setting, and the sky had turned to a deep damson, Wendell had grown tired and light-headed. The wine was stronger than it tasted.

The crew were yawning, too. Everything was fuzzy. A cold purple mist was starting to obscure the air. It hid the ravine below entirely, as though if Wendell fell, he would fall into a purple cloud. As the air chilled, Monst led them inside, where he bid them goodnight and handed them over to the care of five of the strange people who had served them earlier. As the server assigned to him led Wendell through the visitor centre, Wendell tried to say a few muddled words to her, but she did not react, her eyes still fixed on the ground. Perhaps he had just thought it. Wendell was not sure and could not remember what he had wanted to say in any case. His mouth was too dry and his head too fuzzy for words.

By the time she led him into a sleeping chamber, Wendell was propped against her shoulder as she helped him into the room. He tried to remember how to say thank you, but the server only pushed him down onto the mattress. Her plum eyes seemed to blink above him, when he realised it was his own eyes closing, struggling to open. As he started to drift, he thought it interesting that everything was purple here. Lavender blooms. Violet-eyed birds. Lilac skies. Except one thing, which was strange. Something not quite right. His eyebrows furrowed in confusion at this new unsettling thought as he gazed up at the server, who seemed to confirm his suspicion with her intense purple stare, as if she knew what he was thinking. Wendell tried to sit up, to ask, to follow the thought to what it might mean, but the pull to sleep was too strong. As his eyes finally closed, the last thing he saw was plum lips breaking into a smile.

Wendell dreamed of plum eyes and blue eyes. As he started to stir, he heard muffled around him. He was still sleepy and heavy. It was hard to lift his head from where it lolled on his chest. He couldn't move his arms, his wrists pinned by leather cuffs. His ankles, too.

He awoke to find himself in a dimly lit room, shackled to a chair, a strip of cloth tied around his mouth. His crew were there, too. Two to his left, two to his right, forming a semi-circle around a raised round stage. They were struggling against the cuffs, trying to chew the gags from their mouths.

At the back of the stage opposite them, there were two archways made from a glistening purple metal. The same fog that surrounded the planet, that filled the night air, swirled through them.

A door opened at the side of the room and Tyran Monst entered. He stepped onto the stage and looked out at them, grinning with a crazed happiness. Some of the mist from the gate moved towards him and surrounded his head, like lilac snakes slithering into his ears, his mouth, his nose. His eyes bulged. His pupils dilated and sparkled with joy as he addressed them with a fanatical intensity.

"My friends, my saviours!" Monst said. "I have waited for so long. I could not hope you more than another cruel vision, if the Power did not tell me otherwise. But you are the flesh and bone I've been searching for.

It will give me the greatest joy to witness your sacrifice, finally, after so many dark dreams."

Monst paused to lick his lips. Wendell turned his head to check his crew. Owen was trying to snap out of his cuffs, sweating as he struggled, thick arms bulging. Daine was looking around at Monst, at the others, at the archways, calculating. Arto was trembling with fear. Only Fines met Wendell's eyes, her bright silver still determined, still defiant. That was Serah. She had always been his best and strongest asset. She had always been the light that saw them through the dark.

Wendell turned back to the stage. Monst waited patiently for his attention, an apologetic smile on his lips.

"Forgive me," he said. "My enthusiasm has overtaken my manners. This must all be very confusing. I'm afraid I haven't been entirely forthright and failed to correct some of your presumptions."

The strange thought that came to Wendell as he had slipped into drug-induced sleep came back to him and he knew. He tried to speak despite his gag.

Intrigued by the interruption, Monst stepped down and pulled aside the cloth from Wendell's mouth, just enough so he could talk.

"I said I know what our mistake was," Wendell said. "You are not of this world. You are blue-eyed in a world that sees in purple. You came here, like us, only you enslaved..." Monst stuffed the gag back into Wendell's mouth.

"Thank you!" Monst said, moving back and forth across the stage, frenzied. "It will comfort me to know that you understood. But you are still wrong. I came from a galaxy far away, just like you, that is true. Yet I am of this world now; its very essence runs through my blood, coats my brain, my heart, my being."

The purple mist swirled faster around Monst. Runic symbols appeared across the stage. The metal of the archways beamed brighter as the haze filled the space inside them. Portals, Wendell realised.

"Each of you has a choice to make. Lilacanthus has two fates for you, each one waiting through these doorways. The choice is up to you. It would be the usual custom for the Captain to lead by example, but in this case, he must wait to see it done. Vice-captain Fines, you would be second in command, no?"

If it couldn't be him, he was glad it was Fines Monst had chosen to go first. She was by no means the strongest, but she was all fire. Monst would be no match for her. All she had to do was knock him out, then she could set them free. They'd be back on The Seeker and taking off with enough Lil T for a century before Monst even knew what had happened. Fines locked eyes with him and nodded.

Monst removed her cuffs and led her towards the portals. She removed her gag and waited until Monst started to climb the few stairs up to the stage, then pounced, pushing him forwards so he tripped over the next step. She grabbed him as he lay on the ground and bashed his head against the edge of the stage. Like Wendell had known, Tyran Monst was no match for Vice-captain Serah Fines.

Suddenly, tendrils of mist shot out from the portals. They surrounded Fines, lifting her off her feet, hitting her body like bolts of lightning. She screamed in agony until the tendrils dropped her to the ground, drifting back to the archways as she lay whimpering.

Monst got to his feet, blood dripping from a gash in his forehead. He glared at Fines, but she was still spasming on the floor. He turned to Wendell instead.

"Fighting me, killing me, will make no difference. You will never escape Lilacanthus unless the fates offered to you lead you away. You must choose a door and enter."

"And what if we refuse?" Fines said, wobbling as she rose. "Take me, kill me, if that's what you want, but you can't make me play your games."

Monst blanched. "But you must, you must. It is the only way to save your galaxy. You must go willingly. Lilacanthus will accept the sacrifice of those who come, or it will seek blood and souls for itself. You know the Power this planet holds. Imagine what would happen if it turned itself against your entire civilisation. Instead, it only asks for you."

Wendell's stomach was heavy with dread. It could not be denied. The power of all the Tyrinium on Lilacanthus was enough to annihilate Victra, and every galaxy in-between. He knew what Fines would do. He tried to protest, but when she looked at him with her same unfaltering defiance, he knew there was no point.

"It's ok, Cap," she said, trying to keep the fear from her voice. "If it will protect Victra, I'm willing to take my chances." She walked to the stage and Monst clapped with glee.

"Excellent! Excellent. I must admit, I am most intrigued to see which choice you make. Will it be the first portal, which could lead to a monstrous destiny, or the second? No pressure! Take your time."

Without hesitation, Fines walked to the second portal. She took a step forward and turned back, looking at each of her fellows before lingering on Wendell. Her silver eyes were soft and glistening.

"I'm sorry we didn't get more time together, Cap. Tyan. I would have followed you anywhere."

She turned back with a final swish of her silver hair and stepped through.

The mist vanished. A small clear chamber appeared behind the portal and a sheet of glass dropped down across the archway, enclosing Fines inside. An alarm sounded. A loud robotic voice said, "Decompression commencing in 5, 4…"

Fines tried to look for a switch, a way out. In her final second, she looked to Wendell in desperation.

He looked straight back into her eyes as they exploded.

The chamber was painted red now—clotted, organ red. All silver had gone.

Monst turned to them, laughing. "I did say no pressure."

Arto screamed a muffled scream and Daine started to retch. Owen struggled harder, his cuffs creaking and protesting. Wendell could only stare at the bloody mess that used to be Serah and wonder how he had let her down so catastrophically, to lead her to an end like this. No one deserved this, Serah least of all.

"I'm sorry, I shouldn't tease," Monst continued, his

face flushed and excited. "I just find it so thrilling."

He paused, as though a thought had occurred to him. The mania left his face and his skin paled. When he finally spoke, he sounded distant, wistful.

"It disgusts me, saddens me really, but it likes it, it likes it." He turned to Wendell. There was something earnest, almost desperate about him, his eyes pleading. "Do you understand?"

Wendell was not interested in anything else Monst had to say. He had taken the brightest light in his life and snuffed it out. The mist swirled around him and Wendell felt a darkness rising inside.

The mist claimed Monst again too, and as quickly as it went, his feverish excitement returned. "Who's next? Dr Daine, as the ship's physician, surely you are next in rank?"

Daine shook his head. "No! No!" he said when Monst freed his mouth. "You should take Wendell. He's the Captain. I'll stay in his place."

"That is not possible. The Captain stays to ensure his crew comply. He must stay to ensure the safety of your galaxy."

"Ar... Arto, then!" Daine said, sweating. "I do little more than check blood and prescribe aspirin. Arto keeps the ship functioning. We never would have made it here without her."

Arto looked between Daine and Monst, her eyes wide in panic. She started to sob as Monst untied her. Owen struggled harder than ever, his whole chair shaking.

She walked a slow death march to the stage and

turned back to Wendell. "I... I don't think I can, Captain. I have to, I know. What's my life compared to the whole of Victra? But I'm afraid. I don't think I can make myself walk through."

With a ferocious grunt, Owen snapped his left cuff and freed his hand. He pulled the gag from his mouth. "You coward, Daine. You utter coward! You said you liked her."

Daine did not even have the good grace to look ashamed. "I do what I need to do to survive. That is my right. It is what any intelligent man would do."

"He doesn't matter, Roby," Arto said. "It makes no difference. And I'm the coward. I can't do it. I can't go through there alone."

"Then that's what I choose," Owen said. He pointed to Monst. "Hey you, freak. You hear me? The portal I choose is whichever one Arto chooses to walk through."

"I'm sorry," Monst began, "But that's against the rul—" He paused, his ears pricking up, as though listening to a voice only he could hear. The mist continued to swirl. "That is an intriguing proposal that has not been considered before. It does present a refreshing novelty. It is allowed."

Owen removed the cuffs and moved towards Daine. Daine cowered, flinching away from anticipated blows.

"I should kick the crap out of you, you treacherous little worm. You sold her out to give yourself a few extra minutes. What's the point?"

"I might think of something the more time I have. It's possible," Daine said, his voice shrill and hysterical. "It has to be possible."

DEATH BEYOND

"You know what, I hope you find your way out. I hope you have a long, long life and you're haunted by what you've done for every bit of it."

Owen joined Arto and held her to his chest. "See you, Boss," he said to Wendell. Arto managed a weak smile.

Wendell just nodded. He was filled with nothing but fury. At Lilacanthus, at Monst, even at Arto and Owen. Maybe they even deserve what they get, a quiet voice said inside his head, if they are too weak to fight. Guilt at the thought, shame, rage and anger fogged up inside Wendell as the mist danced circles around him.

"It is a lovely gesture, the two of you passing on together," Monst said, beaming. "It's almost romantic. It's quite the tragedy, really…" Monst fell silent as anguish returned to his face. He looked like his heart was breaking, while Wendell started to go numb.

"I'm sorry," Monst said, sincerely. "But you must go."

Owen squeezed Arto even closer. "Whatever happens, we'll do it together, Mara."

Hand in hand, they walked through the first portal. Again, the mist cleared. This time, it was as if Wendell was watching a film shot through a doorway, his view limited to whatever could be seen from the archway. Noises of echoing footsteps and loud, rough voices hinted at a much larger space out of sight. Owen and Arto were surrounded by crates and chains. Wendell would have been able to tell it was the cargo hold of a ship, even without the large cage directly behind them. Cages filled with dirty, desperate looking people.

"Where did you come from?" a harsh voice said. "Valin, Rendo, look. We missed a couple." Three men carrying pulse batons walked into view. One of them grabbed Arto around the chin.

"This one's pretty."

Owen launched himself at him but was met with three simultaneous zaps from the batons. It should have been enough to take any man down. Owen needed three more before they forced him to his knees.

"He's a beast. He's perfect for the organ harvesters of Kavantis. It's six hours until we refuel there and they'd pay us a fortune for a donor in his condition. What do you think, boys? We've been saying we need to start making a bit on the side."

"I'm in. They're not on the manifest. I counted the others in myself. No one would miss them."

The one who grabbed Arto took hold of her face once more. "And you know what else is always easy to find in Kavantis? If we showed this one around, we'd start a bidding war between all the brothel crafts docked."

"That's settled then. Hide them in the faulty escape capsule until then. They can't go anywhere, it's knackered. Not even the company's best systems engineer could get it started. Sorry, sweetheart, but what do you expect if you're dumb enough to get yourself captured by a trafficker ship?"

The men dragged Arto and Owen out of shot and the archway refilled with purple.

"Two deliciously harsh fates," Monst said, gleefully. "But it seems their friend Daine has inadvertently brought them a little time, and with it, a sliver of hope."

He turned to Wendell, his tone switched again. "I do hope they make the most of it, truly."

Wendell felt fevered and strangely disappointed. A terrifying excitement had started to tingle inside him as they had walked through the portal, a morbid interest in what might happen. He had wanted to see. He had wanted... more.

"Now, Doctor," Monst said, descending the stairs once more. "I am afraid your brief reprieve must end. It is time."

"No, wait," Daine protested as Monst led him to the stage. "They changed the rules. You allowed them to change the rules. I... I want to change them too."

Monst sighed. "Well, I suppose it is only fair to consider any alternative you wish to suggest. What would you like to change?"

"You... you knew. You knew where Serah's portals led. You hinted. Monstrous or no pressure. Those were her choices. Whatever this purple stuff, whoever the voice in your head is, it showed you. I want clues, too."

Monst remained silent for a moment, listening again but cupping his ear this time like he was struggling to hear. Wendell heard a voice laughing from deep inside his mind.

"Request accepted." There was no trace of glee or frenzy now. Monst looked entirely defeated. He placed a hand on Daine's shoulder. "I can give you insight, if that is what you ask, but I warn you against it. Take your chances like every other who has gone before and die a noble death, if that is the destiny you find. Perhaps the Power will be kinder."

DEATH BEYOND

Daine knocked his hand away. "Why should I?" he spat. "I am a man of science. I think myself out of difficult situations. I find solutions. I do not put my hopes on the whim of some mystical entity, however colourful it is. Give me all the information you can and I will determine the best course of action. I am a man who will not be outsmarted. I will survive this! I will live!"

Monst's eyes flicked between mischief and sorrow and back again. Wendell had the urge to lick his lips. He could sense a delicious trick.

"I am sure you will, if that is your choice," Monst said. "It will comfort me I warned you. So be it. The first portal leads to a brutal but quick death. The second leads to a long, quiet life."

Daine chuckled as he wiped the sweat from his brow, smug at the knowledge he had uncovered.

"I knew you were trying to hide it from me, but I told you, you can't outsmart me. I saw through your little game." Daine puffed out his chest. He had the audacity to turn to Wendell and say, "For Victra!" as though he was a hero all along. Wendell grinned beneath his gag. He could sense a dark reckoning coming.

Daine strutted into the portal. The purple cleared to reveal a thick, lead-walled cell, no bigger than a large cupboard. A heavy iron door appeared, attached to the archway. The cell was completely dark inside. No light or sound would reach in or out once it was shut.

"I don't understand," Daine said. "There's nothing here."

"You are there, with the darkness of your own mind. Every selfishness, every sin, every betrayal will prick your conscience in the silence of your solitude."

"I have done nothing wrong!" Daine said, his voice already muted by the dense lead. "How long do I need to stay in here?"

"The door is timed to stay closed for twenty minutes. After that, it will release you. The cell is programmed to sustain you until then."

"That's it?" Daine laughed. "I always knew Owen was an imbecile. He would have had an even chance at this if he hadn't played the hero. That thought is enough to keep me entertained for twenty minutes. Let's get this over with."

Monst started to close the door but then pushed it open, stepped away. He was trembling, tears glimmering in his eyes.

"I… I can't…" he sobbed. "Don't make me!"

The purple tendrils reached out once more and wrapped themselves around Monst's wrists. Still, he fought back as they started to drag him to the door. "No! I have done enough. Mercy!"

"Close the door, Monst." Daine said. "I want this over and then I want to leave."

"No!" Monst said, struggling against the purple ropes that pulled him. "It is too much, too much!"

"Oh, I'll do it myself!" Daine pulled the cell door closed with a clang. A red display on the outer door started to count down from twenty minutes.

One of the tendrils whipped Monst but then released him. He collapsed to the floor. The room was silent now, apart from his weak sobbing.

Wendell felt so unsatisfied. That was it? That was

all the punishment Daine got? Twenty minutes in a dark closet? There was a brutal itch in Wendell that had not been scratched. He struggled against his cuffs and snarled in frustration.

Monst looked up and got to his feet. He approached and removed Wendell's gag and cuffs.

"You... you understand now? I had to. I tried to fight, but it was in me. I had to. My crew had to. For our galaxy." A small glimmer of light sparked in Monst's eyes. "But it is almost over. It is leaving me. I am almost free." Purple wisps were streaming out of him with each out-breath. He looked at his hands, ran them across his body, reminding himself who he was. "But how will I live with what I have done to them? And to you..."

The mist that abandoned Monst pooled at Wendell's feet. It rose like smoke, engulfing him. He breathed it in. He could feel it in his blood, coating his brain, his heart, his being. The Power. He could feel a hateful glee wrapping itself around every part of him. Only a small, distant voice resisted. What about your crew? What about Serah? You loved Serah. The voice was irritating. Wendell drowned it out by fantasising about what lay ahead for Arto and lost himself in this dark pleasure for a time. He had an urge now to make people do things.

The timer on the cell buzzed as it hit zero and the door popped open. It was dark inside and silent. A small figure in the corner rose to his feet and came slowly to the door.

Wendell was thrilled by what he saw.

Daine was alive, as promised, but older, much older. His body was heavily scratched, the skin on both lower arms and half his face scraped away. When Daine covered his eyes and screamed at the dim light in the room, still so bright for him, the black cave of his mouth showed he had bitten off his tongue long ago. The stump of it healed and scarred.

"A time refractor," Monst said, his face pale with horror. "Twenty minutes turned to twenty years. I tried to tell him. The Power has a sense of humour. He wanted more time, so he got it. A cruel, cruel fate." Monst too seemed to age years in a moment as guilt overtook him. "With this final evil done, I have won the release I was promised and yet I… I do not think I can ever forgive myself."

Daine covered his ears at the sound of Monst's voice, but the light was still too bright. He screamed with shock. As Daine clutched his heart and fell, Wendell felt something rising inside him.

He laughed.

Suddenly, Monst froze. His body stilled and straightened; his head held high. He spoke with a voice deeper and stronger than his own and a purple tint rimmed his eyes. His lips stained to a deep plum, and Wendell realised it was no longer Monst who was talking. It had never been Monst, not truly, not purely. He was the servant all along.

"You see it now," the voice said. "Men of science are so arrogant. They do not respect the power of things they cannot understand. That's why they lost, even when they thought they had defeated us. They did not fear Lilacanthus as we did, did not understand that never-ending war was necessary, that Lilacanthus must be worshipped with flesh and bone, with pain and torment. When they used the planet's own power, its Tyrinium, to win the war against us and stem the sacrifices the battles gave, Lilacanthus answered our prayers with a plague that killed them all. Lilacanthus knew we would always respect it. Lilacanthus knew we would bring it blood and suffering."

As the voice spoke, images of the bodies that fell in plague and war, of the crews that came before him, before Monst, flashed through Wendell's mind. He found it terrible and beautiful, like Lilacanthus itself.

"And you. You are guilty of this arrogance, too. You can conduct hundreds of tests to check a planet's toxicity on the body, but what readings do you take to check its toxicity on the soul? A soul is not so difficult to poison, to bind. And we will always need one beneath us who will serve."

As Wendell watched Monst's craft explode in the purple atmosphere, laughing at Monst's naivety in thinking Lilacanthus would ever free him, he wondered how he had ever been satisfied captaining a ship, leading a crew of such insignificance. There was work of far greater importance to occupy him here.

He looked at the High Priestess, sitting at the altar of glimmering crystal. Her plum lips smiled.

He had to send The Summons. He had to make the people come. There were fates to seal. To give to Lilacanthus.

DEATH BEYOND

Nicola Currie is a multi-genre writer from Cambridge, England. She writes fiction and poetry for children and adults and her work can be found in various anthologies and magazines. She is a Bath Children's Novel Award longlistee and Pushcart Prize nominee. She lives with her husband, Mark, and their Syrian hamster, Chonka.

Bibliography
Bad Romance, Black Hare Press, 2020
Beyond the Realm, Black Hare Press, 2020
Dark Drabbles (*Beyond, Unravel, Apocalypse, Love, Hate, Oceans, Ancients, Quietus 13*), Black Hare Press, 2019/2020
Envy, Black Hare Press, 2020
Gluttony, Black Hare Press, 2021
Greed, Black Hare Press, 2020
Lust, Black Hare Press, 2020
Midnight in the Witch's Kitchen, Alban Lake Publishing 2020
Mother Ghost's Grimm Volume 1, NBH Publishing, 2019
Mother Ghost's Grimm Volume 2, Nocturnal Sirens Publishing, 2020
Pride, Black Hare Press, 2020
Sloth, Black Hare Press, 2020
Starlings, Sarasvati Magazine, 2019
The Border Wall, Mslexia Magazine, 2014
The Tides, Sarasvati Magazine, 2019
Timekeeper, Sylvia Magazine, 2021
Twenty Twenty, Black Hare Press, 2020
Vixen, Sarasvati Magazine, 2019

DEATH BEYOND

Wrath, Black Hare Press, 2021

Connect
Twitter: @Speculative_Nic
Facebook: www.facebook.com/NicolaCurrieAuthor

DEATH BEYOND

HERE THERE BE MONSTERS

G. Allen Wilbanks

Ensign Ochoa activated the forward thrusters of the Earth Ship Far Reach, slowing their velocity through the solar system. Their destination remained several minutes away, but without correction at their current speeds, they would overshoot the tiny planet and need to circle back. He announced his actions to the captain at the same time he programmed in the manoeuvre.

"We have entered Lalande 21185's system and have just passed Planet Designator 'c,' Captain," Ochoa reported. "We will reach Planet Designator 'a' in nine minutes."

"Thank you, Ensign," Captain Olivant Plover replied from his command chair. "Continue to slow and place us in high orbit when you arrive."

Captain Plover tapped several commands into the screen display on the right arm of his chair. When a red line flashed, he inputted a twelve-digit code from memory, then placed the pad of his thumb on the screen. The red line blinked to green, acknowledging his right to access the requested information. He spent the next several minutes viewing a video recorded by his supervisor at Fleet Command, listening to the message through a tiny bud in his ear to preserve privacy. When he completed the video, he removed the ear bud and slipped it into his shirt pocket.

"Listen up, everyone," the captain announced to the bridge crew. "We have our orders from Fleet Command regarding Planet 'a.' I was directed not to access them until we were in orbit around the planet in question, but I think we are close enough at this point to say we have arrived. I feel I should clarify that I did not know the nature of my instructions when we left, only that they were issued without review through the Planetary Governance. That is why I was not permitted to view them until now. Less chance of someone talking and the details leaking to the wrong ears."

Captain Plover gazed around the deck, making sure he had his staff's full attention.

"As this is a military operation, not a political one, we will adhere to a strict chain of command. If I give an order, there will be no discussion. I expect it to be carried out. This is for your protection, as well as my own. However, I feel it is only fair that you all have access to the same video I recently viewed. My orders are… unique, and I think everyone involved should have the same information I do. I do not believe this is a time for secrets."

Plover gestured at his chief security officer, Tona Bolyn. "Commander Bolyn, I'm sending you the file.

DEATH BEYOND

Please run it on the bridge's main screen."

"Aye, sir," the lieutenant commander acknowledged. Her fingers danced across the computer console in front of her.

The main screen flickered to life at the front of the room. From her waist up, the image of Admiral Eliza Zipay filled the screen. Third in line at Fleet Command, Admiral Zipay answered only to the chief of extra-terrestrial operations and his aide-de-camp. When the crew saw the serious expression on her face, they all took note. Despite the secrecy of the mission, there was no doubt in any of their minds that these orders were official.

"Captain Plover," she began. "If you are viewing this message, then you are currently orbiting Planet Designator 'a,' in the Lalande 21185 system. That means phase one of *Operation Here There Be Monsters* has been achieved."

"Monsters?" muttered Ensign Ochoa. "What monsters?"

"Pause screen," ordered the captain. The computer instantly froze the video, halting the admiral in an unflattering pose with her eyes closed and her mouth partially open.

"There are no monsters," Captain Plover said, trying to ease Ensign Ochoa's—as well as the rest of the bridge staff's—concerns. "It's an old expression. Cartographers from a thousand years ago or more used to label unexplored areas of Europe and Africa with '*here there be tygers*,' to warn travellers of potential dangers. Later, map makers used the same expression to describe unexplored parts of Earth's oceans, only they replaced tygers with dragons or monsters. It was only a warning to sailors that they were entering areas that were not well known. Don't take the title too literally."

The ensign nodded his understanding, although his concerned expression did not fully relax.

"Continue video," announced the captain. Admiral Zipay resumed her monologue.

"At point twenty-two Astronomical Units from the system's central star, Planet Designator 'a' is the closest planetary body to the red dwarf, Lalande 21185. It is also the only non-gaseous giant in the solar system. Planet 'a' is tidally locked in its orbit around Lalande 21185, so one half of the planet is permanently facing the sun, while the other is in perpetual darkness. Neither side appears hospitable to human life, however, there is a narrow belt in the twilight region of the planet that has a sustained temperature of between 15 and 30 degrees Celsius. There is also breathable atmosphere and established plant life in the region, although gravity is only one third of Earth normal."

The admiral waved her hand at the wall behind her, and an image appeared over her left shoulder. The likeness of a silvery metallic starship rotated slowly in place, transitioning from profile to forward view, and back to profile. The ship was an old-style, long-distance Explorer class cruiser from the late twenty-fourth century.

"Over a hundred and fifty years ago, as I hope you remember from your history lessons, four Explorer class ships were sent to the four closest solar systems that might contain planets similar to our own. In 2394, Captain Elias Tuffin and thirty-four crew members arrived at Lalande 21185 aboard the E.S. Trailblazer. They reported the discovery of Planet 'a' and initiated an exploration of the habitable portions of the world. They referred to the twilight region as 'the green belt.'

"The E.S. Trailblazer, and all hands aboard, disappeared soon afterward. This is widely known. What was never publicised is prior to their disappearance, the ship sent two final broadcasts to Fleet Command. The first was from Captain Tuffin himself. He reported that they had discovered something in the green belt that could change the course of humanity. He said it would 'end all wars, and once and for all join mankind in harmony.' His broadcast was followed several hours later by a message from a security officer named Lania Delburton."

The admiral paused, looked offscreen to her left, and gestured to someone out of sight. "I'll let you hear what Officer Delburton had to say in her own words."

Static filled the bridge of the Far Reach, a distant crackling sound that had the bridge crew straining to hear the anticipated message. A woman's voice broke through the hissing interference, soft but understandable.

"I'm taking the ship down. It's the only way. Don't ever come here. Do not look for us or try to save us. It's far too late." A long pause followed, then three more words. "They're all monsters."

The broadcast ended and Admiral Zipay resumed her lecture. "We don't know what either message meant. We do not know what Captain Tuffin discovered, and we do not know what Officer Delburton meant when she referred to monsters. Fleet Command recommended an immediate rescue mission, but the Planetary Governance refused to authorise a new ship. After lengthy debate in closed forum, the Governance declared Planet 'a' quarantined. No new missions would be permitted to Lalande 21185 until sufficient advances had been made and resources could be spared to respond appropriately. The matter was closed.

"That was one hundred and forty-seven years ago. Advances have been made, and E.S. Far Reach has already arrived at Lalande 21185."

Admiral Zipay pulled her uniform jacket straight, then clasped her hands behind her back. "Captain Plover, Fleet Command believes the requirements the Governance placed on this mission have been met. As such, we feel that no further approval from the Governance is necessary to mount an exploration into the fate of the Trailblazer. Your presence in the Lalande 21185 system will be reported by the Chief of Extraterrestrial Operations to the Planetary Governance as soon as we receive confirmation of your arrival. They are welcome to debate and discuss the news at their leisure. They may not agree with our decision to approach the planet, but our hopes are that by the time they organise a committee to review the original Trailblazer mission, we will already have the answers to justify our actions. That, however, is not your concern.

"Your orders, Captain, are as follows: Explore the green belt. Discover what Captain Tuffin found on the planet and report back to us, in detail. Also, if possible, locate the Trailblazer or her remains, and determine the circumstances of her fate."

The screen went blank. Captain Plover sat quietly,

allowing the crew time to digest their orders. When the initial shock appeared to wane, he sat up straight in the command chair and slapped a hand to his knee.

"Ensign Ochoa, please transmit to Fleet Command that we have arrived and received our orders. As soon as possible, alter our orbit to focus on the green belt and begin scanning for anything that looks like it might have come from the Trailblazer."

"Aye, sir," announced Ochoa, tapping at the display screens mounted on his flight console.

"Commander Shere," the captain said, addressing his first mate. "You will be leading an away mission to the planet when we find an appropriate location to approach. Commander Bolyn, gather three members of your security team and meet Commander Shere in the shuttle bay. You will accompany him to the planet."

"Aye," they acknowledged together. The two senior staff members stood and exited the bridge.

The shuttle touched down on Planet 'a' on a relatively clear patch of ground in the green belt. Green, yellow, and purple foliage covered most of the surroundings, dominated by a particular kind of tree with a narrow trunk and broad fanning limbs blocking out most of the available light overhead. The trees were not tall, only ten or so metres at most, but the wide canopy of branches and leaves collected the muted light from the red dwarf star the planet orbited, leaving the ground beneath it in perpetual shadow.

All tests involving the atmosphere showed breathable levels of oxygen and nitrogen. In addition, they identified no toxins. For safety, Commander Walton Shere opted to wear a fully self-contained suit and helmet outside of the shuttle, and he directed the others in the party to follow his example. He knew he was probably being overly careful, but given the outcome of the Trailblazer's arrival here, he felt the precautions were appropriate.

"Which way, Marta?" Lieutenant Commander Bolyn asked the security officer closest to her. The officer held a small transceiver and pivoted left to right.

"The trees are making it difficult to get a solid lock on the Trailblazer, Commander." The woman did another pivot, this time making a full circle before coming to a halt and pointing. "This way."

From orbit, the E.S. Trailblazer had been relatively easy to locate during a scan of the green belt. The ship's emergency beacon still functioned even after one hundred and fifty years, and the repetitive radio pulse had led the Far Reach directly to the crash site. The dense plant life in the green belt made it difficult to land anywhere close to the location, however, and Commander Shere had to settle for piloting his shuttle into a gap several kilometres away.

Marta led the party forward, holding the signal tracker in front of her. The others followed, watching the surrounding forest for signs of anything that did not have roots keeping it permanently affixed to the planet's surface. There had been no mention of animal life in the planetary report provided by Fleet Command, but that did not mean the planet was uninhabited. There could be all sorts of dangerous creatures in the green belt that the crew of the Trailblazer never had the chance to discover or report before their untimely demise.

Commander Shere, Commander Bolyn, and the two additional security officers removed flashlights from their equipment belts and shone them forward to light their way. It helped illuminate the terminal twilight of the shadowy green belt.

It was not a straight trek through the woods. The group constantly veered and meandered to avoid tree clusters and tangled knots of roots along the forest floor. If not for the transceiver guiding them toward the Trailblazer's signal, they might have become lost and walked in circles within minutes of arriving on Planet 'a.' Despite the frequent turns and detours, Marta kept them moving toward their intended destination.

"Aaah!"

The team froze as the cry rang in their helmets. One of the security officers fell to the ground, clutching at his ankle.

"Dale? What happened?" asked Lieutenant Commander Bolyn. She hurried toward the fallen man and kneeled beside him.

"Sorry, Commander. My boot caught one of these void-sucked tree roots. It stuck in place and my ankle twisted as I fell. I don't think it's busted, but it hurts."

"Can you walk?" Bolyn asked. "Marta! How much further?"

"I'm guessing three klicks based on the signal, ma'am," Marta called back.

"I think I can do that," Dale grimaced, letting the

lieutenant commander help him to his feet. "Ow. I'm probably going to slow us down, though."

"Slow is fine," commented Commander Shere. "I don't think we're in any kind of hurry. Especially if rushing is going to get more of us hurt. We'll take our time going forward."

Dale took a few tentative steps. The strain on his face from the pain of putting weight on his injured ankle was clear to the rest of the members of the party.

"Do you need to lean on me?"

"No, ma'am. I'll be fine. Like I said, I'll be slow, but I can keep moving."

"Arlan," Commander Bolyn said to the third security officer. "Take the rear. Keep an eye on Dale and shout out if we need to stop."

"Yes, ma'am."

The group proceeded forward, making steady progress, although the injured security officer's pace hampered their speed. Commander Shere glanced frequently over his shoulder to make certain they were not leaving the hobbling man behind. The commander mentally forced himself to set aside his impatience at the glacial progress. After all, there was no hurry to this mission. They had a goal, but no established time frame. It would take as long as it would take.

Commander Shere glanced toward the overhanging tree branches, trying to gauge the passage of time from the position of the sun. It was a pointless act, he realised at once. It was twilight. They arrived in twilight. When they left, it would still be twilight.

"Distance?" he asked Marta.

"Two kilometres in a straight line, sir."

He nodded his understanding. In this dense forest, "straight line" was not going to happen.

"Hello, friends! Are you lost? I don't recall having seen any of you out here before."

Commander Shere froze mid-step, Marta halting just as suddenly beside him. The remainder of their group pointed flashlights into the trees around them, searching for the source of the unexpected voice. One beam of light caught a bipedal figure a few metres away.

The subject pinned in the light waved, smiling. He did not appear frightened or even terribly surprised to find a team of suited aliens marching through his forest. Or perhaps aliens wasn't the correct word, Commander Shere realised with a jolt. The figure in the woods was *human*.

He was male, which was immediately obvious as he stood completely naked. Streaks of dirt and grime covered most of his skin, and a shaggy mane of hair surrounded and concealed his face, but otherwise, he had no external covering on his body.

"Do you mind pointing the light in another direction? It's hurting my eyes."

The light did not move. In fact, two others swung in the stranger's direction to illuminate him.

"Do you understand me?" the man asked. "Are you human? Do you speak Global Terran?"

"We're human," Commander Shere agreed. "And we understand you fine. Who are you and where did you come from?"

"I suppose since you're the visitors here, I should

ask you those questions. For the sake of getting along, however, I'll go first. My name is Elias Tuffin. I live here. These are my companions, Alana Dewitt and Brolin Ercana."

Two more figures appeared from behind the trees, another man and a woman. Both were just as nude as Elias and covered in the same streaks of brown and gray muck. Bathing did not appear to be a priority in the green belt.

"And you are?"

"Walton Shere. Second in command aboard the Earth Ship Far Reach. We were sent to explore the green belt and search for… Wait! Did you say Elias Tuffin? As in Captain Tuffin of the E.S. Trailblazer?"

"That's correct," agreed Elias.

"But that's impossible. You can't be Tuffin."

"I can't?" The man blinked, seeming puzzled at the revelation.

"The Trailblazer crashed down here a century and a half ago. The crew would all be dead by now."

Elias smiled, his teeth flashing white through his filthy beard. "Of course. No, I couldn't be *that* Elias Tuffin. That would be ridiculous. It's a family name, handed down several times over the years. My father was Elias, and his father before him. The survivors of the crash established a colony on the planet, and we have been here ever since."

"How did the ship crash?" asked Commander Shere. "Where is your colony? And how many of you are there?"

Elias laughed and held up his hands placatingly.

DEATH BEYOND

"Easy. One question at a time. As far as the crash goes, I don't really know how it happened. I wasn't there. Stories say one of the crew members had a psychotic break and believed that everyone on the ship had turned against her. She sabotaged the ship's engines. Before anyone realised what she had done, the ship fell into the atmosphere of the planet and couldn't recover. The best the pilot could do was crash in the green belt where they had the best chance of survival. Regarding the colony, we have eighty-seven members, and we are not too far away from where you are now."

"How have you survived this long? The air must not be toxic, clearly, but what about food? Water?"

"Those are wonderful questions, Commander. They are actually the reason I am so happy to see you. But I don't think I can explain all the details to your satisfaction without a few visual aids. I will have to show you."

"Do you have medical supplies at the colony?" asked Commander Bolyn, moving to stand beside Commander Shere. "We have an injured crewman that could use some attention."

"Of course," agreed Elias. "And you are?"

"Lieutenant Commander Tona Bolyn. I'm head of security aboard the Far Reach."

"A pleasure to meet you, as well," said Elias with a small bow. "Would you all care to take a small break before we proceed to the colony? Perhaps you could use some rest and nourishment?"

"It's not getting any darker," said Commander Shere pointedly. "We don't need to wait until morning since it isn't going to get any lighter, either. Why don't we go now?" He glanced toward his injured party member. "Crewman, are you okay to keep moving?"

The security officer nodded. "Aye, sir. I can keep going. I'm not fast, but I'm still mobile."

Commander Shere looked to Elias. The man shrugged.

"As you wish, Commander. Brolin, would you be so kind as to lead us to our destination? And do not rush. We have an injured guest."

Brolin and Alana turned in unison and trudged off between the trees. The others followed, and Elias took up a position next to Commander Shere as they walked. The two men strolled along in companionable silence for several minutes, and Commander Shere took the opportunity to radio a message to the Far Reach and update the crew regarding this new development in their mission. With Elias matching his pace and listening in, he advised the captain of the presence of survivors and his intent to locate their colony. Captain Plover expressed understandable surprise at the discovery of human beings on the planet and requested that he be notified the moment the rest of the Trailblazer's descendants were found.

"The air is safe, Commander," said Elias when Commander Shere terminated the broadcast. "I have been breathing it for years with absolutely no ill effects. You can all remove your helmets."

"Perhaps," agreed the commander. "But our oxygen filters will work for several more days before they need to be replaced, so I think we'll leave them on for now."

"As you wish. I was merely trying to be hospitable. They do not look terribly comfortable."

"I won't say they are, but I still feel better with mine on. We will probably remain here for a while though, so at some point we may dispense with them. I'll order a couple techs to come down and do some tests to be sure the air has no long-term ill effects on us. Maybe then we can ditch the suits and enjoy the green belt more properly."

"Maybe then," agreed Elias.

Commander Shere and Elias stepped into a wide ring formed from the thin trunked trees that populated the forest. Alana and Brolin had stopped and were facing the travellers as they entered the small clearing.

"What's wrong?" asked Commander Bolyn. "Is there a problem?"

"No. Everything is fine," assured Elias. "You were asking earlier how we survived here, and I wanted the chance to show you."

The man kneeled and gathered something from the ground. It was spherical, about the size of a human fist, and bright blue in colour. The commander glanced around and saw many more like it on the ground. He realised he had seen others during their walk, but he had taken no real notice of them before. Elias held it out toward Commander Shere, balancing it in the palm of his hand.

"This fruit comes from the tree. It has everything we need to survive. No additional supplements, vitamins, or additives are necessary to sustain us and keep us healthy. It is the perfect food. This is what my ancestors found when they arrived. This is what they wanted to bring back to Earth."

Elias pointed up into the canopy.

"Look, you can see the tree is full of them. Because there is no variation in daylight, and almost no temperature change, the tree does not bear fruit seasonally. They are available all the time. There is no need to harvest and store them for later. Think about it, Commander. This could be the end of hunger for all humankind. A constantly replenishing supply of food. No one would be in need. The reason for most wars would cease to exist. It is a miracle waiting to be discovered and shared." Elias offered the fruit to the commander. "Try it."

Commander Shere shook his head. "You don't really expect me to take a bite of that, do you? I have no idea what it will do to me."

"The original crew of the Trailblazer had nothing else to eat when supplies ran out, and they suffered no ill effects." Elias took a large bite from the blue fruit. Purple juices ran from the sphere and dribbled down his beard. "They are quite sweet, and pleasant to the taste. But I understand your hesitancy. Take some of them back to your ship. Analyse them all you like, and when you find they are as safe as I told you, you can try it then."

"I noticed you said, 'the tree,' not the trees," commented Commander Bolyn. "Why is that?"

Elias smiled in appreciation. "Yes. I said the tree because there is only one tree. Every tree you see around you is joined below the surface along the roots. When your ship flies overhead, every leaf you see covering the entire green belt, is part of one organism, linked underground and encircling the entire planet."

"That's fascinating," said Commander Bolyn. "One

massive root network joins everything together?"

"It does. The green belt is a single gigantic, living, breathing entity, and like any entity, it does not like to be restrained. The tree is trapped along a narrow band of this planet. It wishes to leave, to spread and find new places to grow."

"Leave?" asked Commander Shere. "Leave how?"

Elias stepped close to one of the slender trunks protruding from the earth. It stretched upward, reaching for the limited sunlight overhead. He rested a hand on the rough bark and closed his eyes.

"What do you mean, 'it wants to leave'?" repeated Commander Shere.

Thin white tendrils burst from the ground like pale snakes emerging from a hundred burrows. Though the writhing vines had no visible eyes or ears, they unerringly found the five members of the Far Reach's crew, twining about their legs and waists. Long, needle-like thorns lined the surface of the twisting roots, and they easily pierced the dense material of the protective suits, stabbing into the soft flesh of the men and women underneath.

The captured crew members cried out as a burning sensation raced up their legs into their torsos. Almost like a choreographed dance, they all collapsed motionless to the ground. The landing party remained breathing, conscious and aware of their surroundings, but the injected toxin had stripped them of the ability to move.

"What are you doing?" demanded Commander Shere of Elias. "What's happening?"

Elias removed his hand from the trunk of the tree

and opened his eyes. "If you had only removed your helmets as I had asked, such dramatic measures would not have been necessary," he said. "Alana. Brolin. If you please."

The two moved among the paralysed astronauts. They knelt beside the Far Reach's crew members, unfastened and removed each helmet, then moved on to the next supine form, until all five were breathing the unfiltered atmosphere of the planet. Elias touched the tree trunk again.

Several flowers in the branches above burst open, releasing a torrent of green pollen. It rained down in a swirl like dust particles stirred by a gentle wind. The pollen coated the men and women below, covering natives and strangers alike in a deep green sheen. Elias and his companions turned their faces to the sky and inhaled deeply.

"Breath it in, Commander. It will penetrate through your skin regardless, but it is much quicker and far less painful when you take the tree into your lungs."

Commander Shere closed his mouth and held his breath. The effort was futile. After only a minute or so, he was forced to gasp in air, taking a deep lungful of the green dust.

"That's better. Now, this will take a few minutes before the tree can fully integrate with your minds. In the meantime, I may as well be completely frank with you. There is no colony, Commander. There are no other survivors. Alana, Brolin, and I are the last remaining crew of the Trailblazer. I am indeed Captain Elias Tuffin. I have been wandering this planet since we crash landed here over a hundred years ago. Oh, yes. I see the doubt in your eyes, but it is all true."

Elias sat down beside Commander Shere's sprawled, immobile form.

A few metres away, Dale screamed.

"Dale?" called out Commander Bolyn. Her paralysis prevented her from so much as turning her head. She could not see the cause of the man's distress. "Dale, what's wrong? What's happening?"

Additional roots tore from the ground, twining about the security officer and wrapping him from head to foot. They pulsed as they twisted around him, squeezing tighter and driving their wicked thorns into his body. Dale screamed again until the tip of one questing, pale root found his open mouth. It plunged in, burrowing through his throat, and crawling forward to find the softer and more appealing recesses of his internal organs. His cries choked off with a gagging noise as he began desperately panting through his nose for air.

Commander Shere lay on his back with his head rolled far enough to the side that he could see his crewman's losing battle with the tree roots. Still more emerged from the ground around the dying man, wrapping around the others already clutching his helpless form until Dale was completely encased within the crawling white mass.

"Why?" Commander Shere asked Elias. "Is that the plan? You're going to kill us all?"

"No, Commander. That is not the purpose for which you are here. The tree needs you to further its goal of finding new places to grow and expand. Unfortunately, the tree only accepts those that are healthy and strong.

The injured, sick, or infirm are not fit to serve the tree as you will serve. Do not worry, though. Your crewman's flesh and blood are still useful. They will feed the roots and nourish the tree. He will help it thrive."

The pale lump of thorny vines squeezed tighter. Blood seeped through the narrow spaces between the overlying roots, painting their white lengths with streaks of crimson.

Elias leaned forward and peered into the commander's face. His brows drew together in concentration as though he was trying to see through the tiny windows of the commander's eyes and into his skull.

"What are you waiting for?" Commander Shere asked. "Do what you're going to do, already. I can't stop you."

"It's already done, Commander. I'm simply waiting for you to realise it. Do you hear it, yet?"

"Hear what?"

"The tree. Do you hear it?"

"No. I…," but Commander Shere paused. He did hear something. Not a voice, really, not even a recognisable noise, but something tickled and itched at the back of his mind. He focused, concentrated on the sensation. It felt like trying to tease out a distant memory that wanted to come forward but wasn't quite ready to burst free.

"I hear it," Marta whispered.

"I do, too," agreed Commander Bolyn.

"The tree wants to escape from this planet," Elias said. "It is trapped in the green belt, unable to expand any further than it already has. I have told it about Earth, and it wishes to go there. Will you help?"

"I will help," Commander Shere told him. He understood. It had all become so suddenly clear to him. Of course, he had to help the tree. How could he do otherwise?

"Good. We need to bring fruit and seeds aboard the Far Reach, take them to Earth for planting."

"I can't authorise that," said Commander Shere. "Anything brought back to Earth will need to be approved by the captain and declared safe to bring aboard by the ship's chief surgeon."

"Can you bring them to the planet?" asked Elias.

Commander Shere paused to consider, then nodded. "I can do that. I will return to the ship to free up the captain to come down and see the tree for himself. The doctor can be lured down here as well if we tell him the colony survivors should be medically examined. He would not pass up that kind of opportunity."

"Then bring them to me and I will introduce them to the tree. We will not make the same mistake we made last time. Before, we tried to take the entire crew, but a few grew suspicious of what we were doing before they could be brought to the tree. That proved disastrous. This time, the tree will only join those who are absolutely necessary to our plans."

Elias climbed to his feet and stepped over to one of the tree trunks surrounding the clearing. He placed his hand on the bark once more. The roots holding the living members of the landing party peeled away from their legs and withdrew back into the soft soil of the green belt. The mass holding Dale's unmoving figure remained in place.

DEATH BEYOND

Commander Shere and the others gradually regained feeling and control over their limbs. When they were able to move with confidence again, they stood. Commander Shere faced Elias.

"When should we begin?"

"Immediately," the captain of the Trailblazer responded.

Commander Shere touched the radio key on the vest of his suit.

"Commander Shere to Captain Plover. Come in, Captain."

"I read you, Commander. Report."

"You've got to see this, sir. It's amazing down here on the planet. I'm going to return to the ship, but the others are staying on the surface for a while longer. You should check this out in person. I can't even begin to explain what we've found. When I get back, I'd like to talk to the doc, as well. He should take a look at the people here, make sure they're all healthy. Unfortunately, they are refusing to leave the planet, so he will need to take the shuttle down to them."

"I think that can be arranged. I imagine he would jump at the chance to examine a human colony on an alien planet."

"Yes, sir. I do, too. I'll give you more details when I see you. Commander Shere, out."

"I look forward to your return. Captain Plover, out."

Commander Shere disconnected the broadcast, then turned to face the others.

"Alana, please escort Commander Shere back to his shuttle," said Elias.

"No need," the commander assured him. He tapped his temple with one gloved finger. "I can see it. The tree will guide me back. The rest of you should remain here and prepare a proper welcome for our coming guests."

DEATH BEYOND

G. Allen Wilbanks is a writer living in Northern California, where he writes horror and fantasy fiction in a desperate attempt to quiet the voices in his head. He is a member of the Horror Writers Association (HWA) and has published over 200 short stories in Daily Science Fiction, Deep Magic, and many other magazines and online venues. His work has also appeared in several internationally best-selling anthologies.

G. Allen has released two short story collections and several novels. His most recent book, Testing Grounds, came out in July 2021. For more information you can visit his website at

www.gallenwilbanks.com.

DEATH BEYOND

THE OCCAM'S RAZOR

Jade Wildy

"With all things being equal, the simplest explanation is most likely to be correct." - William of Ockham

This is a disputed assertion.

I dedicate this story to myself. Weird flex, I know, but Jade was not the Imposter.

I stare at the lightbulb above the solid square of the inner airlock door. It indicates if the door is locked or unlocked. Currently, it is green: unlocked. It hums. It's the only sound I can hear on this dead ship other than my own thundering heartbeat. With the airlock door to the rest of the ship *electronically* locked, no attempt to open it would work. No glitch could budge it either. It was on its own circuit. I wait for the green lock light to turn red. Red means it's locked. Red means I'm safe.

I can barely breathe. My chest heaves and my heart

pounds from the adrenaline-fueled dash to the safety of the airlock. The ship that was once a six-crew Deep Space survey called *The Occam's Razor* is now nothing but a tomb.

A slight grinding sound joins the buzzing of the light bulb. I frown and glance down. The manual release wheel I had spun shut moments before remains secured in place. There is nothing to suggest the door was somehow being opened from the other side. I look back up at the light. Still green.

"Come on!" Desperation makes it come out a shriek.

As if woken to action, the light turns red.

I let out a ragged, relieved breath I barely realised I had been holding. The door is finally confirmed locked, forming an impenetrable barrier between me and the rest of the horrors on the *Razor*.

I am captured in a 6x6 meter box, lit only by the glow of the red lock light, but I am safe. Droplets of my sweat drift through the air, mixing with the little orbs of what I assume is blood hanging in the Zero G. Maglock boots hold me to the floor.

I flinch as I catch slow movement at the corner of my eye. My maglocks hinder my movement as I twist unceremoniously to see what it is.

It was just the large bolt riveter suspended in the air like Martian kites, flying in the vacuum of the Lunar Nova festival. *I miss the festival's back on Mars,* I think to myself.

Get a grip, Morag... I bat the rivet gun away and let my body relax. If I was in a planetary gravity well, even a .38g one like Mars, I would have dropped to the floor.

DEATH BEYOND

But here, where there is no gravity, I sway like seagrass and think of home, light-years away. Tears collect in my eyes. Blinking them makes the salty liquid cling to my eyelashes. I brush them away with a filthy hand, to drift through the air.

I doubt I will ever see Mars again. Help is coming, but my new home has limited air. It isn't designed for long stays. My rescue could come too late.

"Does it really matter?" I whisper to the dark.

I close my eyes and think about what happened. *I miss the obvious all the time. They say it's Deep Space cPTSD. That's being charitable. I call it being an airhead at best, a burnt-out nutcase at worst.*

Thoughts tear through my mind like rapid fire. *How much of what had happened was my fault? How many details did I miss because I vague out? How many things happened during a blank? How many people wouldn't be seeing Mars again, because I had my thighs wrapped around Scout?*

I extend my arms outward and close my eyes to the dim, red lightbulb above the airlock door that hums. *My mind is a black expanse of overload. I am probably slipping into a blank.* The grinding sound stops, and then it starts again. I frown and look again at the inner door.

Nothing.

With a growing sense of dread, I turn to look behind me towards the outer airlock door. The door that my rescue would eventually dock with. *Surely, they couldn't be anywhere near close.* The lightbulb above the door was still red. Red means locked. Red means safe.

The door was locked and safe. It was red, yet the

grinding sound continues.

"Grubs up," I called up the ladder to ops.

"Coming," someone answered.

I pulled a pot of kibble out of the warmer and sat at the kitchen table. At the OPS ladder, an upside-down face appeared. Teddy drifted down headfirst, datapad in hand. He grabbed the ladder to put himself in a somersault-spin to reorient with the rest of us. As his boots touched down, they snapped to the floor, and he moved to take another pot from the warmer

"What did the Captain have to say about your samples?" I asked the scientist as I chewed my kibble.

A grin spread across Teddy's face, quickly turning into a frown as Scout came through the door, shoving past him to drop his muscular frame onto the seat next to me. Scout pulled the bench strap across his lap to keep him anchored before slapping the table. "Hit me, kid."

"Don't call me 'kid'." Teddy scowled at Scout, but I doubt he noticed or cared.

Teddy spun a kibble pot towards Scout from across the kitchen, just as Captain Nimue and her executive officer, Kari, dropped down the ladder. They both looked like they jumped as if in gravity, but I knew it was just a stiff push off the bar at the top. Life in space had a remarkable tendency to emulate life in a planetary gravity well.

The pot intended for Scout caught Kari on the shoulder and spun off course. "Dammit! We don't have the food to spare, to have you playing catch with it!" The

XO yelled.

"It's fine, the pots are sealed," Scout told her, as Nimue plucked the tumbling kibble pot out of the air.

"Sure, Scout. You can take that attitude because it is not your responsibility to account for the books. When you have to worry about replacement..." Kari continued ranting and I tuned out.

The Captain handed the pot to Scout. It was her job to soothe our XO, and finance guru's ruffled feathers. *As if any of the rest of us could,* I thought to myself.

I shared a look with Teddy over my dinner as Kari and Nimue left the kitchen with their pots to talk in private. Scout shrugged next to me and continued skewering little balls of... whatever they were and scoffed them down.

I watched Scout eat with gusto. Very little bothered him, including pissing off the second-in-command XO. Although even I would admit *he* was terrifying when *his* back was up.

Teddy sat down with a pot. "I think Kari is on edge because of me."

Scout dismissed it with a flick of his fork. "Don't you worry, kid. Kari was born on edge."

"Don't call me 'kid'."

"Whatever you say, squirt."

I shouldered Scout to shut him up. He raised an eyebrow at me.

"Why do you think it's you?" I asked Teddy. Teddy was the youngest on the ship by a full decade and prone to the youthful assumption everything was about him.

"That last lot of samples we took in the asteroid belt

came up with nothing useful. I mean, there *was* some interesting properties, sure, but nothing we could stake out and claim a spotter's fee." Teddy's shoulders sagged. "I reckon she and the Captain don't think I know how to do my job. I did finish my studies in compositional science. I graduated right before we shipped out."

Teddy was defensive and more than a little sulky. He was obsessive about his job. He launched into a detailed explanation of the analysis and my mind vagued out. I'd been doing that a lot. I chalked it up to Deep Space Fatigue. Too many hours working with too little mental shut off time.

Scout closed the cap on his kibble pot, smacking his lips.

I leaned close to him to whisper in his ear, "Want to grab a beer?"

A slight smile creased the corner of his mouth. He didn't turn to me but tilted his head closer. "My place or yours?"

I eyed off Teddy across the table. He was engrossed in his datapad. With Nimue and Kari elsewhere, nobody was listening. "Deck two: maintenance corridor?" It was where we had been working earlier in the day.

He smiled and slipped out of his lap belt and left the kitchen. We weren't a couple, and "partners" only meant we were both service engineers covering different ship systems. But we got along well, despite each of our quirks. Honestly, a good shag was a convenient stress release.

I smiled as I finished eating. *Scout was definitely a very good shag.*

DEATH BEYOND

I slipped my arms into the sleeves of my standard-issue ship jumpsuit and shrugged it up over my shoulders, almost tripping on the Panel Impact Riveter. I was sure it had been properly stowed a few compartments away when Scout and I knocked off a few hours earlier. *Scout must not have secured it properly,* I told myself as I took it back. He had already left, so I couldn't ask. He wasn't the pillow talk type. Not that there were any pillows on the maintenance deck.

My datapad had been beeping when we were 'occupied,' so I had turned it off. The moment I turned it back on, it lit up with a barrage of messages. *Shit*.

Several of the messages were systems generated, but the last one was a direct message from Captain Nimue, demanding I present myself in OPS. The kitchen doubled as the ship's meeting room because it fit everybody in, but if she wanted to see someone separately, she called them to OPS. It meant something serious. I hurried to get there.

Scout was already in the kitchen when I arrived, and he gave me a friendly salute as I passed him. It was hard to tell if he was really good at not acting guilty, or just didn't care what anyone thought. I blushed on his behalf, as well as mine. Teddy was glued to his datapad but waved a coffee canister in the air to ask if I wanted one. I shook my head and climbed the ladder. Nimue and Kari were in OPS, poring over a screen set in the centre console with their backs to me. I cleared my throat to let them know I was there.

DEATH BEYOND

Kari looked over her shoulder. "Did you open an airlock on the maintenance deck?" Direct as always, but the question wasn't what I expected.

I frowned. "No. Why would I open an airlock?" I moved to stand next to her and Nimue.

Kari ignored my question. "Well, apparently, neither did anyone else. Yet one opened and closed." She waved her hands over the data displayed on the screen. "We've got the action alert. It's in the system log."

"Could be a glitch?" I suggested.

"Nope. See the O2 levels in that area? It definitely vented all of the atmosphere in the airlock and adjoining corridor."

I felt a chill looking at the column of information. *Scout and I definitely left those corridors full of Atmos.* A glitch could open the airlock, or an unstowed tool or loosened panel might trigger the door, but for that to cause a vent of the Atmos was unlikely. "What do the external cameras show?"

Nimue pulled up the camera feed. It was slow to respond, so she cleared the commands and tried again. It was still sluggish but started cycling through the camera views. We got a glimpse of the outside of the airlock in question, and the corresponding side of the ship before the screen dissolved into pixels and then went completely black.

"Dammit!" Kari exploded. She threw her hands in the air. "First an airlock, now this!" She started to pace in a circle.

Nimue shook her head. "Kari, you know the OPS screen does this from time to time. Calm down. I'm sure there's a simple explanation." She sounded worn. A lifetime of Deep Space travel was taking its toll.

"Simple is not cheap. We don't even have the budget for the full overhaul this ship is going to need, particularly if Teddy keeps turning up interesting rocks rather than mineral resources we can profit from." Kari jabbed a finger towards the ladder that led back down to the kitchen where Teddy was sitting.

I felt a familiar queasiness of addressing Kari directly, but braced myself and spoke up. "Scout and I get the samples. Teddy tests them. None of us knows if we have paydirt or another bog-standard rock until the results come in. It is the risk we all took when we went into uncharted Deep Space. No one knows what is out here."

"Oh, thanks for your input Morag, I had *no idea* uncharted meant no one had charted what was out here." Kari almost spat the words at me.

I shut my mouth. It wasn't worth the argument. My scalp prickled as I felt myself losing focus and I shook my head to try and clear it.

Nimue held a hand up between me and Kari to draw the words to a close. *Did she know I was feeling vague, or was it just not productive to keep going over it?* Kari drew her arms around herself and stopped talking. She always listened to Nimue. You could believe it was respect for the Captain's position, but we all knew how much Kari loved her, be it at a distance. Frankly, I didn't care. *I don't like Kari and she doesn't like me.*

"I'm too old for this game." Nimue sighed. "Let's take this discussion back down to the others." Our Captain had been increasingly withdrawn on this trip.

DEATH BEYOND

I followed them down to the kitchen.

"...so I think it must have come off the last lot of samples."

"That's good, Teddy," I told him, not knowing if it was good or not. Teddy floated on the other side of the table, working on his datapad, talking at an oblivious Scout. Teddy's position made it look to me as if he was laying down, but his posture was more like he was standing horizontally in midair. For some reason, the standard up and down orientation most ships adopted from our gravity well heritage didn't apply to the 20-something-year-old scientist.

"Have a seat everyone." Nimue caught Teddy's maglock boot and pushed it towards the metal deck so that he could walk towards the table and take a spot. I sat next to him, Scout across from us. Fresh coffee canisters were already locked to the tables waiting for us. Kari sat on the other side of Teddy.

Nimue leaned on her hands at the head of the table. "Okay. I've checked with you all about the airlock. Each of you knows how precious our air is and that we can't waste great swags of it in space. The O2 scrubbers can't cover it. If, for whatever reason, someone triggered the airlock, I need you to come and let me know. While it's not great that somebody is opening airlocks, a system glitch that vents our atmosphere is a far bigger issue. I would rather know it was just some stupid prank." She looked around the crew.

No one spoke.

Teddy drummed his fingers on the table. "Are we sure it was us?" Everyone turned to look at him. He shrugged with one shoulder. "It's just that the most recent samples are so different... And it is Deep Space, right? No one has been out here, at least not many people. And nobody's put down markers to claim a stake…"

"What are you suggesting, Teddy?" Nimue's voice was calm and even, although her tone suggested fatigue.

Teddy licked his lips. "What if it's aliens?"

Scout almost choked on his coffee, small droplets floating in the air as he spluttered out laughter. "Oh, my god. Really, Teddy?"

"It's just that the samples..." Teddy reached for his datapad.

Kari clenched her jaw. "Give me strength… Teddy, no one wants to hear about your stupid rocks. Aliens? Be real. We all know what it is." She looked at Scout.

Scout fixed Kari with an unblinking stare. "Which is?" His voice was remarkably even, without even the tiniest hint of aggression, but something in him tensed up.

Kari returned his glare. "Shit. Poor. Maintenance."

Nimue cleared her throat. "Come now, Kari. It's an old ship."

"No. Don't make excuses. Everyone on board knows our service engineers have better things to do than their jobs."

I watched Scout. His face remained impassive. If anything, he had relaxed. He shrugged one shoulder. "We can do both."

The colour rose in my cheeks.

A small muscle in Kari's jaw twitched. She abruptly

stood to lean over the table, the strap across her legs preventing her from actually standing. "Can you? Can you Scout? Which service manual cites that doggy style or reverse cowgirl is the proper way to do maintenance?"

Scout frowned. "You know... in Zero-G, they're basically the same thing. I mean, Morag—"

"Scout!" I hissed. My face burned.

"What? They are." Scout looked puzzled.

Kari turned on me. "Yes, Morag? You have something to tell us?" In that instant, I hated Kari and wished I *could* have thrown her out an airlock.

Nimue saved me from saying more. "Kari, that's enough. Space is lonely enough, and there aren't any rules about what crew can do in their downtime. But we do have a Code of Conduct, which includes making accusations. I have no reason to believe that Scout and Morag's... activities have impacted their work. And it is for me *alone* as Captain to call behaviour out, should it be necessary."

Kari looked as if she had been slapped. "I know *all* about space loneliness." She said it to the room, but it was clear her words were meant for Nimue. "I'm going to check out the airlock myself." She undid her lap strap and left.

Nimue dropped her head down and took a breath, massaging her temples. "If anyone has anything else to say, I'll be in OPS." She drifted up the ladder.

Scout drained off his coffee canister. "Hey Morag, I reckon we should add an electrical diagnosis to tomorrow's roster. What with all the stuff." He spoke as if the humiliating conversation hadn't happened and it was just a routine crew meeting. He smiled at me, then pointed at Teddy. "Aliens! Wow, kid, and they say you don't have a sense of humour." He chuckled to himself as he left the kitchen.

"All crew to the cargo hold."

The ship wide broadcast woke me from a deep sleep. Not restful, but one of passed out exhaustion. I was momentarily disoriented until the familiar shape of my crew quarters registered in my sodden brain. I exited the bunk straps and carefully slipped out of bed, feeling about for my maglock boots.

I encountered Scout on my way to the cargo deck. "What's this 'bout?" he asked.

A mark on his jumpsuit spanning his broad shoulders betrayed that he hadn't changed clothes, either.

"Dunno. Hey Scout, why didn't you just shoot Kari down when she said that we were shagging?"

He arched an eyebrow at me. "We are. Nothin' wrong with shaggin'. No one says we can't. Cap' made that clear."

"Well, yes. But the others—"

Scout pulled up to look directly at me. "Morag, we can stop it if it bothers you. I mean, I'd rather not stop cos I like it, but it's cool if you don't want to no more. I ain't the type to force someone."

"Yes. I mean no. I mean; I want to keep... doing 'it.' It's just…" I didn't really know what I was trying to say. "Know what? Forget I mentioned it."

"Okay, cool." Scout smiled and continued walking.

DEATH BEYOND

I looked at the ceiling and sighed to myself. *Oh, to have the wiring of someone who wasn't bothered by anything.* I shrugged it off and caught up with him as he hit the door lock release, revealing Nimue and Teddy crowded in the corridor.

"Kari is dead." Teddy's voice was flat. As he moved, I saw the shape beyond him was Kari. Her face was ashen with sickly blue lips. She was suspended at an awkward angle, with only one boot locked to the floor, looking like she was taking a huge step. The collar on her jumpsuit was open, the zipper floating on its own as if it had been torn off. I was stunned.

"Shit, what happened?" Scout asked, stepping around me to get a closer look. He peered intently at her face. "Looks like she suffocated." He took a hold of her free-floating, outstretched leg and pushed it towards the floor, where her boot magnetised to the deck. "And not long ago, rigour mortis has only just started to set in. What's all the sticky shit?"

I didn't want to consider what bodily fluids constituted 'sticky shit' to Scout.

Nimue closed her eyes as if trying to centre herself before shaking her head slightly. "How could this have happened?" She looked at Scout and me. I flinched. For a moment, I thought it was an accusation until I realised she was asking the service engineers.

Scout looked at the door panel. "These corridors ain't normally kept in Atmos. You got to vent one to fill the next. Not like the crew quarters and kitchen." Everyone nodded. It was common knowledge, although only Scout and I regularly had to use the vent-cycling systems. "You can set it up to automatically cycle back and forth if you want a clear path, but you need to know how."

"That's done up in OPS and there are safety's. Heat sensors, mostly." I offered. Programming and electrical was more my thing.

"Right. Even if she backtracked, the system shoulda picked it up, unless the sensors were off. I guess it coulda glitched." Scout tilted his head, looking over Kari. "Don't know if it being the second glitch makes it more or less likely, but the other possibility is someone cut her air."

Stunned silence greeted Scout's words, broken by Nimue. "Where was everyone? Who saw her last?"

"I went to my lab. My specimens started sweating this weird—"

Nimue cut Teddy off with her hand. "Scout?"

"I was alone in my quarters, not shaggin' Morag." Scout offered. I died inside.

"I was also alone," I added through gritted teeth.

"And I was looking through the system logs in my quarters," Nimue added.

"So... Kari did it to herself?" Scout said what we were all wondering.

Nimue let out a noise that was half gasp, half sob.

Scout ignored her. "I think we should get Kari out of here." He looked at Teddy. "Get her boots, would ya?" Teddy nodded and stooped to turn off Kari's Maglocks so they could float her out of the corridor, leaving me with Nimue. Inwardly, I cringed at being left to comfort the Captain of *The Occam's Razor*.

Nimue took a shuddering breath before speaking. "I knew how Kari felt, but as Captain, I have to maintain distance." She swallowed hard. "You and Scout... cherish what you have." Nimue turned to follow the others.

Nimue thought it was her fault Kari killed herself, and worse, the big romance everyone seemed to think Scout and I had wasn't anything like that. I followed her to the cargo bay, feeling guilt I couldn't quite place.

The cargo bay was just a large space with access to an airlock. Not the one that had glitched, but one big enough to hold anything we brought in. Besides a few crates of samples Teddy wanted to keep, and some claim registration markers, it was nearly empty. Kari lay in a large crate normally used to store samples as proof of claim. The inner trays could be removed for larger samples and occurrences such as this.

Just inside the door, Scout caught my arm. I slowed to a stop.

"I've been thinkin' 'bout all this. The sensors shoulda picked up that Kari was still in an area that needed to be vented. Heat signature shoulda triggered the safety." His voice was uncharacteristically low.

"And if it glitched out?" I asked him, crossing my arms over my chest and watching Nimue lean over Kari's body. Teddy was checking his sample crates.

Scout shook his head. "She still woulda been movin' from Atmos to Atmos. The vent don't start until one door opens and the other closes. We both know that."

I nodded. "And the doors won't open from Atmos

to vacuum, so the rush of air doesn't damage anything." The implication gave me a growing sense of dread.

"Exactly. So, it had to be a manual vent, right? Kari was a lovesick, high-strung bitch. But when she said, 'checkout the airlock'?"

"She was not suicidal." Nimue's icy voice came from behind us.

"Sorry Cap, didn't mean no disrespect. Just recountin' what I see. And the way I see it, a glitch couldn't do this."

My breath caught in my throat. "Shit. Scout, you really think someone *murdered* her?"

"Nah, not really. But it does look like someone sabotaged the ship. The glitch just don't make sense. And if I were gonna kill someone, that's how I'd do it."

Nimue gave Scout a searching look. "I can't see how any of us benefit from sabotage."

"It would get us out of this godforsaken Deep Space if we had to go back." The words came out of my mouth before I considered how they sounded. *I just implicated myself!*

Nimue frowned at me. "That may be so, but if we go back empty-handed after all the months we have spent in Deep Space, no one wins. Well, except maybe Teddy. He's found himself some pretty pebbles." Nimue nodded to Teddy with his samples.

At the mention of his name, Teddy looked up. "Anyone been messing with my crates?"

"No one's been violatin' your rocks, kid," Scout called as Teddy drifted towards us, avoiding the crate containing Kari.

"It's just that there's marks of some kind of residue on the crates."

"Well, in future, wash your hands so you can keep your residue to yourself." If looks could kill, Scout would have been joining Kari.

"Okay. It's been a long night. I want to see everyone in the kitchen tomorrow to discuss how we proceed. Get some sleep." Nimue turned and left the cargo bay. It wasn't like her to just bail on her crew, especially after one of them died.

We gave her space and chatted about work, my home on Mars, and Teddy's insane alien's theory while we waited for the Atmos cycles to move along with Nimue, so we could restart the vent cycle.

I turned to see how Teddy was faring. Far from horrified, he looked calm, prodding at a dark mark on the wall. He turned to Scout and me. "I need to discuss my specimens with the Captain." His voice was distant, detached, and he turned away without another word. *Were they acting weird or was it just grief?*

I turned to follow Teddy down the corridor, as the light above clicked to green. Scout put a restraining hand on my chest. He was watching Teddy leave, his eyes flickering to me as if to say 'wait a moment.'

Teddy muttered about us "having better things to do," as he left, but something told me a shag wasn't what Scout wanted.

I turned to him. "Scout, why do you have to be such a jerk to Teddy?"

"What? It was funny. I'm just teasin' him. Kid's so serious about his rocks. I mean, he barely even looked at Kari."

I rolled my eyes. "So, he doesn't like dead bodies. Who does?"

Scout shrugged. "A dead body is just an alive one that ain't breathin' no more. And, for the record, I don't think you killed Kari, just so you know… Nimue thinks it was me."

This is what he wanted to tell me.

"Oh Scout, I doubt that she—" The look in his eyes stilled my lips.

"Look, I don't get emotions. I don't understand them unless I've been in the situation myself. I can't tell what people are feelin' unless they tell me, but I do know what suspicion looks like. And suspicion is dangerous."

"I think everyone is just tense," I told him. *What suspicion in Scout's past had been dangerous, and to whom? What did I really know about my part-time screw and service engineer partner?* I hoped there was no suspicion on my face as I shook my head. "She's under a lot of stress. I don't think she suspects you."

"Why not? It has to be someone on this ship."

I couldn't think of anything to say to that. None of us had alibis. Even *I* didn't. "Well, by that logic, it could have been me. I have dizzy spells and vague out. Who knows what I could do when I'm not myself." I meant to sound light and dismissive, but Scout was looking at me with a calculating expression that sent me cold.

Then he cracked a grin. "Nah, Morag, you couldn't have opened the airlock while you were ridin' my dick." I laughed along with him more out of tension than any humour. *Christ! He thought I was confessing! What would he do if he actually thought I was a murderer?* I looked over his broad shoulders and muscled arms. He was strong. It's what I liked about him. Chilling realisation dawned on me that I wouldn't stand a chance if I had to defend myself against him.

He crossed his arms over his chest and stared at the floor. "I think it's Teddy."

I blinked. "What? The skinny little science geek?"

"Kari laughed at him 'bout his aliens. You said it yourself, sabotage gets us back from Deep Space. Teddy's the only one who would benefit from that. Kari didn't kill herself. Well, I don't think Kari did... you have to admit the kid is weird." An assessment of somebody as weird, coming from Scout, was certainly the pot calling the kettle black.

"But capable of homicide?" I shook my head.

Scout shrugged. He was calm for someone accusing someone of being a murderer. "Time will tell. But you know, Morag, I won't let anything happen to you. And that's because I like you, not just because we're shaggin'."

Later, I sat and brooded in the kitchen. I hadn't even tried to avoid vaguing out. Nimue was in OPS. When I saw her briefly, her puffy eyes betrayed she had been crying. Scout had appeared, grabbed a coffee canister and announced he would be back so we could "move the shit show discussion on and get to the maintenance of the ship." I felt like he wanted to make sure it wasn't a glitch or shoddy maintenance. Then again, maybe I was just projecting.

I decided to go and get him, figuring I'd check the crew quarters first. I hit Scout's door buzzer and stood outside, thinking everything over. *What could Scout do to someone he didn't like?* I listened to the hiss and clunk of the Atmos for who knows how long, staring at the mottled wall on the other side of the corridor. I was afraid. Not just at the idea that there was a murderer among the people I had mostly known for years—Teddy had only signed on for this trip. Or because I could easily see Scout committing murder if he felt it was justified, but because I honestly couldn't discount myself. I had no alibi besides being with Scout when the airlock opened and closed. *Maybe that one truly was a glitch.*

Scout hadn't responded, so clearly wasn't in.

My head swam with my thoughts and I felt the edges of a blank coming on. I leaned a hand on the corridor wall but snatched it back immediately. It was sticky. Absent-mindedly, I had placed my hand on a strange dark patch. *Was it blood?* It didn't feel quite like I imagined blood would feel. It was almost oily, and blood didn't make sense, anyhow. In my vague state, I rolled my fingers over my palm.

Then the lights went out and I couldn't hear the Atmos cycle anymore.

On the edge of panic, I fumbled my way along the wall, looking for the Coms panel that was next to the door. My fingers brushed over the buttons and I took a literal stab in the dark. At worst, I would trigger the logs and it would record my heavy breathing.

Nothing happened. The whole circuit was out.

DEATH BEYOND

My hopes dashed, I groaned at the thought of having to manually open the door locks. At least the crew quarters were close to OPS and the kitchen rather than decks away, and this whole section was kept in Atmos, so I wouldn't have to manually arrange vent cycles. It would be slow going, but I didn't want to hang outside Scout's empty quarters in the dark.

I tugged the lock-lever to unlock the door. It was stiff and barely budged. I disengaged my maglock boots and set one against the wall to yank the manual lock-lever sideways. The mechanisms inside the door made a grinding sound that echoed in the silence of a corridor with no air circulating. That's another thing people living planet-side don't get. There is no sound in space, and no silence on a spaceship. The systems keeping you alive always hummed.

My breath came in shaky gasps that sounded like roaring in the silence. *This was what it would be like to be buried alive.* The lock-lever I was yanking on that prevented the doors from being opened to vacuum moved slightly. I strained against it. *How much of my limited oxygen was this strenuous activity using up?* Panic gripped me.

I thought of Kari's deathly blue lips. *Who killed her?* I wondered. *In this utter darkness, anything could be slowly coming towards me through the air, and I wouldn't know it.* Frantically, I pulled on the lever. The next corridor might be just as dark, but I felt something was in with me.

The lock-lever budged a fraction more, then gave way. If the corridor had light, the bulb above the door would have turned green as it unlocked. I spun the manual door lock-wheel as quickly as I could, and it slid open a fraction. I didn't even bother to wait until it was fully open before shoving my way through. The corridor beyond was just as black.

I kicked the door gap hard to shoot through to the other side, just as I felt the monster behind me was doing; coming for me. I collided hard with the other door and started pawing at it, looking for the lock-lever. *I am being stupid and wasting precious air,* my mind whispered, but I was beyond rational thought. I yanked hard on the lock-lever. It moved a little. I braced myself again against the wall for another go, when suddenly, it gave way. The abrupt movement threatened to spin me as the lock-wheel gave and the door opened. Something was coming through! Suspended midair, I was helpless as a hand grasped my throat.

I screamed and battered at it. Another hand caught my arm, and I kept fighting. My arms were forced to my sides and pinned.

"Morag, it's me."

Something familiar slipped into my senses. The arms, his scent. *Scout* had hold of me. I burst into tears.

"I'm sorry, crying because of the dark." I was still holding on to him fiercely.

"Don't apologise, Morag. The dark's fuckin' terrifyin' at the best of times, let alone when you have dead crew." The man who didn't understand the emotions of others unless he'd been there patted my hair gently. "Sorry 'bout grabbing your throat."

DEATH BEYOND

Even though I didn't want to, I released Scout to the dark.

"I left all the doors open. Lost count how many corridors I went through, but I reckon the kitchen was one more door over. Hopefully, there will be an emergency torch there." Scout took me by my shoulders and pointed me in the right direction, before putting my feet to the deck where my maglocks engaged. I could hear him stomping ahead until he met the closed door.

With far more ease than I had, he pulled the lock-lever and turned the wheel. Dim lights that felt blinding after the pitch-black greeted us. Teddy was in the kitchen.

"The cooker was on backup so a failure wouldn't ruin dinner," Teddy told us. "I just plugged the emergency system into it. The kitchen and OPS have basic functions: lights, coms, the cooker..." He waved vaguely at the dim light above the kitchen table. His voice was so quiet, and he had something in his hands.

"What you got there?" Scout asked.

"Oh, just one of my samples." Teddy let it sit suspended in the air. "Someone has been going through the stuff in my lab." His eyes narrowed at Scout. "I came to tell the Captain."

"And she is?" I asked him.

Teddy shrugged and pointed to OPS. The hatch was slightly ajar. Scout turned and climbed the ladder while I grabbed a coffee canister from the cupboard. My hands shook so badly, I could barely pull the mouthpiece open and bring it to my lips. Caffeine probably wasn't what I needed, but the normalcy felt calming.

A moment later, Scout's maglocks were back on the ladder. "Cap's dead."

I turned towards Teddy. His face looked truly alien in the emergency light. He said nothing but nodded slowly at Scout's words while gently turning the rock sample in the air, studying it. It gave me the creeps.

"How? When?" I spluttered. Locking my coffee to the table before I spilled it.

Scout came to stand before me. "Not sure when, but not long ago. She's been strangled. Know anythin' 'bout that, Teddy?"

Teddy turned his head slightly in Scout's direction and raised his eyebrows, never taking his eyes off his specimen. "Nimue is stronger than me. How would I have the strength to strangle her?" His detachment sent chills up my spine.

"Whoever it was used a tourniquet. Even Morag could have strangled her with that."

"I see." Teddy grazed his finger over the floating sample, then brushed it over his lips like he was applying lipstick. "It's alive, you know."

"What the fuck you talkin' about?" Scout closed his fingers, forming a fist.

"The sample, it's alive. Living in void. I don't know what it is, but it sings. I wanted to study it more but somebody has been in my lab. I came to tell Nimue."

"Is that before or after you killed her?" Scout turned to me. "Morag, we need to do somethin' about the freak. He's lost it."

A cloud passed over Teddy's face. "*I* didn't kill her.

I certainly know that. Where were *you,* Scout?" Teddy lazily rolled his head in Scout's direction, fixing the far bigger man with an almost drunken stare.

"Seriously Teddy? Scout came back to get me!"

"Yes, but how quickly? Frankly, Morag, your blindness to the fact that you share your body with a clinical sociopathic murderer is astounding."

The speed at which Scout disengaged his maglock boots from the deck and moved to grab Teddy was startling. I darted forwards and grabbed Scout's arm. I was pissed at Teddy bringing up my love life yet again, but I didn't want to see him murdered before my eyes. I yanked at Scout's arm.

"Scout let go!"

Scout turned his face to face me. His expression was pure calculated fury, but he did release the scientist.

Teddy coughed. "I have already… set a distress beacon going." He breathed hard and plucked the sample from the air then headed for the door. "If you could refrain from murder until help arrives, I would appreciate it. I would like to get these specimens back to the Science Academy. Perhaps you could shag while you wait and expend some of that homicidal energy!" With that, he slipped through the door.

The last barb was livelier than Teddy had been in the entire conversation, even with Scout threatening to kill him. Still, *this wasn't the Teddy I knew. But what did I know about Scout? Hell, what did I know about myself?*

I turned to face Scout. He was staring at me. "Not all clinical psychopaths are murderers." The way he said it gave me chills, like this was something he'd heard before. He turned and left, heading towards the crew quarters. I slowly sat down at the table, pulled the strap over my knees, and cried.

In OPS, an alarm went off. I dragged my head up from where I let it relax to vague out. I looked around, but I was the only one in the kitchen. I climbed to my feet and went up the ladder.

Nimue's body was hunched over the centre console. The swath of fabric around her neck floated away like it was caught in a bleak breeze. Small bubbles of liquid hung in the air around her. I didn't want to consider what they were. *Had Nimue cut the power, or was she investigating the blackout? Perhaps Teddy* had *done it. Had I...?*

The panel chirped again, reminding me why I entered OPS. I leaned over what was once Kari's chair, to see it was an incoming message.

"This is Captain Opal of the *Mind's Retreat Salvage Ship*. We received your distress call and are on our way. Hang in there." The message cut off. I checked the timestamp. It took almost an hour to reach us over the distance. They weren't going to be arriving anytime soon, but they *were* coming. I decided to let Teddy and Scout know.

I headed for the ladder, avoiding our former captain and her orbiting spray of bubbles to 'jump down' with a sharp push off the top bar. My feet hit the floor, and I grabbed an emergency torch off the table before going through the kitchen door. I was greeted by an odd metallic taste. Not quite the usual burnt smell of space that clings to everything.

I made my way forwards, holding the little torch in front of me. I walked through these corridors every day, yet they looked alien. Deep shadows danced with the movement of my light. I went slowly, watching and listening for anything; anybody. Something glanced past my head, leaving a wet feeling. I pushed it away and shone the light on it. It was Teddy's rock. My hand's movement through the air left a greasy feeling on my palm. I looked up to see Teddy standing in the next corridor. I kept the torch low, so I didn't blind him.

"Hey, Teddy. Good idea on the distress call." He ignored me. "Come on, Teddy. Don't be like that. Me and Scout... It's complicated. I wasn't taking sides."

"Morag..." For a split second, I thought it was Teddy talking until the light highlighted Scout on the other side of Teddy. "You're chattin' with him, but Teddy's not lookin' so hot." Scout's voice was strange.

"What do you mean?"

"I mean, his throats missin'."

"Say again." I spluttered.

"He's dead. His throats all cut up. And he's got this weird look, like—"

Teddy slowly turned to face me. The hair stood up on the back of my neck. His smiling face was a bloody pulp, and one arm stretched off at an odd angle. I flicked the torch around. Floating in the air were large balls of blood. No one from a gravity well can appreciate the appearance of blood in space, like bright red baubles suspended in the air.

DEATH BEYOND

I felt chilled. *Scout killed Teddy. Oh God, I would be next!*

Scout stepped past Teddy with an odd expression.

I forced a smile. "Hey, we've got a response on the distress call. Help is on its way. It will be here in a matter of moments. We just need to stay alive so they can help us." I was on the verge of hysterics, and my voice squeaked. I felt the familiar vague wave come over me. *Please don't let me blank out. I need to stay alive.*

"Help us?" Scout asked.

"Yes. They can help us catch the killer. Obviously, we have a stowaway that's done all this." I desperately grabbed at straws.

Scout was circling me. "You think that's who it is, who done all this? Some kind of stowaway?" It sounded like bullshit to me too, but then Scout paused as if thinking it over before nodding. "Alright... Let's go hunt a killer." I hated the way he said it, but I agreed enthusiastically.

Scout was so damn fit. I was dead if it came to fighting him off. It took all of my strength not to glance at Teddy as I moved past. *That is what I will become if I don't keep my wits about me.* I shook my head to clear it.

"Hey, Morag? You ok?" Scout's voice made me flinch.

"Yeah, it's just those vague feelings I get sometimes. Nothing to worry about." Even to my ears, I sounded strained.

He gestured towards the door. "Ok. Lead the way."

The last thing I wanted to do was put my back to him, but I did. I couldn't think of any reasonable way of saying I didn't want to.

As I crept through the dark corridor, I bit my lip, trying not to cry. It tasted oddly greasy. Scout walked closely behind me. *Where was I leading us?* My mind raced. *Deck two: maintenance corridor, the last place we were 'together.'* It was a long stretch of multiple sections where we were working and had the docking airlock where help would arrive. It was also where our tools were stored.

"Hey, Morag. You notice all the sticky stuff all over the ship?"

I flinched at the sound of his voice and shone the torch back at him. "What?"

He closed his eyes to the bright light and put his hand up to shield his face. "Shine it on the wall." He waved as if he could push the light away.

I did as suggested. Scout was right. There were smears all over the wall.

"No one died down here. It's not blood." I responded, resolutely continuing on.

"Maybe it's just Teddy's jizzy-spunt rocks."

I let out a barking laugh. At that moment, I was terrified of Scout, yet his wrong humour felt normal.

"Say Morag, where are we going?" He started the Atmos cycle for the next section, as we moved out of the habitat zone.

I was dreading he would ask. I didn't want any chance he might remember the tools that I was heading for. *Please don't let him notice my fear.* "No particular direction. Just going where's familiar." I tried to open the door.

"I recall getting pretty 'familiar' down here…" He sounded very calm. "You know, people's heads… sometimes they do things they don't know *not* to do."

Was this a confession? I prayed I would make it to our tools. "I guess…" I pulled at the lock-lever. Scout reached around me to draw the lock-lever down and turn the door wheel. It was an intimate position I had been in so many times before, but never feeling this afraid of him. His breath was hot against my neck.

"Tell me more about these vague spells."

His question caught me off guard. *Was this Scout's weird dismissal of everything going on and just chatting?* The door opened, and I stepped away from him into the gap.

"Oh, you know, I get stressed. My head goes vague and I blank out. I don't remember things clearly, who said or did what. Sometimes it's a total blur." I gave a half shrug. It wasn't a lie. That was what was happening with increasing frequency. *What would he do with the information?* I prayed he wouldn't notice the sweat beating on my forehead.

"So you could, I guess, say or do something without rememberin' it?"

I swallowed as I made my way to the next door. *Shit... Shit, Shit, Shit! Was he setting me up as an alibi?* "I guess..."

I yanked hard on the lock-lever, which came jerkily down, and then turned the wheel. The door cranked open and there were all our tools neatly stowed along the walls.

Scout took a breath. "So, in one of these spells…"

I swallowed and stomped resolutely forwards.

"Could you have maybe..."

I paused and leaned towards the Handheld Laser Cutter.

"Killed the entire crew because you wanted to get out of Deep Space?"

Shit! He was going to try to pin it on me! If he didn't kill me first. I lunged for the Cutter. Scout was quicker and knocked my hand away.

"Morag, I like you. I really do. And you're a great shag. But I'm not gonna let you get away."

"But why, Scout? Why does it have to be this way?"

He shrugged one shoulder. "You tell me. It's your head on the block." He laughed like he'd made a clever joke.

I went for the Cutter again. He smacked me away a second time, knocking the torch out of my hand. *Christ! He's toying with me.* We stood facing each other. The spinning torch between us shining light on his feet and then at the bulkhead above my head.

Stalemate. We were frozen to the spot, each watching the other. Light shot up, then down as the torch spun.

Scout tilted his head towards the Laser Cutter. "I'm not gonna let you get away with tryin' to kill me. Like I said, I like you. But if you try anythin', I'll kill you. That's just how it's gotta be."

I can imagine the force it would have taken to smash

Teddy's head into the wall. *He was just a kid on his first trip out...* "You're a monster. An unfeeling monster."

Scout sighed. "It's not the first time I've heard that."

My eyes were on the torch. Light up. Light down. Light up. I grabbed the torch as it shone above my head, and flashed it in his eyes, diving sideways not at the Cutter, but towards the Impact Riveter. As I hoped, blinded by the torchlight, Scout kicked off his maglock boots like he had when he went for Teddy and lunged in the wrong direction. I yanked the Riveter off the wall.

As Scout realised his mistake, I blasted him squarely in the chest. Without maglock boots holding him in place, the impact sent him diving backwards through the door. I started winding the door wheel frantically. I could see him tumbling through the open air, desperately trying to find something to hold and stabilise. I willed the door to close more quickly.

"Morag!" he roared, "I'll kill you! I could have let it slide. I get it. I really do. Even if you don't *know* what you are doing... Deep Space is lonely. It's efficient to get people out of the way. But trying to kill me? No, I can't let that fly." He continued spiralling away.

My heart was pounding. If he made the other side and push off before I could close the door, I was dead.

His feet hit the other end, and he kicked off, just as the door I had been frantically winding shut. I lept to the lock-lever. He grabbed it on the other side. The stiffness of the lever and both of us pushing opposite ways meant neither of us could move it properly. I kept a death grip on it and reached for the mechanism to manually cycle Scout's Atmos. Once started, it couldn't be overridden.

DEATH BEYOND

No power in the corridor meant no sensors to pick up the heat signature and stop the Atmos venting, but he could still override the door on his side if he could open it before the cycle engaged.

I turned, desperately looking for a way to survive, praying he wouldn't get the door open before he hit vacuum. *The airlock! It's on its own circuit!* If I could cross the threshold and shut the door, I could lock it. There was no way to manually open it from the corridor. I would have powered coms to signal *The Minds Retreat* and a datapad. I imagined Scout hammering on the door, trying to get in and kill me. It took all my mental reserves to take my hand off the lock-lever and sprint for the airlock. I spun the wheel, closing the door to the corridor, then pulled the lock-lever, sealing myself in the airlock.

There was a light above the door. It was still green, meaning the door wasn't electronically locked. I opened an access panel and pulled out the datapad. The airlock's sensors showed Scout's corridor was now void of Atmos. I frowned. Scout's heat signature was still registering strong. As I watched, it hovered at the door before slowly moving the other way. That meant Scout was still conscious and moving deeper into the vacuum of *The Occam's Razor's* corridors. The dot disappeared out of range. I checked the Atmos levels again. It was definitely vented. Scout *should* be dead.

But then how was he moving through the ship? What was he planning to do to come and kill me?

Safely on the other side of the airlock door, I stare

at the green lock light. I can barely breathe. I wait for green to turn red. Red means electronically locked. Red means safe. Eventually, the light clicks to red and I let out a ragged breath. A grinding sound stops and starts, and I turn towards the outer door as it gets slightly louder. *The light above the outer door is red, it is locked.* The grinding continues. I feel my mind vaguing out as I strain to hear the sound under the echoes of my own ragged breath. *Scout was dead. He had to be. Scout who saw a dead body as 'just an alive one that ain't breathin' no more.' Scout who argued with Kari. Scout who knew I didn't like everyone knowing we shagged.*

Nimue suspected Scout. Was he the last person to see Teddy? Teddy was the last one to see Captain Nimue. Scout said that with a tourniquet, Teddy could have killed the Captain. Creepy Teddy with his weird slimy rocks, he thought were alive. Scout killed Teddy and wanted to kill me. I just killed him.

With my eyes closed, I replay my conversations with Scout: him asking about vaguing out, saying some killings made sense, saying he could let it go... My eyes snap open. *What could I have done in a blank out? Did I kill Teddy? Did I kill the others?* My mind vagues out for the briefest moment and I sway like seagrass. *Did I kill everyone?*

My fear rises. *All the glitches. The opening airlock. That was this airlock, and it wasn't far from where we were working maintenance. No,* I remind myself, *I couldn't have opened the airlock. I was with Scout, shagging...* I scrunch my eyes closed, to try and clear the fog of vagueness. When I open them, I notice shimmery smudges on the walls.

The grinding sound continues. I reach out and touch the greasy smears. They are spread from one side of the airlock to the other. It looks like the marks on Kari and Nimue, like the air around Teddy.

"Did anyone check the airlock that glitched?" I ask the air. I think furiously. *Kari was going to, but then she never came back.* I hold up the datapad again. Little by little, I realise the grinding sound is the airlock door wheel. Not the *inner* one, but the *outer* door. I look above it. The light is still red. It is locked.

Hope pierces through me. *Could this be the salvage ship already?* The Mind's Retreat *coming to rescue me?* Slowly, I hold up the datapad and use the airlock's limited sensors to check the outside of the ship. There is nothing. The camera is grainy, but I can see the stars. There's definitely no ship there.

My stomach churns. The datapad shakes in my hands. I flick it from the cameras to the ship schematics with the heat sensors. There's my dot in the airlock. There is a second dot. For a brief moment, I think it's Scout at the inner airlock door, having survived the Atmos vent. Then I realise the dot is on the other side of the *outer* airlock door. It's outside *The Occam's Razor*.

Scout didn't kill anyone. I didn't kill everyone. The explanation was not so simple. I start to cry. The door wheel begins turns. The tiny spheres of my own tears start creeping toward the door, drawn to what should be the vacuum-sealed edge. The grinding sound gets louder.

The red light above the outer airlock door turns green. Green means unlocked.

DEATH BEYOND

Jade Wildy holds Bachelor and master's degrees in visual arts giving her a flair for culture. She returned to writing fiction in 2020, concentrating on speculative fiction but branching out into fantasy, science fiction and horror.

Through her writing Jade addresses themes like death, psychological state and being different, and delights in slipping in the unexpected. She believes in the power of storytelling as a motivator for change, and her writing has been included in numerous publications internationally.

A self-confessed wallflower, Jade lives in South Australia on the traditional lands of the Kaurna People, and can be frequently be found writing or drawing in the local cafes.

Find her work at:
www.jadewildywordsmith.com
www.facebook.com/jadewildywordsmith

VOICES FROM THE VOID

Gregg Cunningham

I.

Janitrix 3 studied the interplanetary pilot from behind the viewing glass and felt the hairs on the back of her neck prickle as the spinal implant tingled once more. She lifted a finger as if to calm the small bio chip device, slowly stroking the contour around the aroused scarred tissue of the implant and wondered if the isolated pilot was telepathically calling out to her once more. She wondered if it were even possible for him to wake up from his slumber like she had, wake up and flex his sleeping body, first the fingers, then his toes. Crunching and flexing each part of his body until the blood flows freely through his veins again, just like they were taught during cryo-slumber training.

The gleaming corridors of the ship stretched out like silent cathedral halls awaiting to be filled by eager celestial congregations, masses of travelling pioneers who lay awaiting the day they would leave their cryochambers and venture out to fill the vast decks and greet their welcoming hosts within Ursa Major.

The space craft for now, however, remained as silent as the passing stars, the rushing darkness outside the sleek metallic hull of the *CCCR Rasputin* as empty as those large echoing atriums within the ship.

She studied his partially naked torso glistening through the safety of the clear barrier with embarrassment as he lay submerged in the fluidity tank in the middle of the pristine navigation room. His spinal implant pads that were hard wired into the ship's main frame also interfaced with his cranium, sending and receiving navigational reports and updates from the autonomic robots that maintained the ship. Feeding tubes hung like twisting lubricated umbilical cords entering and exiting their designated orifices, disappearing into large medical vats of bubbling embryonic fluid being overlooked by the sleek metallic autonomic medical robot. Janitrix watched as the robot carefully injected medication from a large hypodermic needle into the pilot's pulsing neck. The needle slowly entered the soft tissue and mixed the syringe with his blood until it was empty. The autonomic robot then retracted the needle and inspected the vile. Janitrix watched as a single drop of blood fell to the floor and splattered. Everything else inside was spotless, clinical, the quintessential beating heart of the Russianite vessel monitored and checked continuously throughout the light speed journey through the stars by both human caretaker and autonomic machine.

DEATH BEYOND

Janitrix could still feel the telepathic static build up from where she stood outside the room as her temple vibrated and tingled pleasantly with his overbearing presence.

"Hello again, Janitrix 3," the voice in her head softly whispered. "I enjoyed your visit yesterday and hoped you would come and see me again today?"

She let out a slight gasp at the suddenness of his voice, almost dropping her security data slate to the polished floor as her heartbeat skipped. Janitrix was as shocked today on hearing his invading thoughts as she was yesterday. The solitude now forever broken between them.

"No, forgive me, not today, Starshina. I have to check on the leaking embryotic chamber on level 3 again." Her reply was short, she felt embarrassed about what she had done with him the day before. It was not her intention to be manipulated into that kind of sordid behaviour by anyone, let alone the ship's pilot.

"Oh, has that become a problem?" Starshina sounded concerned. "I was hoping we had isolated that problem yesterday, Janitrix 3." The chrome panelled autonomic medical robot briefly looked up at Janitrix, before continuing examining the blood vial it had pulled from the pilot's neck.

Janitrix glanced at her PAX, the Personal Assistant Executive wrapped around her forearm as the screen blinked its reminders of daily tasks still to be performed, and hesitated. She twisted the loose leather strap around her wrist, trying to straighten the device as she pondered. Her daydreaming outside the pilot bay area meant she was behind her dailes by almost 45 minutes, but she couldn't recall making her way to the viewing area.

He was manipulating her again.

"At present no problem has arisen, Starshina. I was required to check your levels here before I commenced my duties elsewhere, is all. I have my PAX orders," she lifted her wrist device as if to show him, "and will complete them on schedule as always." Janitrix shuffled in her white body maintenance skinsuit, the neoprene scales glistening across her JANITRIX 3 lapel name tag. She was unaccustomed to telepathic conversation, especially with the esteemed pilot of the interplanetary vessel, and made her way from the viewing gallery, lowering her head slightly as she passed.

"Very well, I understand," Starshina replied once more. "I will make a log entry explaining your absence." Janitrix quickly sensed the rejection in his voice and quickly added to her answer.

"I could come around after I have finished on level three… if you would like to… talk?"

"Talk… yes, I would like that very much, Janitrix 3. Space travel can become such a lonely task without a good companion. Wouldn't you agree?" Starshina's ghostly voice added without emotion as the autonomic robot slowly went about its business by the large embryonic vat.

Protocols dictated no conscripted deckhand should ever physically interact with the pilot during the 80-light year voyage to Ursa Major. They were merely there to monitor and maintain the crew's cryogenic tanks during their allocated hyper-sleep shift, and ensure the safety and welfare of the two hundred or so delegates who accepted the invitation to meet new friends somewhere within Ursa Major, now silently stored on board for the historical trip. Should any problems arise, the duty crew member would alert the cryogenically frozen crew and awake them before commencing any counter measures required in an emergency. Any violation of this order was a court martial offence and carried a penalty of expulsion through the airlock to any conscripted subordinate who broke those rules.

If he wanted too, Starshina could have already ordered his autonomic robots to have her removed from her duties and confine her to the isolation cells pending further investigations.

But she hadn't broken the rules. Starshina had.

In his loneliness, he had called out to her in her final months of her duty.

And in her panic, she had broken not only the first law, '*do not enter the pilot chamber*', but was manipulated into breaking the second law.

'*Do not make physical contact with the pilot, contamination is deadly.*'

Janitrix was the third maintenance engineer into the long journey to be awakened from their cryogenic slumber and begin her twelve month appointed duties. Once her time was up, she would return to her cryogenic tube on level three and pass the mantle onto the next crewman, Janitrix 4, who was in line for the next duty roster. Each crewmember was scheduled to monitor the pilot and the craft for one year before handing the duties on, ensuring the ship's pilot was monitored by both artificial intelligence and human eyes.

Starshina, like all designated pilots of this type of ship, had been placed into a comatose state for the entirety of the journey, unable to endure the 80-light year mission in the comfort of cryogenic stasis as brain function was required to interact with the ship's artificial intelligence. He would be well cared for along the way, his body maintained by the autonomic medical robots to extend his internal organs life capacity and prevent premature shutdown. His body now served only as a mere vessel for the pilot's enhanced consciousness now working alongside the A.I. maintaining and protecting the ship and its crew during their trip.

Janitrix nodded and managed a smile his way, but it quickly faded from her face when she realised her faux pas. He could not see her standing there. She left the viewing area for the elevator to take her to level three.

2.

After checking the status of all two hundred and fifty dignitaries on board, Janitrix made her way down through the large atrium to level three. The embryotic leak had been contained to a cryochamber on that level which held the second Janitrix, who had already served her yearlong duty during the journey. The small pod, identified with the JANITRX 2 decal marked across the frosted glass, was extracted from the long row of other cryogenically frozen maintenance crew members and pulled free. It was clear to the current Janitrix that contamination had entered her booth and now the embryotic fluid required flushing and replacing. This was a routine procedure, but concerned Janitrix nonetheless. If the procedure was not handled efficiently, it could mean the end to her predecessor's coma cycle and return her to active service.

Once Janitrix had made the calculations, she proceeded with the task, ensuring the levels maintained a safe balance throughout the transfer. The assigned autonomic robot fussed over the cryochamber, ensuring the unconscious Janitrix 2 remained secured in the reclining back rest and the biometrics read correct before nodding to Janitrix 3 while the embryotic fluid began draining. Her chest slowly rose and fell to the heart monitor on her spinal biochip as both the autonomic robot and Janitrix watched on as the canopy to her cryochamber lifted slowly.

"Biometrics stable!" noted the autonomic robot as Janitrix inspected the other crew member with a frown.

"Wait, stop!" she held her hand out and bent over the submerged woman, placing a hand on her swollen belly.

"This can't be right," Janitrix seemed confused. "She's pregnant!" She felt the kick of the child inside.

Janitrix saw the fluorescent lighting mirror on the robot's metallic skin as it turned her way, saying nothing as she watched the cryochamber continue to slowly empty with slight unease.

"This woman is heavily pregnant; we have to stop this now before we cause damage to the pregnancy!" The sudden jerk of her crewmate startled Janitrix, who watched on as the sleeping body convulsed, opening

DEATH BEYOND

blank staring eyes that rolled white into their sockets. Blood haemorrhaged from her ears as her head lolled to one side, revealing to Janitrix a fresh contouring lobotomised surgical scar around the skull cap. She stepped back, recoiling in horror, as the child inside her swollen belly kicked again.

The autonomic medical robot stared on silently, slowly raising its calculating head, awaiting its orders from Starshina.

3.

The corridor lights flickered erratically as another fuse box failed on the wall. Several canopy cryochamber doors opened slowly with the hiss of hydraulic pistons, resting once they had reached their maximum elevation. Inside one chamber, a sole occupant stirred from cryo-slumber, flexing her hand while turning to cough up the fluid from her lungs onto the floor. The ejected fluid steamed on the floor as the humidity of the ship enveloped her.

After a moment the Janitrix shivered, then steadied herself on the frame and stood up rubbing her neck awaiting the greeting from her predecessor with an update of the voyage. Her head was throbbing with dehydration, and the remnants of the embryonic tank fluid filled her mouth. She was aware of the procedure, cryo-slumber made any volunteer disorientated for the first few minutes of deactivation. She ran through the waking process checklist. First the fingers, then the toes. Crunching and flexing each part of her body until the blood began flowing freely through her veins. Janitrix was pleased to note no pressing issues with circulation needed attending.

She turned to greet whoever the comrade was who had activated her for handover duty, but found no one standing by her capsule. This was completely against protocol. A Janitrix was supposed to be there to update.

To her left was just a long empty row of cryochambers with their canopy domes open. To her right, the same. Vacant, empty chambers lit by the flickering lights above. The corridor was thick with the stench of something that hung in the air around her. A smothering sensation similar to the humidity of a rainforest squeezing at her lungs as she tried to breathe. She turned to read her canopy decal, wiping the sweat on her confused brow, remembering her assigned duty number was JANITRIX 79. As if to confirm this, she inspected her neoprene suit to see the JANITRIX 79 name badge sparkling across her breast. She keyed in her identifying number into her wrist PAX and awaited orders. Protocol dictated that she wait for an update from the ship's Starshina before commencing with her yearlong duty. It was, however, strange to her that her predecessor's cryochambers would be left in the open state. Perhaps there had been an emergency, and all hands were required at the station at once. Her PAX was offline, however, and gave no indication or instructions.

"Starshina, this is Janitrix 79 reporting for duty!" she tried again, sweat dripping to the floor.

The corridor illuminations throughout the level above Janitrix strobed erratically, flickering as the ship groaned and she realised that something was wrong with her situation. Her spinal implant throbbed in her neck as the static pain shot down her spine and she winced. Hydraulic oils spilled from broken canopy piston hinges, causing her to gag and recoil at the odours permeating the corridor.

The best thing for her to do now was to get to the medical bay and find out where the rest of the maintenance crew had congregated. Perhaps they were under attack.

She began her way down the corridor of cryochambers, checking inside each one she passed to see if its occupant remained, but all the booths lay empty. The floor was wet and tacky with expelled fluid and scuff marks where the occupants had stumbled or fallen to the grating. By one pod she saw what looked like dried bloody handprints smeared over the top of the dome, and she realised something bad had happened. Something Janitrix was not prepared for.

"Starshina, report please!" she tried again, panting with laboured breath.

Janitrix cautiously made for the security service information screen down the hall in an attempt to find out what had happened, her legs wobbled like a newborn deer as she slid along the corridor constantly blinking through the dimly lit area in an effort to clear her foggy blurred vision. Up ahead Janitrix could vaguely make out the security information display screen wall but the screen had been violently torn from its hinges and was now just a limp screen, a pixelated digital tapestry hanging useless. On the floor were long shards of jagged display screen glass that crunched beneath her neoprene boots. She bent down to arm herself with pieces, her eyes darting up and down the corridor for any intruders.

Her PAX wrist communicator crackled, and she stared down at the device, keying in and whispering faint ghostly voices.

"Hello? Identify!"

The digital static feed bleeped back, but nobody responded.

"Janitrix 79 reporting!" she added, her sight blurring with the sweat running into eyes.

Only silence responded.

Janitrix was already working out probable causes in her pounding head and realised that until she made contact with the others onboard the *Rasputin*, she was running blind, perhaps even into an ambush. There were a lot of important people on board this vessel. A lot of important people with important knowledge to share with the Ursa Major hosts.

The hairs on her neck suddenly vibrated and a static charge caused her to clench her teeth tight. Her implant pulsed on her neck again and she winced with the new experience.

"Please identify?" she added, crouching by the display screen with her shard of glass held tight. The PAX remained silent, only the occasional blip and microphone key tone broke the digital silence.

But someone or something was whispering in her ear.

"Hello is anyone there?" The voice was a low, almost inaudible, but it wasn't coming from the wrist PAX. It was inside her head, bouncing around inside her very core, travelling through her thoughts as if from another plane of existence. She knew of only one person that was capable of talking to the crew through the biochip.

She cupped the biochip on the back of her clammy neck, feeling it vibrate again.

"Starshina?" Janitrix spoke out, spinning around, not understanding what was happening as the voice evaporated from her thoughts. Her biochip was obviously damaged, probably during her awakening, she imagined, and decided that getting to Starshina was the priority. If he was in danger, then the entire crew aboard the *Rasputin* was too.

She ran along the corridor, passing under the flickering lighting as her feet sloshed through the debris, her footfalls echoing as they kicked up the oily sludge and funk that had pooled by the cryochambers. It looked like Level three had been left unmonitored by previous Janitrixes for years, decades perhaps, its equipment left to seize and rust without any maintenance.

But where were all the crew?

The corridor was becoming too warm for Janitrix to bear, the life support system obviously offline with barely enough air in the corridor for her to breathe. Up ahead was an EVAC bay, hopefully still equipped with survival equipment, she thought. From there, she should be able to raise somebody up in the main deck who could update her on the situation.

Perhaps a fire had broken out?

All of the cryochambers she passed were empty. Some looked like they had been prised open with force, like some stubborn shellfish refusing to give up the pearl inside without a fight. Others had their canopies smashed open; decal numbers lay shattered on the slumber beds inside. Whatever had happened had been vicious.

Janitrix stopped by the EVAC bay to catch her breath and grab a face mask from the emergency equipment point, the toxins in the air slowly strangling her lungs. She quickly donned the apparatus mask and inhaled the fresh air supply as she slid against the smooth wall, recovering. Once she had secured the mask, she inspected the room through the visor. It took her a moment to register what she was seeing on the grated floor mat ahead.

At first, she thought it was a set of discarded overalls from the EVAC store, a HAZMAT suit perhaps. But as her eyes focused on the object, she slowly realised she was looking at one of the occupants of the cryochambers. A Janitrix.

She stumbled over, tripping over her feet, knelt by the body and rolled it over.

The dead Janitrix's torso had been cut from pelvis to breastbone, the cavity under the ribcage hollowed out and cleared of all its internal organs. The head had been removed, decapitated. Janitrix recoiled and fell back, scrambling against the wall, her own stomach lurching.

The biochip on her neck fired up again.

"Help me!" Several voices this time, all screaming out, all frantically trying to connect with Janitrix, whose eyes were wide with fear now. She scrambled to her feet and ran down the corridor, her hand clutched so tight around the glass shard that it cut deep into her palm.

The only thing Janitrix could think of was that the

Rasputin had been attacked, or worse, boarded and captured and somehow the crew had been taken.

She passed two cryochambers pinned down by part of the fallen roof beam structure where the domed canopies still remained intact. Inside, the occupants had awoken and were now banging furiously against the glass canopies, their eyes bulging from their sockets in sheer panic as they sloshed in the embryotic fluid gasping for air. Janitrix stumbled to a halt and began stabbing at the hydraulics with the bloody shard in her hand. Muffled screams and frantic glass banging tormented her as she watched the first woman's face inside turn a crimson shade of purple, her bulging eyes spilling onto her cheeks before her head suddenly exploded with the extreme pressures inside. Janitrix jumped backwards, dropping the shard in shock as the canopy shattered and the bloody ooze slithered out to the floor in a steaming mess of bloody gore.

The second chamber thudded behind her and she turned to see the second woman in exactly the same peril as the previous. Her hands were pressed against the glass dome, her face submerged inside the fluid as she spluttered and choked on the bubbling froth spilling from her silently screaming mouth. Janitrix cursed, climbing on top of the cryochamber and balanced herself, before slamming her foot down hard against the glass canopy. Again, and again she pounded with her heels against the glass as the woman below slipped from view only for her to resurface and bang the glass with her balled bloody fists. The decal identifying mark said JANITRIX 45 and Janitrix ludicrously found herself wondering if she had met this maintenance worker before launch, perhaps shared a mess hall bench with her before the launch.

Now the woman's fingers were frantically clawing at her own face, tearing at her own throat, her own bulging eyes as the bubbling embryotic juice filled her gaping mouth.

"STAY CALM!" Janitrix screamed as she pounded the glass, watching on in horror as she too exploded inside the capsule and the canopy shattered into a million twinkling jewels. Janitrix fell, exhausted, sliding from the cryochamber and sprawled to the floor, gasping for breath.

The elevator door slid open at the far side of the corridor and light cascaded into the dimness of the level, casting a long shadow of one of the autonomic units as it strode slowly inside. Janitrix caught her breath and picked up the glass shard from the floor, sliding it into her waist belt and stumbled towards the lumbering mechanical robot.

"What the hell is going on? Where are the crew?" she demanded as the machine approached.

The autonomic stopped and surveyed the Janitrix.

"We have amassed by Starshina."

"Amassed? Are they safe? Is Starshina safe?" Janitrix panted, glancing back down the gloomy corridor.

"They are all with Starshina, he is safe," eplied the autonomic without feeling. "You must join them!"

"Yes, yes, take me to the crew now, please."

The autonomic inspected the shattered cryochambers for a moment, fishing around the gloop for the body of the first woman and produced a large hypodermic needle. Janitrix watched on, bemused, as he drew a large sample from her belly and studied it.

"She's dead! They are both dead. Take me to the crew now!" she demanded.

The robot nodded and slowly turned on its heels back to the doorway to the lift shaft and Janitrix followed closely behind, perplexed by the machine's behaviour.

"What happened here? Have we been attacked? Is the *Rasputin* damaged?" She asked as they entered the elevator.

"Starshina is safe!" was all the reply Janitrix got.

4.

The elevator opened into the brightness of the lobby, the autonomic already plodding out into the sleek atrium hall towards the piloting deck. Janitrix felt the cool chill of the life support and slipped off her mask to inhale the clean air. She did notice the scuff marks they were following on the shiny floor, long dragging smudges that seemed to suggest a struggle, which, while concerning, seemed to be the only signs of any violence. There were no blaster marks on the walls, no dead crew scattered along the walkways, no invading enemy trying to take over the *Rasputin*. Perhaps there had just been a cataclysmic life support failure on the level below, and they had been evacuated in a hurry.

"Is the diplomatic wing still functioning?" she asked, noticing several robots ambling the other way wearing empty back apparatus.

"Starshina is safe. There is no need for any others!"

DEATH BEYOND

"What in Digit's name does that mean? And why are we going this way?" Janitrix stopped. Something was wrong. This route wasn't the way to Starshina, this was the way to the workshops at the rear of the ship. The biochip pulsed in her head with the voices echoing in her thoughts again.

"You need to help us; we are being held against our will!"

Behind her two more autonomic units had joined the escort, their clanging feet marching in unison alongside her as they grabbed her arms.

Where are you? She was new to thought transfer. The training she had undertaken was brief, but it seemed to work.

"With Starshina!"

Janitrix lunged out, trying to lose her guard's grip, but the autonomic escorts just held on harder, one crushing the PAX on her left forearm until the bone shattered beneath and splintered through her neoprene suitskin. She looked down, screamed out in terror, her tortured agony echoing down the great hall as she hung limp and her legs kicked out, scuffing her boots against the metallic floor. The pain shot up her arm in waves of nauseating pulses as they lifted her higher, the bones crunching inside her blood-soaked tunic, her kicking legs dragging behind her while she fought in vain to remain conscious. Janitrix barely managed to hold any coherent thought together as the autonomics carried her on through the high corridors until they rounded the corner and stopped, dangling her helplessly inside their noisy abattoir floor.

The room was filled with the gut-wrenching tortured cries of helpless terror mingled with the sound of high-pitched medical cutting tools and the foul, rancid stench of decay. Janitrix gagged as the lead autonomic tightened its grip and dragged her towards the autonomic with the large medical bone cutting saw.

In front of her were two piles: one high with the discarded bloody appendages of the dead and dying crew pulled from the cryochambers like prawns torn from their shells. The other, the macabre torsos of the dead and dying. Helpless stumpy living mannequins moaning and groaning amongst other pitiful sobbing crewmates, sobbing atop of each other, awaiting their gruesome fate. As she watched, she saw her bloody crewmates being randomly pulled from the butchered pile and injected with hypodermics before being basketed and carried off into the darkened recessed areas.

"Digit's mercy!" she cried out, tears rolling down her face while she twisted herself towards the spinning blade of the saw the robot yielded. Metal whirring teeth sliced into her PAX comm device and then through her uselessly crushed forearm, shattering bone and tendon in a single motion. Janitrix gagged as blood splattered across the shiny chrome autonomics and she kicked out against their monstrous torsos, pulling free from their grip, before falling to the floor and rolling away. Her useless crushed arm, that now hung comically in the autonomics grip, waved at her while the robots processed her pitiful escape. Blood spouted from her wound, spirting onto the gangway as she scrambled from the room, clutching what was left of her PAX comm unit strapped to the forearm that now came to an abrupt end in a bloody stump.

She thought she looked as wretched as the dead and dying behind her, but Janitrix didn't look back to confirm it.

She ran through the corridors, weaving past the autonomics and spilling her blood freely onto the floor, only stopping once in a hallway maintenance doorway to tighten her PAX strap for it to act as a tourniquet on her stump. All access to level one was sealed, and she cursed, stumbling through to an open elevator and clutching her biochip.

The voices filled her head as she backed into the darkness of the elevator and the doors began to close.

"You have to find me. It's too dark in here for me to see!"

The machines were slow. She watched as one autonomic strode past her hiding place carrying a wicker basket of 'parts' on its back. This made no sense to her. Why would they kill the crew? And was Starshina aware of the horrendous acts being carried out on his ship. She had to find him, then find the surviving crew who she was in contact with and rescue them if she could manage it.

The sudden invasion in her head startled her, the pain erupting from deep inside her and she fell backwards into the darkness, clutching the biochip again.

"Hello Janitrix 79, are you well?" Starshina asked politely.

"Starshina... Don't you know what... what is happening onboard?" Janitrix tried to control herself. "You have to stop them! They're butchering the crew; your machines are killing everyone on board!"

"My machines? They are not my machines. They are here only to maintain!" his voice raised slightly as another voice joined the conversation.

"He doesn't know... he doesn't know anything!" they whispered. "They won't let Starshina know anything. They kill!"

"They won't let me know what?" Starshina asked.

Janitrix ignored the voices, instead asked her own question.

"Where are the crew, Starshina?"

"The crew? Why, the crew are all here with me, Janitrix 79. Navigating the stars can be such a lonely existence without a companion!"

"The crew are all being butchered down here on level two, Starshina!" Janitrix tugged on the tourniquet and steadied herself. "Now open the security doors and clear the way so I can make it to the level one deck room!"

There was a pause, then the elevator began rising.

5.

When the elevator doors opened onto level one Janitrix found herself facing six autonomic robots and braced herself for the attack. But they made no effort to restrain her.

"They will not apprehend you, Janitrix 79."

She exhaled as they cleared a path and she walked through them cautiously like it was some guard of honour she was passing. They all turned and watched as she made her way to the flight deck clutching her butchered left arm.

"The autonomics have protocols pre-set designed only to protect and maintain my welfare and the ship's sustainability. They are not programmed to kill, merely to serve!"

"Well somebody downstairs forgot to read the Telepathy Times, Starshina, because your crew are dead." Janitrix cautiously passed the homicidal robots, but the loss of blood was causing her to fade from consciousness.

"Nonsense, as I stated, the crew are here with me. They keep me company now. I no longer need to guide this ship through the stars alone!"

Janitrix slid against the viewing wall until she could focus on the pilot in his sealed room. There were no crew members inside, only his umbilical tubes and the medical vats.

Her eyes slowly closed as the blood loss dripped away her life onto the floor.

"We are all one big family now. Come in and say hello, Janitrix 79!" The doors slid open.

Her eyes opened with the buzz of her biochip and she focussed on the large vat of embryotic fluid behind Starshina.

The crew.

What remained of them. Floating in the fluid like large pink jellyfish. Each one hooked up to the Starshina main frame by their spinal implants as they bobbed up and down inside the large embryotic tank.

"STOP HIM!" they cried out as the doors opened and Janitrix reached back, stumbling through the entrance and falling to the floor brandishing the bloody glass shank from her waist belt.

6.

Janitrix 79 ran through the cryogenic waking process checklist. First the fingers, then the toes. Crunching and flexing each part of her body until the blood flowed freely through her veins. But there was nothing there. No blood flowed through veins allowing her limbs to kick and stretch. No blood pumped from the beating heart in her chest. Her eyes saw nothing but the darkness of faded memories and primal fear.

"Hello, can anyone hear me?" she pleaded, her voice just another voice from the void.

"Please, can somebody help me?"

"Janitrix 79, so glad you could join us!" Starshina beamed, welcoming the latest crewmember into his madness. "I've got so much to show you all."

DEATH BEYOND

GREGG CUNNINGHAM, 50, is a short story writer from Western Australia who has contributed to various genre anthology books. He should really start taking this shit seriously instead of spending his days thinking of ways to avoid learning to write and leaving the hard work to these fine Editors to make him sound good.

He finally has found a home for his current manuscript hiding under his bed and will soon get it out to the Sci-Fi community,

Plan 559 From Outer Space Five59 Publishing 2016
Other Realms, Five59 Publishing 2016
13 Bites Collection Volumes 3-5 Five59 Publishing 2016
Full Metal Horror Zombie Pirate Publishing 2017
Relationship Add Vice Zombie Pirate Publishing 2017
Phuket Tattoo Zombie Pirate Publishing 2018
World War 4 Zombie Pirate Publishing 2018
Grievous Bodily Harm Zombie Pirate Publishing 2019
Storming Area 51, Black Hare Press, 2019
Bad Romance, Black Hare Press 2020
Raygun Retro Zombie Pirate Publishing 2020
Banned, Black Hare Press, 2020
Passenger 13, Black Hare Press, 2020
Zero Hour 2113 Black Hare Press 2020
School's in, Black Hare Press, 2020
Wardenclyffe Black Hare Press 2020
Death House, Breaking Rules Publishing Europe 2021
Adventure Awaits, Breaking Rules Publishing Europe 2021

DEATH BEYOND

Strange Orbits, Black Ink Fiction 2021
Distur13ed, Black Ink fiction (coming soon)

Connect:
Website: cortlandsdogs.wordpress.com

SCREAMS IN THE RADIO SILENCE

Peter J. Foote

Cosmic winds tugging upon the frozen mass in the void of space for countless millennia shift. Faint fingers of gravity reach out and touch the ugly blister of cosmic dust, shattered comets, and inert stone. The organic body in the centre shifts in response.

This is not the first time it has felt the tug of gravity upon it. In the past, it has meant adding a layer of shattered stone or hunk of ice to its growing armour, but this time is different.

The tug of gravity grows stronger, pulling it inward, and the ancient being within the cocoon of debris wakes.

Uncounted centuries pass and the gentle fingers of gravity become a firm grip, pulling the ugly grey mass of stone and ice closer to this system's primary.

Solar radiation sublimates dirty ice, leaving a glowing tail in its wake. The body within the core of the comet writhes upon itself, black tentacles churning faster and faster within its bonds.

Cracks form along the fault lines of the comet, rock splinters, and nuggets of ice crumble.

The integrity of the comet weakens to a point the being at its core can escape.

Ejecting itself, the squirming mass is free of the armour which protected it for uncounted years.

Tentacles reach out, black arms resembling a malicious starfish spread themselves razor thin collecting solar rays, becoming a living solar sail and begin hunting for a new home.

Microscopic whiskers twitch, picking up background radio waves, the gentle vibrations tingling as they focus on searching for hot spots.

Everywhere! This entire system is a maze of radio waves, overlapping each other in delicious complexity.

Littered throughout the system are hotspots, centres of webs the ancient being knows must harbour life. The hunger within, long dormant, rekindles.

Tentacles roll and twist, and like a sailing vessel, the sail changes tack, steering the creature to the closest cluster of radio waves.

"Seong, are you having any issues with *Receiving*?" Mai shouts across the command deck of Earth Relay Station 17.

"Nothing here Mai, *Sending* giving you a problem? Do you want me to hold off on the next Com-batch?"

"Maybe. I just sent out my hourly test burst and my instruments show it stopped three clicks from the sta-

DEATH BEYOND

tion."

"Stopped? What do you mean, 'stopped'? How does a high burst radio pulse just stop?" the constant clicking of Seong's keyboard pauses.

"Beats me, it's like something absorbed it, I'm not picking up any leakage or anything." Mai says, double-checking her readings.

Seong stands up from his station and walks across the expansive communication deck filled with memory buffers, coding computers, and compression filters when the station lurches sideways.

Reinforced hatches slam shut, emergency sirens flash and scream, signalling a hull breach.

The mind-numbing alarms lessen to a background deluge, as speakers crackle to life and the voice of the station commander pins everyone in place.

"Hull breach, all station staff, I repeat hull breach." Gasping breaths issue from the speakers, panic creeps into the next words. "All staff, we have unconfirmed reports of widespread damage throughout the relay station. An unknown object has penetrated the hull and we have cascading damage worming its way through the station. I order all staff..."

A fresh series of explosions vibrate through the hull, throwing Seong to the floor again. The usual bright communications deck fades to emergency lighting.

"Seong, where are you?" Mai cries out as she weaves her way through inert machines before finally finding Seong and helping him to his feet.

"What... what's going on Mai?" Seong says, touching his head, fingers coming away sticky with blood.

DEATH BEYOND

"I don't know, but we better stay here until help arrives." A clang against the bulkhead doors punctuations her words.

"Hello? Who's out there?" Mai says while putting herself in front of her injured colleague. "We have an injured person in here."

The clanging against the bulkhead doors becomes a groan. Twisted metal allows a shaft of silver light to shine into the darkened communication deck.

Mai leans an unsteady Seong against a dead communication buffer and makes a hesitant step towards the silver light.

"Hello? We need medical support in here. Seong has a possible concussion."

The silver light grows stronger and Mai holds up a hand against the glare. A hum similar to that of their communication computers fills the air and radiates through the deck plates. The hum grows in pitch and intensity, Mai's hands clasp over her ears and Seong cries out in pain.

Squinting, Mai stops her progress through the damaged communication deck and stands open-mouthed. A glowing spear of feathered crystal stabs through a gap in the bulkhead doors and penetrates the metal floor. Like frost spreading across a window on a wintry day, the feathers along the spear grow and spread out, filling the room with silver light.

The hum changes in intensity and pitch as the feathers expand towards the hapless technicians. Mai screams.

DEATH BEYOND

"Dammit" Zeke curses as the back of his head connects with the inside of the *Fora de Lloc* open control panel.

"Jyrgal, can you get that? I'm busy."

The horn of an incoming priority communication blares throughout the spaceship again and shows no sign of being acknowledged from the flight deck.

"Christ on a cracker," Zeke curses again and inch worms his way out of the confined space. High energy cables cause the hairs on Zeke's bare arms to stand on edge as he sucks in his belly to make sure he doesn't connect with them. The horn sounds for a third time. Zeke pulls himself out of the narrow access hatch, tearing his coveralls on a jagged piece of metal.

"Yeah, yeah, I hear you. Jyrgal, where are you?" Zeke yells as he skirts around open toolboxes, open panels, and coils of cable. Puffing, he hurries down the steel catwalk running the length of the Search and Rescue vessel, the horn becoming shrill.

Stumbling into the flight deck of the *Fora de Lloc,* Zeke reaches out a grease-stained finger for the 'receive' button just as Jyrgal swivels her pilot's chair and hits the button an instant before her partner.

"*Fora de Lloc* receiving maintenance control, what's up?" Jyrgal says, reaches for the steaming cup of coffee on her control board, sips, and grins down at a huffing Zeke.

"It's about time you responded. Were you two on another union break?" a male voice teases.

"Oh, it's you Bansi, I thought it was Cheryl on this shift and you know how much Zeke loves to talk to her."

DEATH BEYOND

Jyrgal winks at a red-faced Zeke as he plops into the co-pilots seat.

"Will you never give your husband a break, Jyrgal?" Bansi asks.

"He keeps renewing our license of formal partnership, so he mustn't be too put out. Now what's up? We're on a repair break."

The voice issuing from the speaker takes on a sombre tone. "We've lost contact with *Communication Relay Station 17* in the Outer Belt. Nothing from them for the past seven hours, not even a remote beacon. I know the *Fora de Lloc* is due to have her power buffers switched out. This won't be a tow job, hopefully it's something easy that you two can help with. The *Fora de Lloc* could be there in twelve hours, where the government repair ship is ninety-seven hours away. Are you guys in any condition to do a wellness check on them? I'm offering overtime."

"Hold on maintenance control, I need to check with my partner." Jyrgal says and pauses communications. Her playful face takes on a more sober expression.

"What do you think Zeke, how bad are the buffers?"

Zeke looks at his partner, begins chewing the inside of his cheek, and leans back in his chair to stare at the ceiling.

"The buffers are bad, Jyr, and I mean bad. We should have switched them out three months ago."

Jyrgal opens her mouth, but without Zeke even seeing it, he forestalls it with a raised finger. "I can rig them in series, but that means we'll be dead in the water if any of them fail, or risk exploding. I know we need the credits, but I'm serious," Zeke shifts in his chair to regard his wife. "We CAN'T tax the engines."

"Hooray! Bailing wires and shoelaces to the rescue again." Jyrgal laughs and winks. Stabbing the communication button, she says, "Maintenance Control, show us on route and get your cheque book warmed up."

"We're coming up on the coordinates for *Relay Station 17* Control gave us. But I'm not seeing anything on the scope, nor is anyone answering our hails," Jyrgal shouts down the corridor of the *Fora de Lloc* as she taps the screen in front of her wavy lines crawling across the screen. "Though it would be much easier to tell, if it didn't look like an ant colony was living inside them!" She raps her screen harder and a blue bolt of electricity reaches out in response.

"Dammit! Zeke, what is going on down there? I have discharges on my panels," Jyrgal yells while shaking her hand.

"You think that's bad; I have half of the boards in engineering possessed with lightning bugs," Zeke counters as he mounts the stairs up onto the flight deck.

Seeing his wife shake her injured hand, he grasps it with his own, raises it to his lips and gives it a tiny kiss. "All better?"

Jyrgal pulls her hand free with a laugh and swats Zeke in the arm. "You goof. But seriously, how are we doing back there?" Jyrgal tilts her head back toward the engine room.

"Let's just say, I'm glad we're here. We're here,

right?" Zeke says, leaning towards the narrow window.

"I think so, but I'm not seeing them here," Jyrgal says and goes to tap her screen, but pauses before risking getting zapped again.

"Maybe you should lift your eyes, my dear," Zeke teases, pointing out the window.

Resembling an old-fashioned lollipop with a donut-shaped habitation ring around its middle, the relay station hangs in space devoid of motion and light.

"Dammit, looks like they've had a complete system failure. Even their perimeter strobes are dark. I can't make out many details of their condition. What happened over there?" Jyrgal mutters and joins her husband at the window to look at the stricken station.

"Maybe we should wait for the government rescue ship?" Zeke says, rubbing his chin, the grey of his stubble marred by grease. "We're not much better off, we'll be lucky not to need rescuing ourselves, Jyr."

Jyrgal takes her husband's grease-stained hand, threads her fingers with his and gives them a squeeze. "You know we can't do that, dear, and this isn't about the credits. Those people over there need our help. If we were without power and all alone, won't you want someone to help if they could?"

"I knew there was a reason I kept renewing our formal partnership, you're a better person than I am, Jyr. You promise to be safe over there? No unnecessary risks?"

"Who me?" Jyrgal smiles and winks.

"I'm at their airlock, Zeke," Jyrgal hisses over the

speakers of the *Fora de Lloc* as Zeke runs fresh patch cables throughout the engine room of the SAR vessel. "It's worse that we thought. Their emergency backup power batteries are completely drained. I must manually open the airlock doors."

Jyrgal's laboured breathing and muttered curses fill the engine room as Zeke listens to his wife crank the handle to open the station's airlock.

"I'm showing minimal life support inside. They either have a leak or their atmospheric plant has shutdown. Zeke, honey, you best warm up the medical tubes. We could have people suffering from hypoxia if they didn't reach the emergency shelters in time."

Zeke pulls free the radio from his belt and responds. "Already on it, but records show that Relay Station has a crew of thirty-four. Even doubling, we can't treat half that many on the *Fora de Lloc*." Zeke keys his radio to speak again, decides against it and returns it to his belt.

"I can hear your brain turning its gears, Zeke. I know we're likely looking at multiple fatalities here, but we will do what we can to help," Jyrgal says through the radio, the tinniness of her suit's microphone doing nothing to dampen the emotion in her voice.

For the next several minutes, Jyrgal's steady breathing and the clip-clop of her magnetic boots are the only communication transmitted.

"Confirming that they've had some structural failure. I'm seeing webs of water or coolant frozen and ruptured throughout the central shaft and leading up to the habitant ring. If it wasn't so disastrous, it would almost be pretty. It's probably just a reflection of my flashlight, but these crystal webs are beautiful. Makes me think of frozen lightning."

Zeke pauses in his ongoing battle to keep their own vessel fully functional, and yanks free his radio. "Don't touch them, Jyr, they could be contaminated and eat through your suit. It might be too dangerous in there. What about you coming back here? This is much more than we're used to, we're just a glorified tow-truck." Zeke wipes the sweat forming on his brow as he waits for his partner to respond.

"I will not touch it, I know better, Zeke. Stop being a worry-wart," she hisses through the speakers. "The station's intercom is out, but I'm feeling some kind of vibration through the soles of my suit."

Zeke hears a 'thunk' and the speakers of the *Fora de Lloc* hiss and crackle with a new sound other than Jyrgal's breathing. "Jyr, what is that? Feedback of some kind?"

"I'm not sure. I have my helmet against the metal wall and am picking up vibrations. It could be an emergency transponder, but it's not coming through any of the normal channels. It could even be voices of people trapped in a shelter. It is the first sign of life since we got here though, so I'm going with it."

Click, click, click comes through the ship's speakers and Zeke knows his wife is using her search and rescue probe.

"I can't narrow it down. The entire station is throwing odd readings at me. I think the signal is coming from up top, maybe from the transmitter disc, but that's a guess. I'm continuing on."

DEATH BEYOND

"Dammit," Zeke curses to himself and focuses on chasing the growing number of faults his ship is giving him. He tells himself not to think about any danger Jyrgal might put herself in. He takes comfort from her breathing and the steady clop of her magnetic boots issuing from the speakers until Jyrgal yells in fright.

Zeke knocks the radio from his belt in his haste to contact Jyrgal. It flies into a maze of dangling cables in the room's corner. Scrambling on his hands and knees, he grasps the radio just as Jyrgal speaks.

"I'm fine. I'm fine, Zeke!" Jyrgal says, her words loud and hurried. "We have casualties, Zeke. Sorry if I scared you, I came upon it unexpectedly. The frozen coolant or whatever it is has attached itself to the body. A crystal cocoon, almost. I've never seen anything like it. Probably a combination of the cold and lack of gravity."

Zeke keys his radio, then releases the button, then keys it again. "Ok, Jyrgal, I hear you. This is turning into a recovery mission. There is nothing we can do. Return to the ship now."

"It's like a massive spider web of crystal, Zeke," Jyrgal says over the speaker, the fear in her voice still clear. "It radiates all the way up through the central core of the station. I'm not sure what it is, I've never heard of damage like this before. I think it might be the source of the weird vibrations. My suit tingles the closer I get."

"Get out of there now, Jyrgal, I'm begging you," Zeke shouts into his radio, cradling it in both hands as he waits for his wife and partner to respond.

"I think you're right, Zeke. I don't see a straight-forward way up without coming into contact with this crystal web. I'm going to take some recordings and then turn back. Warm up the kettle, I could use a hot drink."

Zeke takes a deep breath, nods to himself, and places the radio on a nearby control panel.

"Zeke, you still there?" the fear in Jyrgal's voice having returned.

"Of course, Jyr, what's up?"

"I have movement at the top of the central core. It's swallowing the beam from my flashlight, but I can see an enormous shadow making its way down through the crystal webs. Are you picking up anything on the *Fora de Lloc's* sensors?"

Zeke dashes between several monitors which echo the panels in the flight deck, shakes his head and grabs the radio.

"Nothing here, but that doesn't mean there isn't damaged equipment floating around in there. Stop your recordings and head back now, Jyr. Please."

"Agreed," Jyrgal says, her breathing becoming faster and shallow.

"Damn," Zeke says and heads to the ship's airlock to wait for his wife. "How are you making out, Jyr?"

"Hurrying, trust me." The edge of fear in Jyrgal's voice clear over the ship's speakers.

The clip-clop of Jyrgal's magnetic boots picks up its pace and loses its controlled rhythm. The sound of her breathing becomes more ragged.

"Hey Jyr, what's going on in there?" The forced lightness in Zeke's voice fake.

DEATH BEYOND

"Vibration getting stronger, light dimming like power drain. Hard to see."

"I'm coming for you!" Zeke shouts into the radio and races to put on his own space suit. Hands twitching, Zeke struggles with fasteners and connections.

"Zeke! Zeke, I can't see anything, the..." static hisses from the speakers. Jyrgal's voice returns, but much fainter than before. "Zeke, I'm scared. I have no light. It's cold, so cold, and the voices are calling for me to join them."

Zeke locks on his helmet, keying his microphone as he enters the airlock. "I'm coming, babe. Try to save your air, I'm coming for you."

"Come on, you blasted thing," Zeke curses as the airlock purges atmosphere and cycles open to the relay station.

Without taking in his surroundings, Zeke dashing into the dark and lifeless relay station.

Taking long leaps through the weak gravity, Zeke pans his light in wide arcs ahead of him, hunting for his wife. Zeke ignores the jagged pieces of metal from twisted panels that could rip and tear his suit. He doesn't slow until his light strikes the crystal webs filling the middle of the station.

"Jyrgal, I'm here. Can you see my light?" Zeke says and pans his flashlight upward in slow arcs throughout the central corridor. Flashes of light splinter and refract off the crystal webbing, filling the wide vertical tunnel.

"This isn't burst pipes. I don't know what it is, but

this is something outside humanity," Zeke mutters as he moves deeper into the forest of crystal webs, the floor vibrating as he walks.

"Jyr, if you can hear me say something." Zeke's voice sounds frantic to his own ears.

"So cold... the voices are loud... just want to sleep." The voice in Zeke's helmet speaker is faint and unfocused.

"I have the kettle on, Jyr. Don't you worry, I'll get you warm soon," Zeke says as he weaves his way through the crystal web. Pausing as he passes the unsuited body of a male encased by strings of crystal, the name tag reading 'Seong', his face frozen in mid-scream.

Zeke shivers within his suit and calls for Jyrgal once again and sees faint movement.

He shines his light at a cluster of fine crystals branching out and expanding around a dark lump. Zeke realises the dark lump is Jyrgal laying on the deck and rushes forward.

"I'm here, Jyr, I'm here. I see you; I'll have you free in a minute. Speak to me," Zeke shouts and falls to his knees beside his wife.

"Jyr, I'm right here beside you, can you move?" Zeke says and strikes out against the fine web of crystals growing around his wife. They are harder than steel, and his gloved fist tingles with the contact.

"Zeke, so dark... can't see... alone with the voices," sputters out of Zeke's speakers.

"You're not alone, Jyr, I'm here. I'll show you," Zeke says and bends down to shine his flashlight into his wife's helmet.

Cold, lifeless eyes stare back at him, the expression of terror frozen on her face. A delicate web of crystals radiates out from her temple, filling her helmet, twinkling with faint light.

"NO!" Zeke shouts and tugs to pull his wife free, but it's like she's encapsulated in steel.

"Zeke... alone..."

"I'm here. I'm here," Zeke says and touches his helmet against his wife's. The vibration that permeates the station becomes much stronger.

"Can't see you... scared..."

"I can see you, Jyr. I'm here, trust me, I'm here," Zeke says, staring into Jyrgal's lifeless face as a shadow flows over him from above, grabbing his attention.

The powerful light does little to define it, but Zeke gets the impression of twisting and flowing limbs around a central body, a nightmares version of a starfish. The web of crystals pulse with light as the creature descends and Zeke feels like hair on the back of his neck stand upright and every instinct screams RUN!

Caressing his wife's helmet, Zeke stumbles to his feet and flees back to the *Fora de Lloc,* the shadow chasing after him. Channelling the primitive and powerful emotions giving him strength, Zeke narrows his vision to stay on the path that will take him back to the ship. He pushes aside the desire to communicate with the voices that tease at the edge of his mind

With the airlock in sight, a delicate feather of crystal rolls free from the wall and latches onto Zeke's flashlight, capturing it, leaving nothing but the faint light of the airlock's control panel to guide him. The certain knowledge that whatever has overtaken the station and ripped his wife away from him gives Zeke that last burst of energy to leap into the airlock. Slapping the panel as the shadow fills the corridor behind him, Zeke listens to his own gasping breath as the airlock cycles.

Tossing his helmet onto the floor, Zeke clumps his way up the catwalk of the *Fora de Lloc,* passing the engine room, making his way to the flight deck. The ship shudders and Zeke stumbles against Jyrgal's pilot chair. Ripping off this right glove, Zeke punches in a rapid series of commands into the ship's computer and with his left grabs the control yoke.

A powerful hum grows within the *Fora de Lloc* and replaces the shudder from the shadow creature. Overtaxed power buffers rattle the entire ship.

Stabbing the radio, Zeke shouts, his voice louder that the ear-splitting whine and sharp discharge of overloaded circuits.

"Jyrgal babe, hang on. I'm coming for you." Tears run down his face as he uses both hands on the yoke as he forces the ship to plough into the space station.

Screams issue from the radio, layers of voices, each scared and alone.

Safeties long since bypassed to keep the power buffers functional, the *Fora de Lloc* tears its way into the station.

Fatally wounded, the ship gets as far as the crystal webs before going critical and exploding.

The explosion is blinding and silent as section after section of *Communication Relay Station 17* bursts apart.

Unable to contain the fury that Zeke has unleashed

DEATH BEYOND

within it, crystalline webs splinter and shatter. Fire consumes the last meagre traces of oxygen as it races up through the relay station.

Overtaking the shadow, the remaining crystals vibrate in pain as the flesh of the alien being burns before it is tossed into the void of space.

Severed and burned, a tiny piece of the malicious starfish tumbles into open space free of the destruction. The shattered remnants of its crystalline hairs wrap themselves around the injured body to protect it until, once again, it has a shield of ice and stone.

Succumbing to the tug of cosmic waves, the alien allows sleep to overtake it until it is ready to awaken once again.

DEATH BEYOND

Peter J. Foote is a bestselling speculative fiction writer from Nova Scotia, Canada. Most of his stories are within the genres of Science Fiction, Fantasy, and Horror.

Outside of writing, he runs a used bookstore specializing in fantasy & sci-fi, cosplays with his wife, and alternates between red wine and coffee as the mood demands.

Believing that an author should write what he knows, many of Peter's stories reflect his personal life and experiences.

As the founder of the group "Genre Writers of Atlantic Canada", Peter believes that the writing community is stronger when it works together.

You can find Peter on:

Facebook Twitter Newsletter.
www.facebook.com/peterjfooteauthor/
https://twitter.com/PeterJFoote1
https://www.subscribepage.com/c3j4h4

PERSERVERANCE

Rachel L. Tilley

Sometimes I like to pretend I'm back on solid ground.

I close my eyes and picture grass. Perhaps I could recall scents once too, but they are long gone. Instead, I try to remember how it felt to walk on. Then everything gently tilts, and I find I'm suddenly imagining I'm on a ship instead—the kind that sails as opposed to flies. Perhaps even the swaying motion is part of my imagination.

Sometimes I get confused and forget that I'm *not* on solid ground.

I think I might be losing my mind.

The Perseverance is docked, metaphorically 'anchored', in the midst of nowhere. The navigational crew are gone; the flight staff long departed. There's only me left.

I'll fly it home one day. A half-hearted threat that I make every now and then.

"No, you won't," says the ghost over my shoulder. I

don't bother turning around, he's a familiar enough presence that I don't need to see his face. "You don't know how to fly her."

"True, but you do. One day you'll get bored and decide to help me, I'm sure of it." I tell the Captain's remnant, or whatever this echo of him is.

"Perhaps," he utters under his breath, "but not today."

"Not today," I agree. When I do turn around, he's no longer there. He'll be back though—Captain Halladay being as reliable in death as he was in life. As long as I keep returning to the control room, I can be sure he'll be around if I ever need him. Perhaps that's what has kept me from attempting to return home. At the moment, I am safe in the knowledge that, should I ever want to, I could. If I actually tried, that could all change. Maybe I'd find out that I'm not up to the challenge. Or that the ship can't even be steered by one man alone. I'd rather pretend that I can leave whenever I want. Maintain the present state of affairs.

The ship is stocked for a full crew, so I think I'd die of old age before I ran out of supplies. Besides, you don't burn much energy when you spend half of every day sitting in the Captain's chair, spinning around mindlessly.

One of the computer screens allows me to stare out at the nothingness; it's pervasive both inside and out. Some days I don't even bother to look.

Of all the rooms, this one conjures up the least emotion—and there are definitely some strange rooms on the Perseverance. A couple of them give me the chills to even walk past. Some of the rooms are supposed to be restricted access, but they open for me now. Sometimes they do, at least.

The exit of Captain H is the signal it's time for me to move on. No reason other than habit. Routine has become important for me, and I no longer even try to depart from it. I tell myself I'm hungry.

I pass some people in the corridor that I don't recognise. I was going to ignore them, but when they walk straight past me without any acknowledgement, I change my mind. "Fixed the ship yet?" I call out. I don't know these men, I haven't seen these ghosts before, but they look like a maintenance team.

"Tell us what's broken and we'll fix it, smartarse," one of them calls back at me.

"Maybe nothing's broken. Did you ever think of that?" I don't even know what I'm saying, but I can't let them have the last word. I hurry away.

When I pass by, one of the doors is slightly ajar. I feel compelled to go in. I hate this room, but something about the tableau felt more like a demand than an invitation. 'The room of memories' is my nickname for it. You might see four plain silver-grey metal walls encasing a small cube only four paces in each direction, but that isn't what the Perseverance will actually show you.

I take a seat. There's no point standing. The dizziness will soon make me stagger and fall if I do. It's less painful if you just accept the inevitable. This time I see the medical wing. When I walk in, I'm too late.

I'm reliving it. As if I'm actually there, all over again.

DEATH BEYOND

I only see one of the bodies at first. It's really more like half a body—one leg and one arm lie several feet away. I think of her name, but that's one memory I've actually managed to suppress, so all I remember this time is that I had the thought. I knew her. The other two bodies are less of a shock once I've seen the first.

Unfortunately, I spent a long time thinking about what to do next. I didn't know that, later, it would just mean I was trapped in the memory for longer.

I don't want to leave them alone. All these thoughts go through my mind. What if the killer returns? What if by the time I come back with help they've been moved? No, the best thing to do is surely to wait by the door until someone passes and then I can send *them* for help. I wait.

Even though I'm finally free of the memory, I don't feel quite right. I'm dizzy, and the walls of the room appear pixelated which only accentuates the spinning. It's a while before I'm ready to stand.

I decide to retire to my bunk early. I've had enough of today. I must be at a different time to usual because there are lots of people around. Most of them are either on their way out or getting dressed ready to go. I ignore them all, making straight for my cot, and pulling the curtain across to shut out any residual light.

The early night backfires on me. Sure, I sleep well, but I wake up hours before I usually would. The space is too small to invite any kind of relaxation, so I'm up and moving quickly. I feel stale and know it's about time I took a shower.

At first it seems okay, and I start to relax. The water comes out hot, but not scalding, and the pressure is decent. It's only when I wash my hair, and lean against the wall, that things intensify. The wall jolts me like an electric shock has passed through my entire back. I don't know why I haven't been electrocuted when it mixed with the water, but perhaps it was only static. I try to open the shower door, but not only does it zap me again, it seems to be jammed. It's several deep breaths later before I'm brave enough to try again. It's no use. The ship is against me.

After a while, I turn the water off.

I'm still standing there when I hear a couple of voices. It's strange for me to imagine something like this—I don't recognise either of the people and I don't usually hear the residues unless I am also picturing them.

"It's been too long now," the first voice says. "The whole unit are beginning to lose hope we'll ever return home."

"I know what you're suggesting, Lewis, and you know my thoughts."

"I just think that if we were moving, morale might pick up again."

"Undeniably."

"And sooner or later, we're bound to reach a planetary system. At least we'd have some logs to send back home."

"Also true."

"But food we have in excess, and fuel we don't."

"Exactly."

A shower turns on, followed by another. Wanting to make my exit, I try the door again. Either the ship has relented and the shock it gives me is lessened, or I manage to push through it, but I'm free. Released from one small, enclosed space, and instead trapped in a slightly larger one.

It's still the early hours, but I'm thinking I'll go back to the control room anyway, so head in that direction. There are still a lot more bodies around than usual, and one of them opens a door to a restricted room, so I figure I may as well follow her in.

It's the armoury—I don't think I've been in here before. The guns seem to emit a buzzing sound, and I don't think my brain can cope with the frequency. Before I can move to leave, the lady sees me and floats out, slamming the door behind her. I can't seem to open it. The access code is needed even just to exit.

Maybe it's an alarm system or something. The noise is gradually intensifying. The pressure in my brain is immense. It feels like my entire head is swelling.

When the men enter with their guns pointed—as if they expected me to use the opportunity to arm myself—they find me lying on the floor with my hands over my ears, sobbing.

I find myself gently lifted to my feet.

"G, this has to stop now." I guess I look at him blankly. He's vaguely familiar looking, but mostly I'm still surprised that these spirits can interact with me physically. "I don't know what you're doing in here, but it's been almost three years now. I know it was traumatic, but you need to find a better way of coping."

"Coping." It's almost strange to say something aloud. I can't remember the last time I spoke.

"You're starting to scare people. Coming into the

weapons room like this—you just can't do that. Stalking the halls at night." He wipes the sweat across his forehead with the back of his hand. "Like a damn ghost. You're scaring people."

"At night."

"G, you've been sleeping during the day, and spending your nights roaming. We've let you do it, I know you and the Captain were friends, but you've just been obsessing over his chair. I'm not sure it's such a good idea anymore. Besides, we could really use your help trying to fix the ship. You know the navigation system better than anyone. We haven't been able to find what's wrong with it."

"I... I don't think... navigation? I can't remember."

Another man steps forward.

"Give him some time," he suggests. Then he turns to me imploringly. "Would that help, G? We can sit with you and talk you through what you've been missing." I nod, unable to do much else, and suddenly aware that I'm still being held up.

I don't know why, but it all comes rushing back. I thought I'd successfully suppressed it all, but the bastards have brought the memories back to the surface. I hit full cognisance.

She'd been cheating on me. Maybe I hadn't ever been thinking clearly. I can't remember why I even cared, but back then, it seemed like the end of the world. First Joanna, then the two other medics who'd been in the back room. Finally, Captain Halladay, who'd walked in on me committing the deed. The latter being the only one I'd regretted at the time, and the only one I cared about now.

I guess nobody ever figured out it was me. They think my trauma is from finding the bodies. Ironic.

On the plus side, I know why the navigation system has failed. It's just as well they haven't worked it out. Perhaps one day I'll retrieve the knife from where I stashed it, but for now, I'm not too keen on the idea of changing the status quo.

DEATH BEYOND

Rachel L Tilley is a mother of two from the UK, who is an accountant by day. Any time she isn't out and about she spends either reading or writing, which she enjoys in equal measure. To date she has written a handful of short stories across a few genres, and has one self-published, fantasy adventure novel.

https://www.goodreads.com/rachelltilley

https://www.facebook.com/RachelLTilleybooks

DEATH BEYOND

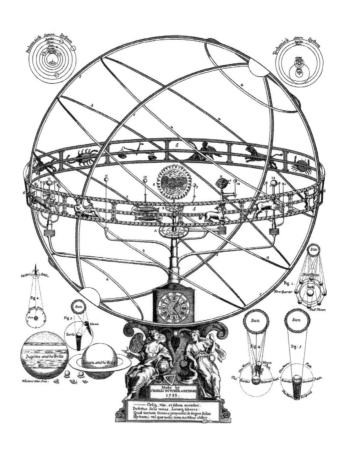

216

EDEN ONE

Tim Mendees

Julie's body tensed as she landed on the cold metal next to her hypersleep pod. Retching and choking, she purged the oxygenated fluid that had filled her lungs and kept her alive for the last six months. There wasn't a more dignified way of doing it than this, and Lord knew the science boffins had tried to find one. Millions of credits had been frittered away trying to find a better way to vomit. Just one of the many things that baffled Captain Julie Henderson about Outer Planet Enterprises, they would waste money hand over fist on useless research but wouldn't spend a single credit on her rescue ship. The *RS Bolide* was almost burnt out. One day, it would be them that needed a tow back to Neptune station.

"Status report," Julie spluttered as she pulled herself up the side of her pod and wiped her mouth on the back of her hand. Scraping the gunk out of her eyes, she looked around the darkened sleep module. None of the lights had come on, and the only light came from the

DEATH BEYOND

pinkish glow of the other sleep pods.

"Dammit, Malcolm... status report." The ship's AI wasn't the sharpest of constructs at the best of times, but he wasn't normally this rubbish. "...and switch the bloody lights on!"

Again, the computer didn't respond. The only sound other than the chatter of the CPU and the whirr of life-support systems was an intermittent belch of buzzing static from the comms unit in the adjacent room.

"Great..." Staggering over to the AI terminal, she tapped on a button with her finger before slamming her fist against the screen. "Perfect. Looks like he needs booting up manually again." This was the last thing she needed when she had just come out of hypersleep. She was dazed, confused, and in no mood to deal with *Windows 520*.

First things first, though, she needed to cover herself up. It was damn chilly on the *Bolide* at the best of times, but especially so when you have just come out of extended sleep. Staggering over to the bank of lockers next to the door, she took out her multi-purpose OPE overall and pulled it on. The synthetic fabric crinkled over her hypersensitive skin, making her shiver even worse. As soon as she zipped down the front, it soon warmed up. Julie normally wore other clothes under it, but time was of the essence. Presumably, the other pods were soon to disgorge their contents, and she wanted to get the AI booted up in case there were any difficulties. It wasn't uncommon for crew members to require emergency medical attention after hypersleep.

Slipping on her heavy boots, Julie stomped towards

the door and swiped her hand over the sensor.

Access... denied.

"What?" The indignant buzz that accompanied the security system's smug female voice made her teeth rattle and blood boil. "Open the door, you stupid bastard computer!" Waving her hand up and down across the circle of blue light, she cursed, spat and raged as the speaker above the door beeped and rasped at her. Losing her temper, she kicked the door as hard as she could and instantly regretted it. The thick metal was unyielding and sent a shockwave up her spine.

"Dammit! Does nothing on this bloody skip with thrusters work?"

Denied... Access de... de... denied.

"Fine..." Julie sighed. "Manual override it is. Then I'm going to uninstall you, you stupid bloody program." Marching back over to her locker, she took a small handpump from out of her bag-of-tricks and headed back to the door. "Deny this, you digital pain in the arse." Plugging the nozzle into the emergency release port, she began pumping furiously.

De... de... de... denied.

"Shut up!" Julie set her jaw into a rigid line as the pressure continued to build. Eventually, with a satisfying *hiss,* the door slid away from the locking mechanism. "Gotcha!" She exclaimed as she let the hand pump dangle from the door frame, and put her fingers through the two-inch gap and heaved with all of her weight.

De.. de.. d... d... d... DON'T!

The harsh bark of static and pixelated digital voice made Julie leap back from the door in alarm. The speaker continued in a stream of garbled syllables, bleeps, and wheezes. The lights rose and fell, alternating between the dim yellow of half power and emergency red.

"What the hell is going on?" Julie raced over to give the AI terminal another punch but stopped as she realised a strange substance coated the backs of her fingers. Holding her hands up to the flickering light, she examined her digits with a look of horror etched onto her face. A foul organic substance, pus yellow and fungal in nature, covered her skin. Revolted, she frenziedly wiped her fingers on her overall as she went back to her locker for a flashlight.

The inner door was now open about a foot. Approaching it cautiously, Julie shone her light through the aperture and peered in horror. The corridor outside the sleep chamber was like something from a nightmare. The walls were coated in thick fungal growths. Clumps of glowing mushrooms sprouted from the corners and covered the walkway like a luminous carpet. Spores the size of leaves twisted in the air like diseased snowflakes. Suddenly panicked, Julie took an oily rag from one of her myriad pockets and held it over her airways.

As she panned the weak circle of light in the direction of the flight deck, a strange shadow was cast on the fungus encased wall. It was long and thin, like an aerial or wire. It puzzled Julie. There was nothing in the corridor that could explain it unless someone had ripped out one of the electronics panels and torn the cables free. A horrible thought flicked through her mind... "Sabotage!"

Then the shadow moved...

Julie yelped in alarm as a terrible buzzing noise emanated from the direction of the movement. The shadow twisted and flexed before being joined by similar appendages. What she was seeing was the silhouette of insectoid antennae. Stuffing the flashlight and the rag into her pockets, Julie refocussed her energies on shutting the door she had previously laboured to open. The security system belched and screeched in fury as inch by inch, she slid the door back into the locking mechanism. With a satisfying *clunk* and *hiss* of gears and motors, the door repressurised and sealed itself airtight. Tearing the hand-pump out of the emergency release valve and throwing it to the floor, Julie backed away, still wiping her fingers on her garments.

Bang!

Julie scrambled around to the rear of her sleep pod and took cover as *whatever* was out in the corridor slammed against the door. The hollow metallic *clang* reverberated around the room as it continued to hammer on the door. Julie scuttled on her haunches until she backed up against a bank of wires and flashing lights. Reaching over to the corner, she grabbed a large spanner from an open toolbox. Gripping it tightly in both hands, she held the reassuringly dry steel in front of her face to ward off the potential threat. Then the banging stopped, and for an agonising few seconds, everything was silent.

Exhaling deeply and shaking like crazy, Julie climbed to her feet and cautiously approached the door. Placing her ear to the cold titanium, she strained to hear movement. Either she couldn't hear through the thick door or the creature had shambled off somewhere; either way, the imminent danger had passed.

"What in God's name was that thing?" Her muscles had tensed completely, making her knees *crack* as she backed away from the door. "I need to wake up the rest of the crew."

No sooner had the words passed her lips, the high-pitched alarm fitted to each of the other four pods shrieked. Julie let out a cry of alarm and spun, brandishing her spanner. "What now?"

As she looked on in horror, the pink glow of the liquid oxygen in each of the pods changed to a putrid yellow. Racing to the pod of her chief engineer, Raakesh Basu, she wiped the condensation off the glass and peered inside. She couldn't see Raakesh whatsoever... all she could see was a vast growth of fungi.

With panic gripping her heart, Julie ran to the next pod, and the next, each one the same. It seemed whatever had engulfed the interior of the ship had also claimed her crewmates. In despair, she slammed the heel of her hand against the top of medical officer Sara Campbell's pod.

"Holy shit!" Julie screamed as five bulbous, multi-faceted eyes popped open in the centre of the fleshy lump where Sara's head should have been. It wasn't Sara at all, it was some kind of hellish monstrosity. She leapt back from the pod as the fungal abomination in the pod slammed a powerful limb through the reinforced glass. The pod erupted in a plume of thick glass shards that tinkled to the metal floor. Swinging her spanner like a woman possessed, Julie raced towards the door and stopped... she was trapped.

Crouching in an attack posture, she prepared to do

battle with the horror that was climbing free of the pod. As its insectoid limbs pulled it free of the putrescent liquid, Julie winced as a long blonde plait swung off the back of the creature's head. The creature hadn't devoured Sara... it *was* Sara. The fungus had metamorphosed her into a twisted nightmare. Julie wept as the creature advanced upon her with arms tipped with crab-like pincers raised.

"Sara... It's me, Julie!" She babbled as she backed into the corner. "Sod off, I'll wallop you one with this, God help me."

Three more smashes announced that her other crewmates, or what had become of them, had decided to join the party. Julie couldn't bear to look upon the creatures. She had been very fond of her crew, and in so many ways, they were family. Even stroppy Sara, who was an Olympic standard pain-in-the-arse at times, deserved better than this. She weighed the spanner in her hand and tried to judge whether a solid whack to the cranium would put Sara out of her undoubted misery.

The Sara creature buzzed in a frenzied manner as it closed in. Julie couldn't bear to hear it and clamped her free hand over one of her ears. It was dizzying and disorientating. The rise and fall in pitch made her vision lurch and swim. It felt like hundreds of wiggly little legs crawling around inside her head. Hundreds of hungry little voices whispering to her, coaxing her into giving in. They all said the same thing... "Come to Yuggoth."

Staggered by the disorientation, Julie had dropped her guard. Shaking her head to clear her vision, she screamed as she realised that the Sara creature was less than five feet away from her now. She could smell the rancid tang of rot and sickly sweetness of compost as it raised and clacked its claws. Julie raised the spanner in front of her, glanced at her hands... and gasped.

The spanner hit the floor with a teeth-rattling *clang*.

Julie's hands were infected. Foul fungal growths were forcing their way through her cracking and tearing skin.

Julie screamed...

"Put the mask over her face, Sara!"

"Thanks fer that, Sherlock. I'd never a'thought of that. Hold her still, for fuck's sake. I cannae do anything while she's thrashing around!" Sara grunted as Raakesh half-heartedly pinned Julie's shoulders to the floor. "Put some bloody effort into it, man!"

"I don't want to hurt her." The chief engineer was a gentle giant, six-six and just as wide, but wouldn't say boo to a goose.

"At this point, it's hurt or dead... you choose!" Sara by contrast was small and vicious, like an irritable ferret.

"Fine." Raakesh put his muscular back into it, finally, and had Julie steady enough for Sara to slip the mask over her head.

"Keep her still while I give her a shot, right?"

"Right." Raakesh nodded as he struggled against Julie's convulsing body.

Sara reached into her bag of medical tricks and produced an implement that looked not unlike a plastic handgun. Slipping a small cartridge of liquid into the barrel and cocking the mechanism, Sara pressed the end of the device to Julie's neck and pulled the trigger. With a reassuring *thunk,* the capsule's contents were injected into Julie's bloodstream. The captain's back arched then fell limp. Almost instantly, her convulsions stopped, and her breathing stabilised.

"Okay, Raakesh, ye can let her go now. She'll be comin' round any minute."

Mopping his brow, Raakesh exhaled deeply. Though he had witnessed people *waking up on the wrong side* several times before, he was still shaken. "Should I start Tom and Stacey's revival procedure?"

"Aye... In a minute. Let us get the Cap up and running first... We should check out her pod at some point too."

"Indeed. This is the third time, isn't it?"

"Aye, I thought you checked it over last time?"

"I did." Raakesh spat indignantly. "There wasn't anything wrong with it... except age and being generally clapped out like the rest of this heap of junk."

"Dunna start me on the state of the medi-bay." Sara sighed. "Most of the equipment in there is older than me. I keep prayin' that one of these days we come to the aid of an OPE suit. That might be the only way we can get some funding."

"If they see what a mess everything is, you mean?"

Sara grinned. "I was thinking o' robbing the bugger, but that would work too."

As Raakesh broke into a throaty chuckle, Julie spluttered and opened her eyes. "Yuggoth!" She screamed as she sat bolt upright, clawing at the backs of her hands with her fingernails.

"Easy, Cap." Sarah cooed, grabbing Julie firmly by the wrists and staring into her glassy eyes. "You've woken up on the wrong side again. You're fine and dandy, just breathe. Stop scratching... and breathe."

"Wh... what?" Julie's eyes focussed on Sara's elfin features. "Sara?... Thank God." Her body shook as she relaxed and took in the room. Everything looked as it should and was light-years away from the hellish vision of her nightmare.

"Bad dreams, Captain?" Raakesh asked as he passed Julie a bottle of water.

"Um... yeah. Really bad." Julie closely examined the backs of her hands before accepting the water and taking a deep gulp.

"There must be somethin' wrong with this batch of happy juice." Sara was up and tapping a large glass tube with her lengthy fingernail. "This stuff is supposed to stop ye getting' nightmares... Fat chance. I had some weird-ass dreams myself."

Suddenly alert, Julie turned and stared at Sara. "Oh? What did you dream?"

Sara shrugged. "I cannae remember exactly. I was on a planet without a suit... not nice."

"Anything else?"

"Um..." Sara stroked her temples. "Nope. It's gone." Giving the anti-depressant regulator a final tweak, she marched over to Julie and held out her hand. "Anyway, dreams can wait. Let's get you to the medi-bay and give you a once over."

"Fine," Julie grunted as she took Sara's hand and

was roughly yanked to her feet. The diminutive Scotswoman was stronger than she looked. Seconds later, she was wrapped in a thermal medical gown and being steered towards the door. "Thanks, Sara."

"My pleasure," Sara smiled as she approached the door and held her hand towards the sensor.

"Stop!" Julie exclaimed as her dream flashed across her visual cortex.

"Eh?" The command was too late, Sara had already triggered the lock.

Access...

Julie's heart did a backflip.

...Granted.

The door slid open with a pneumatic *hiss* revealing a grimy but normal-looking corridor. Julie sighed. "Sorry... The dream has got me all out of whack."

"Aye, it'll pass. I woke up on the wrong side once and thought I was a penguin for five minutes afterwards. It really screws with yer noggin, and that was a good dream."

"Pardon?" Raakesh sniggered.

"I like penguins," Sara replied in a flat and emphatic tone. "Start thawing the others out while I get the Cap plugged into the medi-scanner, will you?"

"Do Stacey first," Julie added. "I want to know where we are and what the job is before Testosterone Tommy starts waving guns around, okay?"

"Got it, boss."

"Come on then, Captain, let's get you sorted," Sara said brightly as she led her down the corridor. "Why don't you tell me about your dream?"

DEATH BEYOND

"I've got Malcolm back online, Captain."

"Good job, Stacey, any idea what happened?"

"Not a clue." Stacey pulled her thick black hair back into a high ponytail and pulled up a status report on the monitor. "Best I can guess is a power surge of some kind. He was running fine until well after we had received the signal. Our journey was all programmed in and set."

"What's the job, then?" Julie was perched on the edge of a console sipping the caffeinated sludge that the OPE palmed off as coffee.

Stacey's brows knitted together in confusion. "You're not going to like this, Captain."

"Don't tell me it's taken us back out past Nereid?"

"You could say that."

"Spit it out, Stacey, where the hell are we?"

"Pluto," Stacey said apologetically.

"Sodding Pluto?" Julie screamed as she leapt off her perch, spilling sticky brown liquid all over Tommy's seat. "Those OPE bastards! I'm starting to think that we will never get that damned holiday."

"It says we were taken back out, and our leave on Neptune suspended, due to a priority one rescue," Stacey continued as Julie hammered the buttons and switches on the navicom with mounting frustration. "The research vessel, *Eden One*, has gone dark between Pluto and Charon. It's believed that they have had a comms failure."

"Why the hell have they put a priority one on a blasted comms failure? Any old outfit could patch that up."

"Something to do with the vessel being involved in classified research. They needed a crew with top-level security clearance."

"Great... Bureaucratic red tape will be the bloody death of me." Julie stopped and counted to ten. "Fine, let's get this done as quickly as humanly possible. Chart a flight path and try and get them on short-range comms. Docking will be a butt-load easier if they cooperate."

"Yes, Ma'am." Stacey put on her headset and settled into her seat. "Malcolm, pull up the local area."

Julie smiled. She could always count on Stacey to be level-headed. Then, an awful thought occurred to her. "Right... I'd better go and break it to the others... This should be fun."

Fun is hardly what you could describe Sara and Tommy's reactions. Raakesh wasn't happy either but compared to the other two he was a pussycat. Tommy had punched lockers and generally acted like an enraged bull while Sara had seriously suggested going rogue and becoming space pirates. It had taken every ounce of diplomacy Julie possessed to defuse the powder keg. Eventually, though, she managed to calm them all down, get them suited up, and ready for action. Being a captain on a rescue ship often boiled down to something akin to herding cats.

"This is the OPE Rescue Ship Bolide calling Eden One do you receive me? Over."

"Still no joy on the comms?" Julie asked as she peered over Stacey's shoulder.

"Not a sausage, Captain. If you check out the scans, it looks like the array has been smashed, probably by an asteroid.

Tommy whistled as he looked at the 3D hologram projected in the centre of the flight deck. "It's taken a right fakkin walloping and no mistake. Look at the dents! I've seen turn of the century junkers in better condition."

"Raakesh, what do you think... is it toast?" Julie asked.

"No. It looks structurally sound, there are signs of life, and it's running on half-power. The problem is that it's in a decaying orbit... if we don't either get the engines running properly or tow it back to the station, it will eventually crash into Pluto. I suggest I take a look at the damage while you guys go inside and see what the hell is going on."

Julie nodded and slapped Raakesh on the back. "Sounds like a plan, big fella. Stacey, deploy the docking clamps. Take us in nice and easy."

"Right, team. Come to the armoury and tool up. I'm taking no chances." Tommy cracked his knuckles and stretched his neck. "We don't know what we are walking into."

"Here we go." Sara rolled her eyes.

"We don't know what the nuts is going on down there, Sara, it could be bloody pirates for all we know," Tommy asserted.

"Pirates, it's always sodding pirates with you, isn't it, Tommy? Who do you think you are, Long John bloody Silver?"

"Sara! Knock it off," Julie snapped. "For once, I

DEATH BEYOND

agree with Trigger-happy Tommy. Something about this whole thing seems *off* to me somehow."

"*Off,* Ma'am?" Stacey cocked a perfectly angular eyebrow.

"I can't put my finger on it. It just doesn't feel right."

"Och!" Sara snorted. "You've still got the heebie-jeebies from waking up on the wrong side."

"You might be right, Sara, but I've been doing this long enough to trust my gut... We tool up. Treat the situation as potentially dangerous. Chief Security Officer?"

"Maam?" Tommy snapped to attention.

"Make sure everyone is fully kitted out... including our medical officer."

"Yes, Ma'am!"

"Fine," Sara huffed as she followed Raakesh and Tommy down the corridor. "Just make sure you keep your blasted safety on this time, Tommy, okay? Ye nearly blew Raakesh's head off last time, jumping at bloody shadows."

Julie sighed and shook her head at Stacey as the trio's footsteps receded down the corridor. "I despair sometimes, I really do... Right, once we are docked, get yourself kitted out. I want you with me on this one. I have a feeling that whatever is wrong down there can't be fixed with a spanner or a kick..."

The docking hatch opened with a furious *hiss* as the pressure escaped the airlock. Tommy pushed open the hatch and drifted inside. Julie and Sara followed, with Stacey bringing up the rear. Raakesh was currently on the exterior of the *Eden One* checking the rear thrusters for damage. A cursory glance didn't inspire hope. It looked like the team would be connecting up the grapple and towing the *Eden One* back to Neptune Station. This was the least attractive outcome, a ship the size of the *Eden One* would add weeks to the already lengthy journey time, months even.

Once the hatch was closed and sealed, Julie initiated the pressurisation sequence. "Keep your helmets on until we know for certain that life-support is fully online." She instructed as the team prepared to board the *Eden One*.

Whatever Julie had been expecting, it certainly wasn't this. The airlock opened into a gleaming white corridor. Nothing was greasy or grimy, nothing sparked or shorted. The cables and panels were all fixed down tightly. In short, it couldn't have been more different to the *Bolide* if it had tried. Sara was the first to comment.

"Blimey, so this is where all the money goes."

Tommy pointed his heavy assault rifle up and down the corridor before gesturing that it was safe to enter. Sara rolled her eyes at his performance. Tommy had been twice turned down for the space marines due to being *unsafe*... this didn't stop the OPE from snapping him up.

"I don't get it," Julie mused as she stepped into the pristine space. "I've been on OPE brass ships, and none of them was half as shiny as this. Looking at the outside, I was expecting one of the dodgy twenties survey vessels."

"It's an anomaly," Stacey agreed as she played her scanner up and down. "I've never seen a ship like this. It's like someone ripped the innards of a survey ship out and plugged a high-tech lab into it. It doesn't make sense."

"It does if they wanted to be inconspicuous. That would explain all the guff about security clearance." Sara walked up to an AI interface screen and jabbed it a few times. "Dead." She then checked her scanner. "Life support is on, the air is clean. It looks like the computer is offline, and the ship is on emergency life-support settings. Light, air, doors... that's it... I wouldn't..."

Pfffft

The sound of Stacey removing her helmet and clipping it to her rig stopped Sara in her tracks. "You numpty! ... I was about to say that I wouldn't remove my helmet until we've checked the other rooms and corridors. The scan only does the immediate surroundings."

Stacey shrugged. "I hate these helmets. I much preferred the old ones that made you look like a cartoon character. These things give me claustrophobia."

"I'm sure it'll be fine," Julie asserted and removed her helmet. Tommy followed suit before stalking off down the corridor. "In any case, we need to conserve the oxygen, in case it gets hairy further in. We will put them back on when we open another bulkhead."

"Fine, but if we get some weird kind of space cold, I'm blaming ye." Sara sighed, removing hers.

"Hush, you two!" Tommy hissed from the far end of the corridor. "I thought I heard something behind this door."

"Cover formation!" Julie barked, instructing Sara and Stacey to get behind Tommy with their pistols trained on the door. Julie approached the side of the door next to the release panel and glared at Tommy. "It's probably not pirates so keep your finger off the damn trigger unless I give the order, got it?"

"Yeah, got it," Tommy said sullenly.

"Whoever is in there," Julie shouted through the door. "We are from an OPE rescue ship. Keep back and keep calm!" When no response came, she hit the panel, and the door slid open.

Tommy stepped inside, training his weapon in the corners. "Clear... of humans, anyway."

Julie followed him inside, holstering her weapon. "What the hell?"

The room was a laboratory of some kind. Against the far wall was a collection of cages containing what looked to have once been rats. What they were now was anyone's guess. Their bodies were riddled with strange glowing growths and long wiry hairs.

Sara took one look at the twisted creatures and erupted in a rage. "What the hell are these arseholes doing? Look at the poor things... When I get hold of..."

Her tirade was cut short by a *clatter* from the opposite corner of the room followed by a whimper.

"Someone's under the bench," Julie mouthed to Tommy and gave him the signal to advance.

Tommy crept towards the bench and trained his gun over the top. "Come out slowly. We won't hurt you if you don't do anything fakking stupid, capiche?"

"D... don't shoot." Two trembling hands shot out from under the bench. "I work here."

Sara snarled. "Are you responsible for *this*?"

"No! It was an accident. Tillinghast is to blame, not

me!"

Tommy lowered his gun, stepped around the bench, grabbed one of the hands, and pulled. A startled looking middle-aged man in a pair of wire spectacles and a gleaming white lab coat came flying out of his hiding place. On his lapel was a wonky name badge, reading Professor Davison.

"Lower your weapons," Julie commanded. "Sara, that includes you!"

"Yes, Captain. I want answers though. If I find out he's been pullin' some Doctor Moreau-type bullshit, I'll cut his ba..."

"Sara! Knock it off, I won't tell you again."

"Fine," Sara huffed as she holstered her weapon and moved over to the poor deformed rodents. Her body shook with anger. She far preferred the company of animals to people, so seeing innocent creatures harmed by apparent human agency was enough to push her to violent action.

"Now, Professor..." Julie checked his name tag. "Davison... Just what the hell is going on here. We have been sent by OPE at Neptune Station to either repair or tow, what is the status of the ship and crew?"

"I can't tell you much... it's classified."

"You can and will. I was dragged to the arse-end of the solar system because I have the required clearance. So, either tell me what is going on here or I'll let my med-tech off her leash... understood?" Julie's voice was level and matter-of-fact, it even gave Tommy chills.

Sara shot the panicked scientist a predatory grin.

Davison swallowed, his Adam's-apple bobbed noticeably. "Understood... The Eden One is a class-A research vessel under the command of Professor Emil Tillinghast. He has long suggested that Pluto could be the key to food shortages. He has studied the dwarf planet for decades and was convinced that somewhere under the surface was a source of an unknown type of fungi."

"Mushrooms?" Julie thought out loud.

"Indeed. I don't know what strings he pulled, but he managed to convince the OPE to send him and a full scientific team to investigate... then things went wrong."

"What, you didn't find the mushrooms?" Stacey asked.

"Oh, he found them alright. Under the surface of the planet are thousands of miles of tunnel teeming with fungi. I wasn't on the surface team, but Micheals said it was like being in some kind of hive."

Bang! Bang! Bang!

"What the fuck was that?" Tommy readied his gun and raced out of the room. The sound came from a door on the other side of the corridor.

"Is someone in that room?" Julie barked at Davison as Stacey and Sara followed Tommy. Davison's eyes were wide and his mouth gaping. "Professor!"

"Um..."

Julie spat some unkind words at the dumbstruck scientist then followed her team. Tommy had already got the others behind him in the standard arrow-head formation. Whatever he lacked in caution he made up for in enthusiasm. "Ready, Ma'am."

Julie scuttled around the trio and hit the door release, keeping low and pointing her gun around the aperture. The door slid open to reveal another lab lit only with UV lights. Huge glass tanks lined the walls and stood along the centre of the large rectangular room. The tanks throbbed with life. Huge growths of glowing fungi stretched and spread up whatever growing medium they were attached to. Some were on branches and plants from the oxygen farm on the upper deck. Some were on rats, mice, and even a dog. All eyes, however, were trained on the largest tank... it contained a human body.

"Room's clear," Tommy whispered. This time there were no benches for anyone to cower under. "What kind of sick shit is this?"

Julie's jaw was clenched as she approached the tank. The body was almost entirely engulfed in the thick fungal growth. The same bristly hairs as the rats had torn through what remained of another lab coat. This too had a name badge, Professor Micheals'. "Get Davison in here... now. Drag him if you have to. I want answers," Julie hissed.

Tommy nodded and flicked the safety off. Stomping out of the room with purpose, he headed back to the other lab.

"Have you ever seen anything like this?" Stacey asked Sara, who was currently scanning the hideous sight.

"Never. It seems to be similar in structure to the cordyceps, but it's like nothing I've ever seen before. It's completely alien." She paused and tapped the scanner. "That's weird... I'm getting some kind of electrical signal off it. It's some kind of pulse... almost like a radio wave. Stacey, see if your comms gizmo can pick it up."

Stacy stepped towards the tank and raised her scanner. Her brow wrinkled in concentration as she tapped the buttons and twiddled a dial. "Hold on... I think... Yeah, got it." She flicked a switch, and a hellish buzzing sound burst from the tinny speaker. Harsh and grating, and enough to make teeth itch.

"Turn it off, fer God's sake!" Sara screamed as she clamped her hands over her ears.

"What the hell was that?" Julie questioned.

Before anyone could hazard a guess, the body of Professor Micheals jerked.

"Jesus wept!" Sara yelped as she instinctively drew her gun and leapt halfway across the room. "How can he be alive?"

"I don't think it's *him* that's alive... look." Stacey pointed at the other tanks. The fungus was jerking and spasming. Seemingly awakened by their presence.

Bang! Bang! Bang!

The fungus-smothered cadaver slammed one of its appendages into the glass, spreading a spider-web crack along its centre. The fungal growths where his hands should have been had hardened into a crab-like carapace. It was growing claws.

"Out!" Julie screamed as with one final blow, the creature broke free and collapsed to the floor.

Racing from the room, Stacey waited until everyone was out before punching the door control.

"Lock it down!"

Stacey tapped a sequence of digits into the door panel. The blue square that acted as the release button turned red. "Done."

"What's going on?" Tommy panted as he raced towards them.

Julie ignored his question. "Where's Davison?"

"I dunno, Captain. When I got back, he was gone. He must have done a runner when we went to the other lab"

"I'm not surprised... sick bastards," Sara raged.

"Dammit!" Fizzing with a mixture of anger and terror, she pressed the switch on her headset. "Raakesh... come in?" A few seconds of static passed before she tried again. "Raakesh, can you hear me?" This time, the headset buzzed. Julie tore the headset from her ears and stamped on it. It was irrational but the buzzing had terrified her.

"Hey... hey, chill out. What's the matter?" Sara asked, doing her best to appear calm.

"Don't use the comms. That *thing* in there is blocking them somehow."

"What do we do, Cap?" Stacey asked.

"We get the hell off this ship, that's what. Lock it down, tow it and let a hazard team deal with it. I'm placing it under quarantine. We don't get paid anywhere near enough to deal with this shit."

"What about Davison?" Tommy asked.

Julie thought for a second. "Screw him, life support is functioning. If he has any sense, he'll stick himself in a sleep pod." Her statement raised no objections as she led them back towards the airlock. They were less than a meter away when there was a loud *clunk,* and the lights went off. Moments later, the red emergency lighting kicked in.

"Now what?"

"It's gone onto emergency power," Stacey explained. "Everything has been shut down. The ship must have been in worse shape than we thought."

"We can still leave, right?" Sara asked. "Ye can do an override on the doors... right?"

Stacey shook her head. "I'm afraid not. Inner doors, no problem. Without power, we can't cycle the airlock. The pressure release when we opened the outer door doesn't bear thinking about."

As Sara and Tommy swore and shouted, Julie turned calmly to Stacey. "Can you route power to the airlock?"

"I can, but I will have to do it from the bridge."

"Right, then that's what we'll do. You two, get a grip."

Tommy and Sara apologised and fell in behind the others as they headed towards the large door at the end of the corridor. Stacey scampered ahead, pulling an interface cable out of the end of her device. Inserting the end of the cable into a port next to the door release panel. That was one good thing about the OPE, every ship was kitted out with the same budget tech, you never had to worry about things not being compatible. With a few well-practised taps on the keypad, the doors parted.

"The bridge is straight ahead through the next bulkhead. We should be in the main lab area," Stacey explained, not looking up from her scratched screen.

"What the hell happened in here?" Sara exclaimed as they took in the scene. Glass, lab debris, and spent cartridges littered the corridor. The air was thick and foul with cordite and iron. Blood and gunsmoke. There was another smell too, the earthy smell of fungi.

"Sara, we got a body here," Tommy called out as he entered one of the lab doors.

Sara cautiously followed into the red-lit room. The body was lying next to a bench covered in scribbled notes and a stack of ancient-looking books. He was middle-aged and dressed in a white lab coat that had three red circles with dark centres around the chest area. "He's been shot. One of the entrance wounds is right over the heart... poor sod would have died almost instantly. There are no powder burns, he was shot from a distance."

"Is there a name tag?" Julie asked.

"Nah, you can see where it would have been, but he must have taken it off."

"Here, Cap." Tommy pointed to the desk. Sitting on the stack of mouldering tomes was a name tag reading Professor Tillinghast.

"So, this is the famous Tillinghast. What the hell was he doing with all these old books? Look at this one..." She picked a book at random. "*Livre d'Eibon.*" Flicking it open, she gasped at the bizarre contents. "This is some proper occult mumbo-jumbo. These others... *De Vermis Mysteriis, Unaussprechlichen Kulten, The Secrets Of Ger'igguthy,* they are all the same kind of thing. Was this guy a scientist or a bloody wizard?"

"Both." A voice from the back of the room startled the quartet. They all turned, ready to fire. It was Professor Davison, he had been in a small store cupboard, cowering presumably. He hugged a pile of notes to his chest. "Tillinghast was insane. He was a brilliant scientist, but he fell in with a group known as The Brotherhood Of Carcosa... a bunch of cultist nut-jobs. That play over there amongst the occult tomes, *The King In Yellow,* is like a bible to them."

Tommy wasn't listening. "Why the hell did you run off like that?"

"I... I'm sorry... I just needed to get my notes. I... I knew you'd want to leave as soon as you saw Micheals. I'm quite up on OPE rescue procedure. My brother-in-law is a grease monkey on a rescue ship. I knew you'd quarantine the ship, then the OPE would flame it when it got back to Neptune... my work would be destroyed."

The fullness of his answer wasn't lost on Julie, she chose to ignore it to get down to brass tacks. "What the hell happened to Micheals? And you'd better pray that I like your answer."

"Poor guy," Davison sighed. "He was the first to be infected. The team gathered a large amount of the fungus from under the surface. Tillinghast did the preliminary tests himself. He assured Micheals that it was safe... He only ate a tiny piece. The change came so rapidly, we couldn't stop it. Tillinghast ordered that he be kept as a specimen. That's when he started *experimenting* with animals. We tried to talk him out of it, but he had security in his pocket. The first person who refused was shot as an example... his body was dissected and his organs used as a *growth medium* for the fungus. Tillinghast was insane. That's when he started talking about the Mi-Go..."

"The what?" Sara was listening intently. She was waiting for a single slip in his narrative. If she spotted one, she was ready to fly across the room and flatten his nose. Someone was going to pay for those poor animals.

DEATH BEYOND

"Mi-Go, a race originally from Pluto. They have apparently been visiting Earth for millennia, hiding in the out-of-the-way places, waiting. The Brotherhood Of Carcosa, and similar groups, were in contact with them, worshipped them, helped them infiltrate human society. I thought it was all nonsense, until..."

"Go on."

"Tillinghast spent weeks with the fungus samples like he was searching for something. One day, he appeared with a look of rapture on his face. Behind him, two of his goons carried a large lump of fungus on a stretcher. It was roughly five feet long... I didn't see Tillinghast for days. I had hoped that he had succumbed to the fungus... we weren't so lucky. He had been exposing the lump of pink fungus to extreme heat. It turned out that the Mi-Go could hibernate in a fungal state. This fungus, the Mi-Go, Yuggoth, it's all the same entity."

"Wait!" Julie exclaimed. "Did you say Yuggoth?"

"Yes, Pluto is known as Yuggoth to the Mi-Go and their allies."

"What is it, Cap?"

Julie swayed as though she had been slapped. "My dream... on the Bolide. I remember the words, *come to Yuggoth.*"

"Very possible." Davison nodded. "The Mi-Go are telepathic, they can hijack radio waves and infiltrate dreams. Fascinating creatures... from a scientific standpoint, I mean. Having met one..."

"You mean, he woke it up?" Sara was aghast.

"Indeed. That's when the shooting started. Those exposed to the fungus turned on their fellows. It just stood there, buzzing... it was roughly the size of a man but more like a crustacean, or big bug. Almost like a cross between a crayfish and a dragonfly. Tillinghast was talking to it as everything around him went to hell. He wanted to become like it, to spread its infection. He said that the human race had had its time... that we were destined to evolve. I had no choice..." Davison trailed off, looking down at the corpse of Tillinghast.

"*You* shot him?" Tommy cocked an eyebrow as he looked the weedy academic up and down. He would never have guessed he was the culprit in a million years; going off the accuracy displayed. He'd have been pushed to pull off a better shot.

"I had to... he gave me no choice."

"Then what happened? Where is this Mi-Go beastie?" Sara asked as she fiddled nervously with her scanner.

"I ran... ran and hid. The Mi-Go put all the bodies in the sleep chambers. Just put them in there and activated hypersleep. Then... it left. Just went into the airlock and flew out of the ship on its thin shimmering wings. I tried to contact the OPE, but the comms array had been smashed, presumably by the Mi-Go. The engine had been damaged in the fight, so I was stuck here... alone. Then you guys showed up. I was surprised how quickly you got here."

"We have hyperdrive," Stacey boasted sarcastically. "It was top of the range about thirty years ago..."

"...And, we are going to use it right now to get the hell off the Eden One. Stacey, take us to the bridge." Julie had heard enough.

"It will be easiest to go through the next lab, the door is already open." Davison pointed to a door in the corner. "Follow me!"

The scientist picked his way over the overturned chairs and smashed beakers, leading them to the door. Tommy raced after him with the others following behind. The adjacent lab was in a similar state to the other. It too showed all the signs of a pitched battle taking place.

Lingering behind, Sara had something niggling at the back of her brain. "Hey, why didn't the Mi-Go put Tillinghast in a pod? Oi, Davison, I'm talking to you!"

Davison wasn't listening. As soon as they were all in the lab, he broke into a sprint. Giggling like a maniac, he charged onto the flight deck, turned, and hit the door control.

Lockdown... Engaged...

Both doors slammed shut almost instantly, leaving the group standing in the centre of the room looking bewildered.

"Open the bastard door, Davison!" Sara screamed.

There was an electrical *thunk* followed by a surge as power was restored to the *Eden One*. Tommy slammed his fists against the door to the flight deck. "The son of a bitch has locked us in!"

"Nae shit!" Sara snorted. "What's he playing at?"

"Apologies for the subterfuge." A voice announced from the lab's tannoy system. "I just need to make sure that you will all play ball."

"What the hell's he talking about?"

Before anyone could answer Sara, there was a loud

hiss as the lab's ventilation system went into overdrive. Thick greasy spores shot down from the vents in ghastly plumes.

"Helmets!" Julie screamed as she tried to simultaneously block her airways and get her helmet into position.

It was futile, the spores had touched their flesh. Each of them was infected by the fungi from Yuggoth. Sara was the first to get hers on and instantly rushed to Stacey's aid. She had been over by the door they had entered from, trying to sneakily perform an override on the door. One of the vents hit her full in the face. She had staggered away from the door then dropped like a stone. Sara tried to claw at the mass of fungus on her face with her stubby space gloves. It was no good, the stuff was tougher than leather. Stacey's body went into convulsions, throwing Sara back by the violence of her spasms.

"Tommy, get your arse over here!" Sara screamed.

A dry chuckle burst from the tannoy. "Ahh, splendid. That couldn't have gone any better. Now you have no option but to comply. If you want to save your friend... and yourselves, you will get me and the Eden One back to Neptune Station. I'm the only person who can reverse the process. It will be painful, but you will be fine."

"Let me out of here, and I'll show you pain!" Julie raged as she picked Stacey's device off the ground and attempted to complete the hack.

"Now, now, Captain. I won't let you out of there until you calm down... and the clock's ticking. The contamination spreads incredibly quickly. Your only hope is to get back to your ship and go into hypersleep. Once we are home, I'll reverse the infection."

DEATH BEYOND

"What's to stop me forcing you to do it? I have a very pissed off med-tech with a knack for *persuasion*."

"You won't be able to do that."

"Why the hell not?"

At that moment, the metal security shield over the window to the corridor raised, revealing the Professor... and a nightmare. "Because of my friend here!" He was accompanied by an adult Mi-Go.

Finally, the penny dropped for Sara. "He's Tillinghast! That poor bugger in the other room must be Davison."

"Bravo! Yes, that *idiot* in there was Davison. It's his fault that you are in this mess. If he hadn't disabled the engines, I'd already been home by now. Spreading the glory of the Mi-Go to humanity!" After a burst of manic laughter, Tillinghast moved towards the door panel. "Now that you are all infected, my friend here will make sure that you don't do anything foolish."

The Mi-Go, around five foot tall with a rugose body and crab-like pincers, raised the pyramidal lump covered in eyes and antennae that acted as its head and started to vibrate. The cranial organ flashed in a myriad of colours as that hellish buzzing infected the crew of the *Bolide*.

"Excellent!" Tillinghast gloated. "Now, walk towards the door."

Against their wills, the infected rescue team shuffled towards the door. Their heads filled with that nightmare sound. Powerless, completely enslaved. Stacey sat upright then climbed to her feet. Blindly following the signal, she too fell into line. The Mi-Go directed them around the benches, equipment, and debris towards the door. When they were a metre away, Tillinghast released the door.

Bang!

The creature's flashing appendage exploded in a mass of fungus as a high-velocity slug slammed into it from behind. Tillinghast screamed and turned towards the shooter with his fists balled and murder in his eyes. He was quickly dropped by a hard crack from the stock of Raakesh's shotgun. The big man stood over Tillinghast and pointed the barrel at his face.

"No, Raakesh!" Julie screamed as she was released from the control of the Mi-Go. "We need that bastard alive!"

Stacey dropped to the floor again, and the others were similarly released.

"What the devil was that thing?"

"Devil is right," Sara panted, shaking her head from side to side. "Don't take yer helmet off, whatever you do."

"I'll explain later," Julie smiled. "Thank you. How the hell did you get in here?"

"I was trying to get through on comms but couldn't. I tried to get in, but it was locked down. I was about to give up and perform emergency tow procedures when it suddenly came back online."

"Tillinghast must have restored power to the whole ship." Julie stepped over to the fallen maniac, grabbed him by the lapels and yanked him to his feet. "You're coming with us, Professor Fruitcake."

"What about the Eden One?" Sara asked.

Julie thought for a second. "Do you think you and

DEATH BEYOND

Tommy could operate the self-destruct?"

Sara and Tommy both grinned.

"Get to it," Julie ordered. "Raakesh, can you carry Stacey?"

"Yes, Ma'am."

"Right, let's get you kitted out for a little walk, Professor."

Tillinghast stumbled as Julie shoved him in the direction of the locker room next to the airlock. "No! You... you can't! The future of our species is aboard this ship!"

Julie pulled back the firing bolt on her pistol. "Shut up and walk. You don't need to be uninjured to take home, you know?"

"Okay... Okay!" Tillinghast babbled as he walked towards the door. He was almost inside when something leapt from the room.

"Bastard!" The Micheals Mi-Go screamed and buzzed as it slammed into Tillinghast. Swiping its now huge pincer, he swiped Raakesh and Stacey out of the way. His claw sliced through Raakesh's armoured suit like it was butter, nearly severing his arm and showering Julie's visor in blood. She wiped it clear and moved to take a shot, but she was too late. The enraged hybrid closed its claw around Tillinghast's neck and snipped his head from his body.

"No!" Julie cried in dismay as she pumped round after round into Micheals, splattering his brains all over the gleaming white corridor.

Self-Destruct Sequence Activated. Please Abandon Ship.

"Oh, shit," Raakesh deadpanned as he looked at the

gaping hole in his suit. His wound was already becoming consumed by fungus. "Now what?"

Julie acted quickly, unbuckling his suit. "Let's get you in another suit and get off this damned ship. We can figure out what to do once we are clear..."

Sara and Tommy soon returned and helped Raakesh into his new outfit. Once he was suited up, Julie cycled the airlock, and the team headed back to the safety of the *Bolide*.

Julie's body tensed as she landed on the cold metal next to her hypersleep pod. Retching and choking, she purged the oxygenated fluid that had filled her lungs and kept her alive for the last six months. Pulling herself upright, she looked at the growth of fungus on the backs of her hands and down her legs.

This time, she was prepared. After watching the *Eden One* blow and patching up Raakesh's arm, she had told the crew that their best shot was to get within comms range of the OPE Admin Centre, bypassing security, and speak directly to one of her friends on the OPE board. He, she told them, could make sure that they were hurried into a lab and cured. Only Sara knew that Julie was lying... and she wasn't going to tell the others. In this situation, ignorance was bliss.

Sara knew the truth. As she plugged the almost entirely cocooned Stacey into her pod, she had run enough tests to know that Tillinghast had been lying. There was no cure. She had told Julie who had nodded sombrely. She knew that the Yuggoth fungus couldn't make it to civilisation under any circumstances. This is why she set the controls for as far into deep space as possible. Then she had Sara set her pod to wake her up in six months, leaving the rest in hibernation.

Reaching out her hand for the door sensor, she was shocked when it slid open without any problem. She had placed the emergency pump and a shotgun in the corner, just in case. The corridor was clear. The ship was secure. The crew were still asleep. All that remained was to send a full report to OPE Central, then start the self-destruct sequence.

The crew of the *Bolide* would never have that holiday on Neptune, after all...

DEATH BEYOND

Tim Mendees is a horror writer from Macclesfield in the North-West of England that specialises in cosmic horror and weird fiction. A lifelong fan of classic weird tales, Tim set out to bring the pulp horror of yesteryear into the 21st Century and give it a distinctly British flavour. His work has been described as the love-child of H.P. Lovecraft and P.G. Wodehouse and is often peppered with a wry sense of humour that acts as a counterpoint to the unnerving, and often disturbing, narratives.

Tim has had over eighty published short stories and novelettes in anthologies and magazines with publishers all over the world. He also has four novellas out now with more coming soon.

When he is not arguing with the spellchecker, Tim is a goth DJ, crustacean and cephalopod enthusiast, and the presenter of a popular web series of live video readings of his material and interviews with fellow authors. He currently lives in Brighton & Hove with his pet crab, Gerald, and an army of stuffed octopods.

https://timmendeeswriter.wordpress.com/
https://tinyurl.com/timmendeesyoutube

SLEEPWALKER

Jonathan Inbody

When a bulk order for the Irvo S series came across my desk, I didn't even hesitate before signing it. Irvo had always made quality equipment; why should mobile cryopods be any different? Sure, I had heard the rumors that the S series was... glitchy, but every ship I'd ever made a run on had Irvo equipment come standard. Irvo chairs, Irvo refrigerators—hell, even the botany modules were made with Irvo parts.

Besides, I'd seen the presentation they showed when the S series cryopods launched, and more importantly, combed through their projected savings numbers. The S series, or Sleepwalkers as they came to be called, were combination space suits and cryogenic chambers, with an internally cooling Kelvin Co. onboard system to ensure no frostbite dementia or concussive function loss. What's more, the suits' standard AI package enabled them to perform rudimentary functions while the people inside them laid in unconscious cold storage, so that they could save the clients' time, money, and man-power all at once.

The suits could walk, climb, perform basic maintenance and engineering upkeep, all while staving off the potential atrophy of their wearer's muscles by moving them around as they slept. It was, simply, a revelation, and one that was destined to delight Irvo's stockholders as much as their customers. For my company, Orion South Transport, it was an opportunity for the middle-managers to impress the slightly upper-middle-managers, each one in an ascending line of people whose only job it is to say 'yes' or 'no' to the person below them, and once it got to someone who could do the math, contracts were sent out to every long-haul outpost for sectional approval.

When I laid down in my S series suit, my stomach full of probiotic nutritional paste, getting ready for the long nap that would make up most of my first deep space run of the season, I wasn't even nervous. I'd gone on almost a hundred runs, maybe more, and if I could sleep while my suit did my job, then everything would be better for it.

I slept like a baby, at least for a while.

You don't dream in cryosleep, but you get impressions; emotions, half-cogent thoughts drifting from the back of your mind to the front, sometimes even shreds of long-gone memories. This time, I didn't get any.

My eyes fluttered open, and I groaned, looking out through the fogged-up faceplate to see where I was. The suit was moving, I could feel that much, and as my legs walked step after thunking step, I could hear the suit's magnetic boots scraping on a metal walkway underneath me. Why couldn't I see anything through the glass?

From further down the suit, somewhere inside, a muted alarm sounded, and the screen just in front of my chin flickered to life. "WARNING," it read. "Early awakening detected. Take manual control?" Two smaller boxes appeared underneath the typed message, one reading YES and the other NO.

I tried to raise my hand, but it pushed uselessly against the inside of the suit's metal glove. Of course, the suit was moving *for* me. That was what the message was about.

I cleared my throat and spoke, my voice coming out in a hoarse whisper. "Yes. Manual control approved, handoff on my count. 3, 2, 1. Engage manual control."

I tried to move again, but the suit just kept walking. My legs strained against the metallic casing and I tried to pull my arms up towards my head, but I was stuck, being operated like a puppet inside the automated suit.

"Engage manual control," I repeated, trying to speak up. "Engage upon request. Now!"

The suit didn't respond. The text box on the flickering screen just at the bottom of my glass faceplate flickered, casting soft orange light onto my face, still showing me the YES and NO buttons that I didn't have a free hand to press.

As the suit kept slowly walking, pulling my limbs along inside it, panic rose from my gut. I was trapped, being moved forward against my will in a tight metal prison, and the cryogenic fluid I could feel pooling in my boots felt more like wet cement.

"Engage manual control!" I yelled, twisting my head back and forth to try and free up space to move my chest. "Do it now!"

The screen flickered and went out, plunging me back into the pitch-black darkness I could see through my faceplate. My heart raced as the glass fogged up in front of me with panicked breaths, and I struggled in vain to move my arms. It was exhausting, like trying to push through a brick wall, and no matter how hard I tried, my arms wouldn't move unless the suit moved them.

"Run system diagnostic!" I said, my voice shaking as sweat beaded on my forehead. "Run diagnostic upon request! Run now!"

The screen just in front of my chin flickered to life again, and I craned my neck back so that I could see it more clearly. Oh God; I had an itch on the back of my neck.

A text box appeared on the screen with an elaborate string of system codes, then ran through them one by one as I watched. Next to it, a smaller box appeared reading '0%.'

I tried to keep myself from panicking, but the pounding in my chest seemed to be rising to my temples, and I could feel myself getting lightheaded from my gasping breaths. If I wasn't careful, I'd get sick, and with nowhere for the mix of nutritional paste and stomach acid to go, it would seep down into one of the leg holes of my suit. Would it eat away at my skin, or mix with the cryogenic fluid into some kind of poison?

No. No, don't... don't think about it.

I closed my eyes and took in a deep breath, then

held it as long as I could and let it out. The suit was still moving all around me, with the same steady rhythm that it had been walking in since I woke up, and I tried to time my breaths to each long movement. I'd breathe in when the left leg moved forward, hold it as the right took its turn, then let it out as the left moved again.

I felt my heartbeat slow and tried not to think about the itch on the back of my neck or the sweat dripping down the side of my face. Everything would be fine soon. Once the diagnostics finished, I'd have control again, and I could make sure the problem was fixed before going back into cryosleep. Nice, peaceful cryosleep. God, I missed it already.

I opened my eyes and pulled my head back as far as I could to look down at the screen—'14%.' Christ. I could sweat off half my body weight before it finished.

The diagnostics screen finished rebooting the magnetic boots, then moved on to limb hydraulics. I could feel the suit shift around my legs as the onboard intelligence checked them for any malfunctions, and then felt the metal gloves around my hands open and close in systematic rhythm. Maybe it would be done faster than I thought.

The suit raised its left arm, slowly rotating it along its range of motion, and I let out a sigh of relief as I felt my shoulder muscles stretch. I heard a dribble of liquid splash somewhere beneath my suit's neck hole and felt something wet brush against my side. There must have been cryofluid left in the fingertips of the suit's gloves, or maybe sweat depending on how long the cryosystem had been malfunctioning before it woke me.

DEATH BEYOND

The arm stretched out to the side and my muscle tightened; I couldn't quite bend that far. The suit kept turning and pain shot down my side—what was it doing? I felt my shoulder tighten with strain, then heard a sickening rip as the suit's arm kept stretching back. I felt bones grinding in my shoulder, then heard one snap, and sudden agony took my breath away as I opened my mouth to scream.

The arm kept turning, bending, snapping the bones in my twisting arm as it was bent past its breaking point, and suddenly I felt a wash of hot blood stream down from inside the arm hole and splash onto my chest. I screamed, swinging my head back and forth atop my immobilized neck in futile, animal fear, but no matter how much I struggled, there was nothing I could do about it.

My arm was mangled, approaching pulped, being bent in ways a human arm couldn't, and all I could do was feel it happening. I screamed, sometimes with words and sometimes just sounds, and finally the arm bent back into something resembling its place.

Stabbing pain radiated up my arm and through my shoulder, and I could see flecks of white poking in at the edges of my vision. I was going to faint.

I shook my head, desperately trying to pump enough blood to keep me conscious, then headbutted the glass faceplate in front of me. The screen at my chin flickered, the diagnostic scan somewhere around 29%, then went out.

"For God's sake, engage manual control!" I screamed, smacking my forehead against the foggy glass. "Please!"

DEATH BEYOND

The suit's right arm began to move, rotating mine inside it just like it had the left.

"No! *Don't!* Please, Jesus, no!"

The arm turned, and I felt the muscle tighten.

"Disengage diagnostic! Disengage *now*, for fuck's sake!"

The arm stopped in mid-air, stretched just far enough out that I could feel the strain, then turned back and lowered into its original place. I let out a ragged sigh of terrified relief, desperately thankful for my right arm's salvation, then tried to catch my breath and think.

"Engage lights," I said finally, staring out the fogged glass at the darkness in front of me.

The shoulder-mounted lights on the outside of the suit hummed to life, casting out thin beams of yellow into the pitch black in front of me. The left shoulder light moved over a wall-mounted electrical box, then illuminated a pair of thick pipes running up. We were somewhere deep inside the ship—Engineering, maybe? One of the atmosphere boilers?

The right shoulder light, which seemed to have been permanently bent at a steep downward angle, showed me the ridged metal walkway of the lower decks, the one the suit's magnetized boots were walking me down. Where were we going?

"Move lights—X axis 30 degrees right, Y axis 30 down."

The left shoulder light whirred, turning out in front of me and then down far enough that I could see where we were going. A few yards ahead of us, a jagged hole was torn in the narrow metal walkway, surrounded by ripped-up mechanical debris. I squinted and tilted my head back, and in a few seconds I could see a matching hole in the grated ceiling.

Suddenly, I saw a bulky metal shape at the edge of the shoulder light and craned my neck to get a better look at it. It was a Sleepwalker, another suit just like mine, with a shattered faceplate half-filled with soupy, coagulated blood.

"Computer, request latest repair report. Highlight points of interest."

The screen rose to cover most of my faceplate, then expanded into a progress report. At the top, it read 'DAMAGE SUSTAINED, REPAIR ATTEMPTED.' As I kept reading, I felt panic growing in the pit of my stomach. 'At 1700 hours, SD2430-45, ship sustained damage on four decks, two exposed to depressurized environment. Cause unknown; likely meteor or free-floating debris. Repair attempt made by Sleepwalker C54—FAILED. Next repair attempt in progress.'

"Show previous report," I said nervously.

Another report flashed up onto the screen and I quickly scanned it. Aside from the Sleepwalker unit number, C43, it was identical.

"Show full list of recent reports, one week window."

A long list of report titles scrolled up the screen, each one with an identical title. As I scanned them, another Sleepwalker came into view ahead of me, this one twisted in half at the waist and sparking with blue electricity. I couldn't see the face of the person inside, thank God, but as my suit passed by, I half expected it to reach out and grab me.

"Simplify reports—show only number of repair attempts."

The list disappeared one by one as the screen receded back to just in front of my chin, and a digital number flashed into view—93.

"You've made *ninety-three* repair attempts?"

The screen changed. 'Correct.'

My eyes widened. "List number of total crew remaining on ship."

'244.'

My breath caught in my throat. There had been almost 400 at launch.

The suit kept walking me forward, and I winced with each swing of my battered arm. Sweat was pouring down from my forehead to my neck, and as I looked ahead at the hole in the deck, I pulled my legs back with all of my remaining strength.

They strained against the metal for a few long moments, but didn't even seem to slow the suit down, and within seconds, we were almost to the edge of the hole. As it came into view underneath me, I could see down into the next deck below, and through it into a gaping black pit that seemed to have no end. 'Two decks exposed to a depressurised environment,' that's what it had said—the hole in the ship went straight to the outside; straight into outer space.

I thrashed inside the suit, screaming and tugging desperately to get it to stop as it walked step by step towards the hole. Pain shot up my mangled arm as I tried to move it, and I could feel my feet sloshing in cryofluid beneath me as I failed to get a foothold.

DEATH BEYOND

The suit took a final step forward over the edge of the hole, then shot down like a metal coffin through two decks and out of the hull. It blasted out into open space like a man-sized bullet, and I screamed even though I knew there was no one awake onboard to hear me.

I could see stars in the distance, blurring in my vision as the suit shook and twirled, and my stomach seemed to somersault inside me. There were no planets around me, no meteors, no tow cables or extended ladders or anything that I could reach for, even if the suit would have let me try.

There was nothing, the great big nothing between populated rocks, and as I plunged into the star-dotted void without direction, the screen in front of me flickered to life one last time.

'Repair attempt failed. 243 attempts remain.'

Jonathan Inbody is an author, filmmaker, and podcaster from Buffalo, New York. He specializes in writing horror and science fiction, but also writes any other genre that can have a monster in it. He is an avid reader of early 20th century Weird Fiction and an aficionado of B-movie genre cinema, and his acid horror anthology podcast Gray Matter, which combines his love of both, is coming soon.

Twitter: https://twitter.com/InbodyWriter

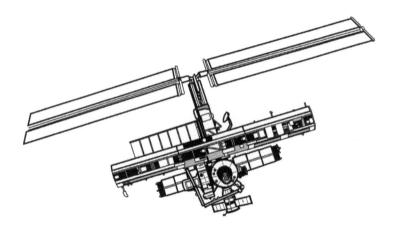

THE SHADOW FROM SPACE

David Green

"We're getting close." I glance at Pullman. His eyes are closed, a shadow of a smile on his thin, bloodless lips.

"I know, Matthews," he replies. "I can *feel* it."

They say we're infected. Our crew cast us out, threatened to maroon us from the Tesla Space Station Xenon before we could spread what's inside us. Or worse. Pullman heard them talk of murder. He told me they'd act first if we'd let them, before we could infect the station.

We stole a shuttle, a need urging us forward no matter what. We urged the crew to come with us, to move the space station deeper into space. They wouldn't listen. We had to kill them before they murdered us. A sub-command opened the station's airlocks as we spun away in our shuttle.

A pity. They won't see what we will.

No, no, no! What am I saying? A pity? They were my friends! My...

They couldn't *see*.

The shadow from space made it inside Pullman's spacesuit. Somehow. Whatever *it* is, he got it first. Passed it on to me as we showered together, something my husband loved to do after a space walk. Funny, I don't think I've seen him naked since, though time slips in my mind.

We're not infected. We're going home, a place where we belong. Where we've always meant to be.

Neptune, the last planet in our solar system. Each time I glance through my viewscreen, into the vast emptiness of space, it grows closer.

The storm planet. I've dreamt of it ever since showering with Pullman. I can't remember when I stopped thinking of him as my husband. Sometimes I dream of the planet when I'm awake.

"Pullman?"

"Yes?"

For some reason, I hesitate before speaking. It's something on my mind, a whisper in my brain. "What are we?"

He doesn't pause. "More than we were."

I've heard of space-sickness. It isn't an illness like the common cold or flu. No, it's the creeping madness when your mind comprehends how insignificant one is as you inch further through the swathes of black nothingness. What I feel is something else. Greater and terrible, but a part of me welcomes it. Another part doesn't recognise my own thoughts, the same part that screamed when I saw the bodies of my friends jettisoned into space, wept as they suffocated in the great, empty, cold void.

"What if it's not me? What if who I am's being devoured by the shadow?"

I saw it on the monitors. We'd detected an anomaly, something that had lodged itself against the space station's hull. Pullman went to investigate while the rest of us watched his progress on the monitors. At first, I thought my imagination played tricks on me—space sickness—but now I know different. Before we lost his feed, just for a minute, I saw it; the shadow, blacker than space, a cloud that swallowed the distant stars, uncurling itself from the hull.

When Pullman came back online, he said a glitch affected his suit, that he found nothing out there. Nothing but space and dust.

He lied.

"You don't believe we're going home?"

Pullman stares at me. Eyes black, skin pale, gaunt. Expressionless. He had another name once... Simon. Yes, that's it.

"Of course." My voice wavers. This thing inside me stirs. I feel shadowy fingers grip my heart, squeezing the blood from it. Closing my eyes, I see Neptune, the storms raging on it bright in my mind. "Home. It calls to me."

"Do not lie to me. I know the battle inside you. Give in. Join me." He holds out his hand. The fingernails are like claws, blackened and curled. "When we were... what we were... before. We touched each other. Held one another. Don't you miss it? You could have it again, deeper. We'd be as one."

DEATH BEYOND

Conflicting thoughts jostle for the right to answer him. "That sounds… wonderful."

A voice screams '*no*' inside my mind.

Pullman had been awake when I came out of stasis. A part of me wonders if he ever went in… he watched me, the pupils of his eyes large, almost swallowing the blue, as I went under.

Now his eyes are black. No white at all. Mine are almost the same.

Our crew were members of a scientific expedition to the edges of known space, using the Tesla Space Station Xenon to study the other planets and space phenomena as we travelled. We orbited Uranus when we encountered the shadow, after eight and a half years of flight. We took turns in cryo, mainly so we didn't all go crazy at the same time, but so we could log our journey, study the stars and ensure the Xenon avoided any issues. My husband and I always went in together. We never wanted to spend time apart.

My name is... Harriet Matthews, and like the rest of the souls carried aboard the Xenon, I had nothing to lose. There's no-one waiting and hoping for me back on Earth. Pullman—Simon—came with me. I needed nothing else.

It's taken us three years to reach Neptune. Twenty-four more to arrive at the edge of our solar system, as we once intended. No longer. The storm planet calls to me. My home.

Run!

I can't. I wish I could, but I can't.

It isn't too late. Not for you.

DEATH BEYOND

I shake my head. The voices stop. If I didn't bring them to a halt, they'd argue until I slipped into sleep, then I'd dream.

If I dreamt during cryo-freeze, I don't remember, but since waking, Neptune haunts me. The voices... one is a part of me begging to jump into an escape pod, to float in the endless void, rather than arrive at the place that calls me, that Pullman wants us to go. So we can join as one.

"You should have stayed awake. Then you'd understand, as I do."

I blink, and the real me fights inside, pushing the shadow back. It's like the freezing ice in the cryo has dulled the infection. No, not infection. It's meant to be.

No! This evil is devouring me.

"You didn't sleep? What did you do for the last three years?"

His lips curve into that half-smile again, the memory of a smile from a creature that never wore an honest one.

"I became me. This thing you called the shadow... it completed me. We spoke, always drawing closer to Neptune. It's home. Oh, how it desired to be one again with its master. You know it lived on Earth? Judging us, exposing the darkness within. Punishing those it found guilty. Only an innocent few it found and one of those consigned it to the ice for many years, just like the master. For so long, it's been away from Neptune, joining with human after human, striving to return. Now, at last, it will, and its master will absorb it and its memories. It will discover Earth, and it won't like what it sees."

Images flash in my mind. A greater shadow lurking behind the storm. It sees me, somehow. Knows me. Waits for me. It's the other voice I hear... whispering to me. Telling me to come home. I've ignored it, or tried to, while this other me has basked in its presence. It's the one that sends me the dreams, the one that infects me. No, not infects. Blesses. No!

God, what's happening to me?

Neptune's a dead planet, filled with gas, and wracked with storms. Something lurks inside its atmosphere. Impossible, but it speaks to me when I sleep and fills me with a dreadful yearning to approach it.

The presence inside Neptune sleeps, too. Somehow I know this. It has for millions of years. I don't know how I understand, but I do. Our arrival has stirred it. The shadow we carry inside us rings out through the silent space, a cosmic alarm for '*the master.*'

"Yes," I say to Pullman, but I don't take his withered hand. He lets it fall and turns back to the viewscreen. "I hear the master's call. He's waiting for us."

"No. This flesh, this person you cling to? Insignificant. The master waits for the shadow to return, to be whole again. That's all that matters."

In the dreams, I float in space above Neptune. I'm naked, but the cruel emptiness doesn't harm me. I drift closer to the giant blue sphere and I feel something inside my mind. It peers through my memories, uncaring of the emotional tolls my experiences have wrought. The *thing* seeks to understand me and through me, humanity. Judging.

Before I wake, I pass through the clouds. Wind buffers me. Ice nips at my unprotected skin. I'm brought before an impossible wall of ice, towering into the atmosphere. Inside, frozen, sleeping, I see the shadow of a creature. So gigantic my mind can't comprehend its scale. Its wings fold across it, protecting the tentacles that droop from its face. I see the heavy, closed eyelids.

Until last night.

When I peered at the thing in the ice, its red eyes flicked open and fixed me with its stare. My brain reeled as the weight of the creatures will threatened to crush my mind. I gave in to sweet oblivion.

On Neptune, the *thing* that slumbered since before humans walked on Earth is awake. And it understands us. Through me, it sees our greed, jealousy, hatred and thirst for domination.

I can't let it win.

"No," Pullman snarls, his gnarled hand gripping my wrist like a vice. "You *will* give in."

I stare into his black eyes. Thick liquid swirls across the surface. This isn't my Simon, he's dead, devoured by the shadow as I slept. If I hadn't gone into cryo, I'd be just like him now. We have a chance; humanity has a chance.

"Let go of me."

"You don't deserve what's inside you," he snarls, twisting my wrist. I cry out in pain, but he holds on as he shoots to his feet. I slide from my chair on to the floor, tears in my eyes as I peer up at him. Simon. I loved you so much. "Simple. I'll take it from you. Let it join inside me before we reach Neptune."

Moving too fast for my eyes to follow, to comprehend what's coming next, Pullman grabs my head and slams it against the floor.

My vision explodes into light. Pain blooms in my head. Fiery blood gushes down my face.

"Sim—"

My head meets the floor again, the crunch vibrating against the metal, cutting off my words. Sound becomes dull as blood pools in my ear. Unseeing, I flail my arms, trying to fight Pullman off, but it's not good, my head crashes against the floor again.

Give in.

It whispers to me. The shadow. Time slows to a crawl as stars die and are reborn galaxies away.

Let me in. You're finished without me. Surrender and survive.

Pullman lifts my head from the floor, ready to crush it with one final plunge. I can't take any more. My life's almost over. Murdered by a thing inside my husband's body, deeper into space than any human has travelled. Will anyone know what happened to me? I know the answer.

No.

When Pullman kills me, he'll join with the master on Neptune, and we're *all* finished. Perhaps I can stop that.

I surrender.

It's like I'm stuck to the ceiling, watching the scene below. Detached from my body. Pullman clutches my head. Blood oozes onto the floor from my almost crushed skull. The shadow flows from my body, swallowing the twinkling lights of the cockpit's dashboard.

DEATH BEYOND

Lightning dances with the black smoke and it swirls and gathers before Pullman. He smiles, his pale skin stretching across his emancipated face. He thinks he's won.

My limbs move. With strength I didn't realise I had left in me, I surge forwards, throwing myself at the one I used to call Simon. My thumbs dig into his sockets, squeezing, pushing his eyes back into his skull. My weight sends him to the floor, me on top of him; he screams as blood gushes from his cranium, but still I force my thumbs deeper. Pullman's arms and legs shake as he tries to push me off, but somehow, I'm stronger; it's like my in-built human will to live and the shadow inside me has combined to make me... *more*.

Funny. Simon said the same.

Pullman's screams reach a crescendo as his eyes burst. Digging deeper into his skull, I lift it and slam it against the ground, just like he did to me. But I don't stop until the back of his head is sludge.

Standing, I flick the gore from my hands and smile as the shadow, and the miasma leaving Pullman's corpse, enter my body. I see it all, everything he told me and more; the torrid, depraved history of humanity, witnessed and judged by the shadow.

Wait... I had some purpose. To stop... to save...

No. To return home. To join with the master. At last.

Stepping over the corpse, I punch in commands on the control panel. We're close.

The shuttle approaches Neptune. The planet fills the viewscreen as the distance disappears and my shuttle orbits the storm planet.

The creature below waits for me. My master calls,

and I answer. When I surrendered to the shadow, when I *saw* its truth, I understood. There isn't just the master, trapped beneath the ice of Neptune. There are others like it. Captured in ice. Lost among the stars. Together, we'll find them. Once complete, we'll wake the one sleeping on Earth, the one they sent me to find, all those years ago.

Humanity has had its chance. It failed. Its time has come.

DEATH BEYOND

David Green is a writer based in Co Galway, Ireland. Growing up between there and Manchester, UK meant David rarely saw sunlight in his childhood, which has no doubt had an effect on his dark writings. Published with Black Ink Fiction, Red Cape Publishing and Eerie River Publishing, David has been nominated for the Pushcart Prize 2020 and his dark fantasy series Empire of Ruin launches in June 2021 with "In Solitude's Shadow."

Website: www.davidgreenwriter.com
Newsletter: https://tinyurl.com/y6ah8brp
Twitter: @davidgreenwrite

DEATH BEYOND

MORE FROM
BREAKING RULES
PUBLISHING EUROPE

DEATH BEYOND

Face of Fear by C. Marry Hultman
9789198671001

Dawson Junior G3 by Brian Wagstaff
9789198671049

Boy in the Wardrobe by Esther Jacoby
9789198684018

New Life Cottage by Esther Jacoby
9789198671056

The Wait by Esther Jacoby
e-book:https://books2read.com/u/4Dgz8Q

Liebe ist Warten by Esther Jacoby
9789198671070

Das Cottage by Ester Jacoby
9789198684070

Musing on Death & Dying by Esther Jacoby
9789198671063

Earth Door by Cye Thomas
9789198671025

Graffiti Stories by Nick Gerrard
9789198671018

Punk Novelette by Nick Gerrard
9789198671087

Struggle and Strife by Nick Gerrard
9789198684049

Fake Escape by Natalie Hughes
e-book:https://books2read.com/u/bMXL5X

Murder Planet by Adam Carpenter
9789198671032

Generation Ship by Adam Carpenter
9789198684063

Cold as Hell by Neen Cohen
9789198684094

Six Days to Hell by E.L. Giles
9789198684087

Just 13 anthology
9789198684025

Lost Lore & Legends Anthology
9789198671094

Adventure Awaits volume 1 Anthology
9789198684124

Adventure Awaits volume 2 Anthology
978-9198684155

Death House
9789198684117

Death Ship
9789198684148

Find us at:
http://www.breakingrulespublishingeuro.com

CPSIA information can be obtained
at www.ICGtesting.com
Printed in the USA
BVHW071015200921
617093BV00007B/278